Kelli Hawkins writes novels for adults and children as well as reports for a private investigator. Over the years she's travelled whenever possible and worked all kinds of jobs: she's been a political journalist, a graphic designer, a mystery shopper – even a staple remover. She lives in Newcastle with her two teenagers.

Keith Hawkins writes... for adults and children...

KELLI HAWKINS

OTHER PEOPLE'S HOUSES

HarperCollins*Publishers*

HarperCollins*Publishers*

Australia • Brazil • Canada • France • Germany • Holland • Hungary
India • Italy • Japan • Mexico • New Zealand • Poland • Spain • Sweden
Switzerland • United Kingdom • United States of America

First published in Australia in 2021
This edition published in 2022
by HarperCollins*Publishers* Australia Pty Limited
Level 13, 201 Elizabeth Street, Sydney NSW 2000
ABN 36 009 913 517
harpercollins.com.au

A catalogue record for this book is available from the National Library of Australia.

ISBN 978 1 4607 5923 3 (paperback)
ISBN 978 1 4607 1294 8 (ebook)
ISBN 978 1 4607 8675 8 (audiobook)

Cover design by Mark Campbell, HarperCollins Design Studio
Front cover images: Residence with pool by Koen Van Damme/stocksy.com/
    1426597; body by shutterstock.com
Back cover image: Residence with pool by Koen Van Damme/stocksy.com/
    1030123; hand by shutterstock.com
Author photograph by Jennifer Blau
Typeset in Bembo Std by Kirby Jones
Printed and bound in Australia by McPherson's Printing Group

For Asha and Dusty.
And especially for Matt. We miss you.

PART I

FIRST
OPEN HOUSE

SATURDAY, 5 JULY
MORNING

I pulled over just in time. Opening the car door, I leaned out and breathed heavily, staring at the asphalt. It felt like my intestines were being yanked around my insides by a sadist jerking on a string.

In short, I felt like shit.

My stomach heaved. The contractions were remarkably like childbirth. To distract myself I compared the two types of pain. The ferocity. The lack of control over bodily functions. For a moment I almost convinced myself this might be worse than the twelve hours prior to Sascha's birth.

A needle-stab pierced my lungs: nothing to do with the hangover.

Sascha.

I hugged the pain to me, unwilling to let it go.

After a minute or so I sucked in the clean winter air and sat up, squinting at my surroundings through watery eyes and a curtain of lank unwashed hair.

Turramurra: one of Sydney's most desirable suburbs, filled to the brim with mortgaged-up bankers and lawyers. Houses here had landscaped pools and attached cabanas, tennis courts, long gravel driveways with turning circles for Range Rovers. I peered around, trying to imagine living in a place like this.

I couldn't. The wide-lawned suburban street was so quiet. *Too quiet*. Even the usual 24/7 drone of traffic chugging up the Pacific Highway just a few blocks away was somehow inaudible. It was like a scene from an early episode of *The Walking Dead* – when everything was still orderly and beautiful and ominously serene. I pictured dead-eyed zombies lurching from behind the nearest house to converge on my car, all grasping arms and bloodied mouths.

Don't be stupid, Kate. Are you still drunk?

Maybe I was. I started to calculate just how much I'd had the night before then didn't want to know. With a jolt, I realised I shouldn't be driving and made a mental note to watch out for RBTs.

I gathered my hair into the best ponytail I could manage, ignoring the tremor in my hands. My nausea had eased, thank God, but I knew the reprieve would be brief. I stared at the ground again, revelling in what a disgusting human being I was. Wallowing in it. Rolling around in my own disgustingness like a dog in the remnants of a dead animal.

Never again. No more drinking.

I burped, grimacing at the taste – wine, with sour overtones. The bitter, chemical aftertaste of the previous night's takeaway pizza was in there somewhere too.

Not tonight, anyway. I swear it.

Even as I made the vow, another part of my brain chortled and rolled its eyes.

July fifth. Probably not the best day to try and give up the grog.

Today was the anniversary.

Ten years.

* * *

I scrounged through the junk crammed into the centre console of my car. With the least manky tissue I could find I wiped my eyes then blew my nose. Back inside the car I grabbed the bottle of Coke sitting on the passenger seat, the weak sun through the window just warm enough to fog the plastic. The lid hissed open and I took a couple of big gulps, the hit of sugar and caffeine making me groan. I peered at the dashboard. 11.27 am. After swigging one more mouthful, I screwed the lid back on, slammed the door shut and turned the key in the ignition.

Two left turns down empty streets and I was there.

A disproportionately large number of cars and people congregrated around a well-kept Federation-style house marked by a For Sale sign. A modest house, by Turramurra standards. A flag poked from the side of the sign at a 45-degree angle, flaccid in the morning stillness. Two small Open House markers skewered neighbouring lawns, complete with arrows, though they were superfluous given the crowds.

Most prospective buyers appeared to be families, which wasn't surprising. I double-parked in front of a nearly identical house across the road as a family approached their Kia Carnival, the parents dressed in conservative smart-casual Saturday attire, their punchy-kicky kids still in muddy sports uniforms. I rolled my eyes as the mother brayed for the children to climb in to the *carn-i-v-aah-lay*, her futile attempt to make the people-mover sound sexy. Other families swarmed across the lawn like invading troops, the parents squinting up at eaves and pointing down at footings as though they knew all about eaves and footings and weren't actually lawyers and IT professionals who spent their days in boring meetings or staring at computer screens.

The For Sale sign was dominated by an enormous photo of a professionally styled, neat-enough but otherwise quite ordinary master bedroom.

So.

The house would be crap.

If that dull room was the home's best feature there'd be nothing better to see inside. I found my scribbled list of houses under the Coke bottle. Condensation had made the paper soggy, but it was still legible.

65 Waratah Dr. Turra. 11.30–12. McQuilty RE. $1.95m+

I eyed the house again, snorted. *Too much.* They wouldn't get more than $1.7. Not even in this market. It didn't matter. Not to me anyway.

That wasn't why I was here.

And I wasn't here officially, either. Yes, I worked at a real estate agency, but just in marketing. Writing flowery copy, laying out ads for the newspapers, that kind of thing. I didn't need to be here for work.

No, I attended open houses for other reasons entirely.

I climbed out of the car, the thudding in my head picking up pace and potency as I straightened. A flash of silver in the footwell caught my eye and I almost bent down to pick up the blister pack of paracetamol before cursing out loud, remembering I'd popped the final two at last week's opens.

'McQuilty Real Estate,' I cursed, pulling my hair free from the elastic and attempting to tame the frizz with my fingers. 'Please don't be Renee.'

I shoved the list into the back pocket of my jeans then joined the hordes advancing up the white pebble driveway, crunching with each step. Tiny white stones spilled onto the grass lining the drive. I shook my head.

Idiots.

At the front steps the crowd slowly fed through the entryway. Everyone paused obediently, reciting names and phone numbers in exchange for the chance to stickybeak through the home of a stranger. Maybe some of them were even serious about buying it. An Asian couple ahead of me spoke to one another in what might have been Mandarin. The small child between them was so bundled up in a parka and puffy pants it looked like a colourful little sausage and could have been of either sex.

'Hello and welcome! Can I have your name please?'

That tittering voice. Renee.

Dammit.

I contemplated heading home, tempted to the car by the memory of sugary, lukewarm Coke. For a moment I wavered, visualising my apartment; imagined sitting on the lounge under a doona watching *Friends* reruns. Then, as I vacillated, the Asian woman moved to her left and I could see the darkness of a hallway through the wedged-open front door. Murmuring seeped from the building, frustratingly muffled. I paused, still undecided. Then a high-pitched giggle, the creak of a closing door.

Even an ordinary home could house extraordinary secrets.

My heart beat a little faster. I hadn't let Renee scare me away before. I would stay.

A couple of mobile numbers later it was my turn.

'Welcome! Can I —' Renee's maroon-lipsticked smile became a flat burgundy slash when she glanced up from her iPad and saw me. 'Oh, it's you.'

'Hi Renee. Great day for it.' I had tried for cheerful bluster but came off sounding meek and insipid. My smile slipped a little.

Renee fashioned her mouth back into a semblance of a smile, but it didn't reach her eyes. Renee Crowley saved her full-wattage beam for those she deemed worthy. And to be worthy in Renee Crowley's eyes meant one thing only – you might buy a house. And since Renee Crowley did not believe I would buy a house from her today – or any other day – I could hardly blame her for her lack of warmth.

Particularly since she was correct in her assumption.

A nobody, Kate, that's who you are.

Mind you, I'd attended eight open houses before Renee remembered my face, so for a while there I'd been one of the smiled-upon. Until some local gossip nattered in her ear; filled her in on my … *history*.

Told her about the *incident*.

She looked at me differently now. Like the rest of them.

Dr Evans, the sad-eyed psychologist I'd been referred to afterwards, had attempted to teach me a four-step plan to help deal with the judgement – or pity, as the case may be – of others. Like all the therapy I'd attempted in the years before I gave it away, it had proved useless. Dr Evans didn't get it.

No one did.

Pity was annoying, but I could deal with that. And the judgement. Well, I deserved the judgement.

I deserved it all.

'Kate, isn't it?'

She got my name right.

A sudden rush of pleasure filled me, followed by irritation for being grateful Renee-fucking-Crowley remembered my name.

Dr Evans would not approve of my neediness.

'Yes. Kate Webb.'

'And a mobile number for you, Kate?' Renee asked, her index finger poised mid-air, the lacquered, claret-coloured nail somehow managing to convey her disdain.

We both knew she would never call. To her, I was a number on a spreadsheet she'd give the owners to prove what a fabulous job she'd done enticing potential buyers inside their home.

I rattled it off anyway.

'Lovely. Take your time.' She turned towards the next people. 'Good morning. Welcome to 65 Waratah Drive. Can I have your name, please?'

I'd been dismissed. But instead of being pissed off with Renee, a familiar buzz spread through me. The thrill of a new house and all its buried secrets. Like that first sip of chilled white wine on a summer's afternoon, anticipation raced through my bloodstream; this was the drug that kept me coming back for more. The front door loomed, with all its promises. Promises of lives lived, of children growing and grown, of nightly dinners around a kitchen table. Of scuff marks on walls and broken light fittings and empty picture hooks. Everyday stuff. Family life.

Beginnings.

And endings, of course.

My pulse quickened as I walked through the front door.

* * *

The hallway was stifling and smelled like biscuits. Bloody stylists: always insisting on that just-baked biscuit smell. That, or freshly brewed coffee. I supposed it was better than the heady scent of cat's piss or overcooked vegetables. And, yes, some houses did smell that bad.

The Asian couple were in the first bedroom, so with impeccable real estate etiquette I waited my turn in the hall. After a minute or so they emerged. The child – I still couldn't tell if it was a boy or girl – twisted back to look into the room, tugging so insistently on its parents' hands it was almost horizontal. As they dragged it away, the child started to wail and the parents shushed it and dragged harder.

I entered.

It was a child's room. Colourful letters on the wall above the single bed spelled out FLYNN. Other than this personal touch all character had been sucked out of the room in favour of good taste. Neutrals, with 'pops of colour'. In this case, royal blue and fire-engine red. For a boy. Obviously. A throw rug lay across the end of the white metal-framed bed, too artfully messy to be anything but staged. Toys, the retro kind adults adored but children didn't find interesting – not compared to iPads and gaudy plastic shit from a discount store, anyway – were arranged on a white bookshelf. Collectable miniature robots had been positioned up high to protect them from grubby hands. A tiny Guns N' Roses t-shirt hung on a hanger like artwork to target the cool-young-family-moved-to-the-suburbs-but-haven't-lost-their-edge demographic. A wooden train track had been set up on the floor near a child-sized tepee – for that hipster touch.

Nothing in this room spoke to me of Sascha. Or of 'Flynn' for that matter. This was a stage-set masquerading as a child's bedroom. Still, I started searching it.

Moving swiftly, I pulled open the top drawer of the bedside table. Empty. Nothing in the lower two either. I spun around to the built-in wardrobe. The door glided open on silent tracks. Empty again, but for a couple of taped-up wine boxes marked

Kids Books and *Stuffed Toys* – annoyingly sealed up with masking tape. I slid the door shut.

Two small boys tumbled past me as I left the room, yelling 'bags this one' at the same time. One burrowed under the throw rug as his placid mother waited in the hall for me to exit. She gave me a 'boys will be boys' shrug and a beatific smile.

There was no sign of the Asian couple with their gender-indeterminate child in the hall or the next room. This one was a teen girl's version of the previous room. White, aqua and yellow. Cool and calm. I grunted. No stinky t-shirts. No blue-tacked 1D or 5SOS posters in sight. Or whatever boy band girls were squealing about this week.

Bedside table, empty.

Built-ins, empty – save for half a dozen hangers at one end. Nothing for me here.

Damn, damn, damn.

I left the room and crossed the hall, hearing 'Choo-choo' and the sound of clattering trains from Flynn's room. The mother was probably letting the boys destroy the toys for five minutes' peace while she texted her friend about their lunch date.

Next, the master bedroom: white doona on the bed, grey throw rug across a corner, a single geometric-patterned aqua cushion among an excess of white ones. It looked exactly the same as the photograph on the sign, though much smaller when not seen through the wide-angle lens of the camera. But it was the generic black and white wall art that really gave me the shits. Three side-by-side typographic works, each one a single, apparently handwritten, word.

Imagine. Dream. Love.

Yawn, more like.

I'd seen the same prints in three houses in the past six weeks. The artist in me cringed.

By now I didn't hold out much hope. The owners had moved on, taking their personalities with them. Nevertheless, I started on the room. Methodically I slid open drawers, checked behind the bedside tables and peered into the wardrobe. I experienced a moment's excitement after touching something soft at the back of a high shelf. An ordinary men's tennis sock, white, hardly worn. For a moment I considered it, but it was too new.

I'd keep looking.

The sound of someone exaggeratedly clearing their throat made me thrust the sock back, squinting my eyes as my head pounded with renewed urgency. I turned, attempting nonchalance. An old man, tall and somewhat stooped, blocked the doorway. He wore a light-blue cardigan and beige pants and his face was tanned and grim, as if he usually spent his days gardening or bushwalking and was not happy about being in a stranger's house on a sunny Saturday morning. His frown of disapproval split his forehead in two.

I risked a hesitant smile. 'You've got to check out the storage, don't you?' I said. 'Some of these older places have bugger-all storage.' I waved a hand vaguely at the wardrobe. 'This one's not too bad, though.'

His expression didn't change. I excused myself and walked to the door. He stepped aside to let me pass, mouth downturned. A dumpy woman stood behind him with a mildly confused look on her face.

'Having a bit of a snoop, wasn't she?' the man commented to the woman – his wife presumably – not bothering to lower his voice.

My face grew hot as I hurried out.

Next was the living room, which, along with the kitchen, formed one large open space. A renewed blast of biscuit smell – chocolate chip – did nothing to help my latent nausea, so I tried to breathe through my mouth. A TV cabinet stood at one end of the room; a pair of light-grey lounges and the kitchen bench at the other. The open-plan layout told me the house had been renovated; the all-white kitchen was modern enough to suggest it had been quite recently. Renee should know better, I thought tetchily, cursing the fluoro brightness of the room for amplifying my hangover. White kitchens were all the rage. She should have put a photo of this room on the sign out front.

Automatically, I revised my assessment of price. Maybe they'd get $1.8.

Several couples wandered around, some with bored children in tow. One man measured the lounge with a tape measure before his partner shook her head and sighed. Another couple whispered as they peered into the pantry. Perhaps it was too large, or too small – who knew? Others examined the walls and floors. Even the ceiling. No chance for me to search here. I ducked around the L-shaped bench to the kitchen sink where a window overlooked the back yard.

I sighed. It was more of the same. Not the sort of yard where I could picture Sascha digging in the dirt or calling for me to come and see a grasshopper he'd found. Too generic. Disappointing. The lawn was neat, with an older but freshly painted garage to the left and tidy, if uninspiring, gardens around the perimeter. More ridiculous white stones covered the driveway. The temporary absence of a Hills hoist could be deduced by a hole in the centre of the grassed area. Let's face it: no one wanted to imagine hanging out washing.

They were buying the dream, darling.

I didn't bother going outside. I could see from here the back yard would be as devoid of mementoes as the rest of the house.

Time to go.

* * *

I walked back down the hall into a cloud of Chanel No. 5. My stomach started to do the little fluttery thing I knew well. I breathed shallowly, trying to stem the wave of nausea. Renee's chirruping from the front door stopped me. I halted just out of sight and eavesdropped.

'Thank you, and what did you think of the house?'

'Well, it isn't really my cup of tea. We're looking for something with a little more ... *charm*, you know? And a pool, of course – or at least the space to add one. The children are adamant we must have a pool.'

I couldn't see the woman who spoke but I guessed she was the wearer of the Chanel No. 5. Her vowels were strangely rounded, like she was auditioning for the role of Eliza Doolittle in a school play but couldn't get the accent right.

'Mmm, I see,' Renee replied, her words dripping with fake sincerity. 'Ah ... I'm sorry I've forgotten your name?'

Typical Renee.

'Tammy.'

'Well, Tammy, we do have a number of other properties on our list at the moment —'

'Oh, I think we've seen everything available in this area. We've been back in Sydney for a couple of weeks now. We've lived in London for the last five years' – that explained the odd accent – 'and I've been desperately looking for somewhere. We just *adore* this area. My husband starts work in the city soon and we want to get settled as soon as possible.'

'Oh, Tammy! How lovely for you to be searching for a home on our beautiful north shore. It's so leafy and quiet. Just perfect for families. Do you mind if I ask what your budget is?'

'Well, luckily for us the pound goes a long way at the moment. My husband's given me a budget of four point five. Perhaps a little higher if I can persuade him I've found the perfect home.'

Renee's long pause somehow managed to broadcast her happiness. Her next words were hushed. 'Tammy, you might be in luck. Something new has just come on the market. Today. We are only showing it to a select few at this time. Open houses will start next week. The owners have decided to go to auction, but it could sell before that, given the current market, so if you are interested …'

'It has a pool?'

'Yes, a gorgeous pool. Oh, it is nothing short of stunning, Tammy, honestly. It has the charm this house …' – she stopped theatrically – 'sadly, does not. It's in your price range and more to your taste.'

'That sounds great. I'd love to have a look.'

'Wonderful,' Renee said, drawing the word out. 'One of our senior agents, Roger, is taking care of the property. He's arranged a VIP open house today at three, I think. Just let me find the address, I'm sure he texted it to me earlier.'

I stepped around the corner.

Renee had her phone out and talons scrabbling. She glanced up then hastily shifted her focus back to her phone, addressing me at the same time. 'Oh, Kate, I didn't see you there. I was just talking to Tammy. She's looking to buy a home, a *family* home, in the area. She's come from *London* recently.'

She made London sound like heaven. Or an orgasm.

The Chanel lady – Tammy – looked me up and down, apparently not impressed by what she saw: a middle-aged woman with a sheen of sweat, wearing unfashionable jeans, a navy sweatshirt, no makeup and holey Converse sneakers. My hair was in its usual state, somehow both frizzy and lank.

Tammy, on the other hand, looked as she smelled. Expensive. In a show-off-y but casual way. Pearls, crisp white shirt, jeans that couldn't be more different from mine. Probably Gucci or some uber-cool brand I hadn't heard of. Blow-dried hair, full makeup. What did surprise me was that she had two children with her. They'd been so quiet I hadn't noticed them. The boy was about eight and the girl a couple of years older. The children, almost as neatly dressed as their mother, were ignored by both her and Renee. I'd never seen such silent, well-behaved children.

It gave me the creeps.

Sascha had been a quiet child too, though I couldn't ever remember him standing so still and mute. Mind you, he'd been younger than these two when …

I buried the thought, mentally shovelling dirt over it to keep those ghosts firmly entombed. This wasn't the time or place. I'd think about Sascha later, when I was alone in my apartment with a large glass of wine.

We all stood silently for a long moment. Tammy looked from Renee to me with a slight frown.

Renee caved first. 'Can I help you with something else, Kate?' she asked, her polite smile for Tammy's benefit not mine.

'No, thanks, Renee. I'll be off.'

I squeezed past Tammy and her silent children – her perfume so strong I held my breath lest I vomit all over the polished timber floor – and out into the fresh air, but then I moved to one side, head cocked, listening.

Renee gave Tammy the address. I raised my eyebrows.

The house was on one of Wahroonga's hoity-toity-est streets. Something about the address rang a bell in my jangling brain, but I couldn't put my finger on what, or why.

'The Harding house,' Renee sighed. 'You will just *love* it, Tammy.'

* * *

The Harding house.

I was unable to subdue a smug little smile as I put two and two together in my hungover brain and realised Renee was talking about *the* Harding house. I'd heard of it, of course, as had most people on the north shore.

Now I understood her reluctance to say the address in front of me. Renee believed I wasn't worthy, that the Harding house was too good for me. I couldn't disagree with her.

But that didn't mean I wasn't going to be there on the dot of three.

I tuned back in. Renee asked her golden-egg-slash-new-best-friend about hotels in London. She was travelling to Europe next year and was dying to stay somewhere *delightful*. On the Thames and near Harrods, if at all possible – did Tammy perhaps know of anywhere like that?

The lawn was empty now, most of the oglers having raced off to their next open house. I crunched back down the pebbly driveway. Partway along I stopped, staring down at the smooth white stones. Stones like this made a mess of a lawn within days. I'd bet money that this morning the current owners had been out there picking them up from the lawn and putting them back on the drive, swearing at each and every pebble as they did so. I bent down, plucked one at random and flipped it over and over again on my palm, considering.

It was lovely and smooth and so, so bland.

Perfect.

With a sense of satisfaction, I slipped it into the front pocket of my jeans and continued to my car.

I reached for the Coke bottle. A couple of centimetres of stale black liquid sloshed around the bottom of the plastic container. I finished it off in two greedy mouthfuls. It was warmer than last time, and pretty flat too, but that didn't stop me. My car's dashboard clock said it was 12.08. What to do until 3 pm?

Lunch?

The brief thought of food was immediately replaced by sudden, intense nausea. I flung open the door and repeated my earlier head-between-knees scenario, retching violently then spitting foul-tasting saliva onto the tar at my feet. And I knew – again, from far too much previous experience – the vomiting phase of this hangover was done.

Thank-fucking-Christ for that.

I sat up, wiping my smiling mouth with the back of my hand, light-headed with relief, knowing I would feel normal again soon. As I pulled the door shut I glanced across the street. Renee stood at the boot of a silver BMW, the open house flag in her arms, a small sandwich board at her feet. She stared at me, her mouth twisted into a moue of revulsion, eyes boggling like a character from a cartoon.

My face flushed red and hot. I sank into my seat, removing my hand from my mouth like I'd been slapped. Renee swung back to her car, placing the items into the boot hurriedly before marching to the driver's side. She sped off without looking at me.

Great. Another reason for Renee to hate me.

I glanced down at my spittle-flecked sweatshirt then at my shaking hands, surprised by how puffy and veiny they were. How old. My nails were bitten as usual, and one hand was marked by a shallow scratch I couldn't remember getting. A drunk's wound. I grabbed the wheel tight to stop the tremors. My skin shone with sweat, my knuckles taut and white. In fact, my whole body looked foreign to me, which was weird as I'd been putting on weight fairly steadily for years now. I guess in my mind I was still a skinny gymnast with a six-pack and muscular calves. The waistband of my jeans cut into my flab. I undid the top button, enjoying the release of flesh that spilled out and over the denim, then felt repulsed by it. Repulsed by my own body. As if in response, it growled, a long, low animal sound. Suddenly I was starving, nausea gone.

Fuck Renee.

I needed food.

I shrugged off my earlier worries about RBTs, deciding fried chicken was worth the risk. My stomach groaned and gurgled as I drove down the highway to the nearest drive-through. I took my oily box of chicken and parked in an alley behind a Chinese restaurant. When only bones and gristle lay on the greasy napkin I leaned back, trying to work out if I felt better or worse.

I couldn't decide.

Setting the alarm on my phone, I napped until the beeping woke me. I blinked and was startled by an elderly Chinese man watching me with impassive eyes. He wore a bloodied apron and perched elegantly on a milk crate at the back door of the restaurant, a cigarette dangling from his slender fingers. My eyes felt gummy, and drool had leaked out of one side of my mouth. I wiped it away and wound the seat back up, averting my gaze. The man's innate dignity made me feel even crappier. I surreptitiously buttoned up my jeans, hoping he couldn't tell what I was doing, then started the car and drove off.

I'd left myself half an hour. As I approached the house I put the window down to disperse a couple of fried chicken farts, hoping to get them out of my system. The last thing I wanted was to add 'stinky farter' to my list of the day's embarrassments.

But when I pulled up at the Harding house all thoughts of farting vanished.

I fell in love with the place.

SATURDAY, 5 JULY
AFTERNOON

The Harding house was perfect.

Sitting in my little yellow Hyundai with ten minutes to kill, my eyes roving over each brick and tile, mesmerised by the symmetry of the house, but also the imperfections that somehow made this house perfect, I knew – *I knew* – this was it. This was the one. And even after all that went down later, I still believe the Harding house is the most exquisite home a person could ever have or want.

The Harding house, or Highfields, as it was officially called according to the sign, was a landmark in Wahroonga. It had been in Brett Harding's family for generations. Everyone was shocked that he would even think about selling it. Of course, I didn't know all this at the time. My first thought on seeing the Harding house in the flesh – well, in the bricks and mortar – was, *Why, oh why, would anyone ever sell a house like this?*

The house was old, though I couldn't have guessed at a date. Despite attending open houses most weekends over the past couple of years, and despite working at a real estate agency, architecture wasn't really my thing. But I found out from the slick, glossy brochure I got my hands on later that the house was Georgian Revival, built about 1930. The façade was reddish brick, double storey and rectangular. Pleasingly symmetrical, there were three windows along the top floor, balanced on the ground floor with two windows and an impressive porticoed front door. Each of the five windows was charmingly framed by deep-blue shutters. The roofline was steep, the tiles neatly capped by a chimney – like the cherry on an ice-cream sundae.

From the street you couldn't see much of the house at all, just glimpses of red brick through the hedge of leafy camellias. To get to the Harding house you turned down a long driveway, entering through handsome wrought-iron gates, which today stood open. The long, cobblestoned, slate-grey driveway finished at the front of the home in a turning circle that wrapped around a central garden bed of hedge and white roses. The garden beds on the outside of the turning circle were landscaped, though not in that overdone way of so many show homes. These gardens screamed – or I should say whispered – good taste.

The Harding house was worth a fortune; that was obvious immediately. There were bigger and more ostentatious houses on the north shore, but this was something special. The perfect family house. It was the sort of place I'd envisaged Peter, Sascha and me living in one day.

Back when I still had a family.

I pushed the thought away and sat in my car for a long minute, drinking in the beauty of the house, nervous at the thought of entering. This time I agreed wholeheartedly with Renee; the Harding house was too good for me. Too perfect for me to soil with my farts and my fat presence. With my old clothes and unwashed hair and greasy fried-chicken fingers.

Too perfect for my … *searching*.

I almost started the engine up again and drove straight home. And what if they'd renovated badly? Minimalist, like the last house? Or, even worse, decorated in the 1980s?

It was, however, the thought of what I might find inside that kept me from leaving – that made me desperate to enter.

A car door slammed and I twisted around in my seat, startled. A blue Lexus pulled up behind me, as shiny and modern as if driven straight from a car lot. In seconds, a tanned face filled my window. The face was classically handsome, clean shaven and oozing with an excessive confidence that marked him as a real estate agent. His thick dark hair was neat, with grey streaks at the temples. The grey gave him a distinguished air, in that annoying way that only seemed to work for men. And then the face grinned at me, displaying a few wrinkles in the corners of his eyes and the whitest and straightest teeth I'd ever seen. I desperately hoped the stench of my farts had dissipated.

'Hi there, I'm Roger Bailey. McQuilty Real Estate.' He paused, waiting. Before I had a chance to reply, a dense cloud of aftershave wafted into the car like a low-lying fog, as if catching up to him. *My God.* Any lingering odour would go undetected by this man – or by anyone within a ten-metre radius – unless they had the nose of a bloodhound. I held back a cough.

'Oh, um, hi Roger. Nice to meet you. I'm … Tammy.'
Shit. The real Tammy had better be running late.

'Well, hello there, Tammy. Great to meet you too. Renee told me you'd be coming. So you're the lady from London then? Back in Australia for good, I hear?'

'Ah, yes, that's right,' I said, trying not to squirm.

'We have several interested buyers coming along today, though it looks like you and I are the early birds,' Roger continued with a smile. 'If you'll wait a moment I'll check everything's ready and give you a wave when I'm done. And perhaps … can I ask you to move your car just a little bit further around the circle? Thank you so much, Tammy, I'll see you in a moment.'

Roger walked towards the house. I put him at about five or six years older than me, maybe fifty, but he was in great shape. Trim in his expensive suit. Striding off in ridiculously shiny black shoes. Was he the type to shine them himself? Maybe. Why had I never met Roger before? I'd heard his name mentioned by other agents, including Vivian, my boss, so it seemed odd I'd not attended an open house he'd run. Maybe he only sold homes like the Harding house. And homes like the Harding house weren't open for inspection to the general public, that is, plebs like me. Most of them were shown *by appointment only*.

Why not this one, then? The question intrigued me but I had no answer.

Roger bounded up the front steps and consulted a piece of paper before pressing buttons on a keypad near the front door. He stood back, staring at the door. It swung open before him as if unlocked by the power of his gaze. I had a tantalising glimpse of the graceful curve of a staircase; of gleaming parquetry floors.

No keys needed at the Harding house.

Roger crossed the threshold then spun to face me.

Shit, he asked me to move the car.

I moved along a few metres, as close to the outside of the turning circle as I could, then wound the window up, got out and locked it, shoving my keys into the front pocket of my jeans with the pebble I'd collected earlier. The bonnet was pleasantly warm under my arse as I waited and, breathing in deeply, I wondered if it was possible for the air to be both sweeter and clearer here than it was in the rest of the suburb.

With the Harding house, anything seemed possible.

Roger opened the door and waved me in with one hand. In the other he held a mobile to his ear, and he mouthed *sorry* with a polite smile/half-grimace before turning his back to me. I bolted over to the house and up the front steps, farting once more on the way. At the front door I untied the laces of my scruffy black Cons then slid them off. It hadn't seemed necessary to remove them at the last place, but they certainly didn't belong in the Harding house. I was pleased to note I'd worn socks that matched and were free from holes.

'But, Steph, you know I planned to take the girls to the aquarium tomorrow,' Roger was saying as I straightened up and walked inside. He used a tight, unhappy voice I wasn't meant to hear, but since he was all of three metres away and the house was silent and empty, of course I heard every word. I peered around, trying to give him privacy. 'But … Yes, I realise that,' he continued with a glance my way, though I ignored him now.

I was too busy marvelling, slack-jawed, at the sight before me. *The Harding house.*

From the sweeping staircase to the gorgeous furniture, it was totally, absolutely perfect. The entryway was the height of two floors, enhancing the sense of space. Warm light from the second storey window filled the area, but gently; there was nothing harsh about the Harding house. Nothing that jarred or unsettled. White walls made everything feel fresh. Under my socks, the intricate parquetry floors were elegant but not fussy. It felt like a Goldilocks house to me: just right.

I exhaled, the mess of the morning slipping away like a bad dream.

Then Roger spoke, pulling me reluctantly from my reverie. 'Yes. Yes, I understand things change but —' he said in that same strangled voice. 'Of course not. Can't you do it another time?

Yes. Fine, OK. Whatever.' Roger yanked the phone from his ear and spun back to me, annoyance writ large all over his face. But he was a professional. A moment later his white-toothed grin was back. 'Sorry, Tammy. That was my wife. We're just ... we're going through some ... having a few ...' He faltered, the mask slipping. 'We're in the process of separating. I was supposed to have my kids tonight.' He shrugged. 'Things change I guess, don't they? OK, then. So, welcome, Tammy!' His voice returned to the slightly obsequious but somehow still condescending tone used by most real estate agents. 'Can I get your number please?'

I gave him my doctor's phone number, which was the only one – other than my own – I could remember. No one else had yet arrived. Perfect. I knew the real Tammy was bound to be here soon, so I'd better make the most of the calm before the storm.

First the kitchen. With its de rigueur whiteness, it should have been disappointing – like the house that morning – but authentic touches of warm wood, stainless steel and bursts of colour made it work. A KitchenAid mixer in apple green sat on the white benchtop. The blond timber bar stools under the island bench appeared handmade. A toddler-sized fiddle-leaf fig in a yellow ceramic pot by the door looked so healthy I thought it must be fake, but one touch of a deep-green leaf confirmed that life very much flourished in the Harding house.

Next to the kitchen was a sunny conservatory with glass walls overlooking lush green lawns dotted with trees and surrounded by garden beds. You couldn't see any neighbouring homes. To an apartment-dweller like me that in itself was the epitome of luxury.

The gorgeousness continued, room after room.

A formal dining room that appeared well used; a living area with the most comfortable tartan lounge imaginable (yes, I sat on it); a home theatre with armchairs for eight; a marble bathroom that remained understated; then, to top it all off, a library – all dark wood panelling with walls of books like something out of a novel itself.

I circled the room, trailing my hands along the spines of the books, then reluctantly departed, making my way back to the kitchen. No biscuit smells here. The Harding house didn't need cheap smoke and mirrors. I walked over to the sink and kitchen window. Trees waved in the breeze. Perched cheerily on the windowsill was a cactus in a terracotta pot; a prickly pear, with flat, spiky pads arranged like a rabbit's face complete with lopsided ears.

I hadn't seen a prickly pear for years. Not since …

Then it hit me.

The cactus in the terracotta pot was the same as the one my husband had been carrying on the day we first met.

BEFORE

'Come on, Katie, it's just a housewarming party, for fuck's sake. Don't make me go on my own.'

And so Jenna guilted me into it. She was always trying to drag me out to meet people.

You need to be more sociable, Katie, she'd say, like I had some sort of problem.

Why it was important to be sociable all the time I didn't know. Nothing wrong with a bit of alone time, I'd always thought. And I wasn't much of a drinker; a couple of vodka cruisers would last throughout a *sociable* evening back then.

We were flatmates and teachers straight out of university – I taught art, Jenna English and history. At Green Hills High where we both worked, the girls wore undies-revealing skirts and swore more than the boys. The boys sported untucked shirts and spent all their money on, or stole, the latest $200 sneakers. I wasn't a particularly idealistic teacher, having gone back to uni to do my DipEd after a year of trying and failing to kick-start a photography career, but I turned up each day and tried to be better than mediocre. A tough ask at Green Hills High.

I examined Jenna's face, recognising her I-won't-take-no-for-an-answer pursed lips and set jaw. I sighed and nodded, giving up and already regretting it.

So on that warm summer evening we caught the train to Central, then walked to an apartment in Surry Hills, carrying plastic bags that clinked with each step. We heard the festivities from a block away, music thumping down the street from a four-storey building in a slowly gentrifying street. The hosts were colleagues of Jenna's brother, a journalist for some niche-market magazine, and they had a reputation for cool parties and big drinking. Jenna was stoked we'd been invited.

'Finally,' she squealed, grabbing my arm as we approached the building, making me totter on my unfamiliar heels. 'I need a fucking drink.'

I expected a bouncer or at least to be buzzed in, but we wandered through the open front entrance and up three flights of stairs. The front door to the apartment was held open with a brick. From inside came laughter and shouting voices laid over the bass and drums of some indie band I didn't know.

'Oh God,' I muttered.

Jenna looked at me sharply. 'Don't be like that, Katie. Just relax, have a couple of cruisers and enjoy yourself.'

I nodded and tried to smile. 'Yeah, no, it'll be fun.'

'Damn right it will be.'

Jenna set her bags on the floor and ran her fingers through her long red hair. Parted to one side, it hung in soft waves past her shoulders. Jenna's skin was pale and smooth and she wore a one-shouldered top to show off her collarbone, far sexier than my plain black singlet.

She smiled at me, picked up her bags and strode in, entering the party as she always did: first, and as the centre of attention. I hung back, biting at a fingernail. I heard her greeting partygoers over the music. 'How the fuck *are* you, Paul? Jase – it's been ages!' I thought about turning around but knew she'd be really pissed off if I did. Besides, the trip home would take hours and I didn't want to do it on my own. I ran my fingers through my unruly hair and followed her in, a fake smile on my face, trying to emulate her confidence.

The flat was enormous. Industrial chic, they'd call it, with a touch of the shabby too. Lots of exposed brick, wooden floors and high ceilings – but with op shop furniture that had seen better days punctuating the space at random intervals. It was cool though, so cool. I had no idea people just a few years older than us could afford something like this right in the city. How much money did journalists make? It was all open plan, except down one end, which I assumed had been partitioned off as bedrooms. Against the nearest wall a couple of trestle tables were littered with alcohol empties of every description. Half-drunk bottles of soft drink, bowls holding just a crisp or two and a melting tub of ice indicated the party had been going on for some time.

Groups of people were clumped together, beers and cigarettes in hand. I stood alone with my plastic bag for an age before marching over to the drinks table. I busied myself pulling cruisers out and setting them to bob in the sloshing ice. I kept one, twisted the cap off and sipped the lolly-sweet liquid. I glanced around for Jenna, but she'd disappeared. *Fuck.* I picked up a soggy salt and vinegar chip from a bowl and held it as I tried to decide what to do. An enormous black cockroach crawled out from behind the bowl and I let the chip fall to the table. The creature scurried off and I suppressed a shiver.

Perhaps there was more than a touch of the shabby to the place.

'Excuse me,' a voice said from behind me and I turned towards it with relief. A tall man with Slavic cheekbones and dirty blond hair was smiling at me like we were sharing a private joke. It was as if I'd conjured up my very own Prince

Charming. 'I need to put this cactus somewhere,' he continued. 'Any ideas? I fear for its safety tonight, despite the hardy nature of the plant itself. Any suggestions?'

I belatedly noticed he held a terracotta pot with a cactus in it. The cactus looked like something from a cartoon – several spiky oval pads randomly stacked on top of one another. A thick red ribbon was tied in a bow around the pot. 'Oh. What's that for?'

He gave a sardonic grin and my heart beat a little faster. 'It's a housewarming present for these jerks. Don't know why I bothered; they won't even notice it once it's on the roof garden.'

'There's a roof garden? Is that part of the apartment?'

'It's technically for all the residents, but, yeah, it's pretty much theirs. Want to have a look?'

'Sure.'

I followed the man through the crowd. He didn't speak to anyone but seemed comfortable here. A bald guy waved to him from the lounge and a thin woman with a hard face blew him a kiss then stared at me with an expression I couldn't decipher. I walked faster to keep up, enjoying the feeling of belonging. He looked just as good from behind, his legs long in dark jeans and shoulders broad in a white shirt. I spied Jenna in the kitchen as I passed, laughing with a group of men. My rescuer turned to make sure I was following, and smiled. My stomach fluttered. Boys at art school had never had that effect on me.

We wove between partygoers and through a glass door to another stairwell, this one outside. The muggy air smelled of the city – of petrol and pigeon shit and faintly of garbage – but it was welcome after the cigarette fog inside. Metal stairs spiralled up, making me dizzy just looking at them.

The man started up, his shoes clattering on the steps.

I followed, more tentatively. Each step was perforated by dozens of holes so I tiptoed, scared they might trap my stilettos. Calves burning, the railing cool under my sweaty hands, I focused on the stairs. When the rooftop arrived I wasn't ready, almost stumbling as the floor flattened out. A hand grasped my elbow, steadying me.

'Whoa there. We made it. You OK?'

The warmth of his grip made me blush. I glanced at his amused face, embarrassed, knowing I'd be beetroot-red. 'Uh-huh,' I managed.

He released my arm and I glanced around. There were taller buildings nearby, but the roof still provided a spectacular view of the city. The sun was low and lights were just becoming visible in surrounding high-rises. Underfoot was dirty cement and more cement fenced us in, graffitied with colourful tags and other spray-painted art: a wonky purple peace symbol, the Aboriginal flag and a three-eyed cartoon fish with a happier expression than you'd expect such a creature to have. Potted plants took up most of the space. Some were huge enough to be considered trees, other smaller pots huddled together in groups, mirroring the party inside. A rusty wrought-iron table with two non-matching chairs sat nearby.

The man put the cactus on the table with satisfaction. 'At least they'll notice it there when they come up here nursing hangovers tomorrow.'

'It's pretty,' I said, though I wasn't a big fan of cacti.

'Yeah, they're my favourites. Especially these prickly pears. They're so sculptural. And easy to look after too, of course.'

He smiled at me again and I was aware of how much quieter it was out here. The sound of city traffic seemed to come from far away. Music from below floated up, the thudding beat echoing the pounding of my heart.

'Incredible view,' I said, turning away to cover my uncertainty and walking over to lean on the concrete wall. 'Is that the harbour?' I wasn't too familiar with this part of the city, but was pretty sure I could see lights glinting off water between two skyscrapers.

'Yes.'

His whispered voice came from just above my head, giving me goose bumps on the back of my neck. I had to stop myself from turning around.

'You can see the tips of the Opera House sails if you look that way,' he said, his hand reaching past me to point them out.

We stared at the sails in silence for a moment, watching the city lights shining off the white tiles. I wasn't sure if the silence was comfortable or not.

'What's your name?'

The intensity in his voice made me swallow. I twisted around to look at him. Up close, his eyes were very blue, the planes of his face more pronounced. He would be magic to photograph.

'Katie.'

'Hi Katie, I'm Peter.'

'Hello,' I said instinctively in a timorous voice, immediately regretting it.

He grinned. 'How do you know Mick and Jason, Katie? If you don't mind me saying so, you don't seem to fit in here.'

I squirmed under his scrutiny and cleared my throat before answering. 'I'm here with my flatmate, Jenna. Her brother Taj is friends with them. We're both teachers.'

'Ah. Well, that makes sense. You don't seem all that … cityfied.'

I felt a bit defensive at that. 'I'm from Sydney. I've lived on the north shore all my life. Pymble.'

'Pymble, hey? Come on, that's deep suburbia. It's hardly the city, is it?'

'No, I suppose it isn't,' I smiled, conceding the point. 'Where are you from then, Peter?'

'Well, I grew up in a town outside Melbourne. Came here for work. I'm a sub-editor. That's how I know these cowboys.' He turned and rested his elbows on the concrete. 'They do the glory work, get the by-lines and talk about how they're going to win Walkleys. I fix all their crap.' He smiled at me. 'Do you know how many journalists don't know the difference between "*you're* going to the shops" and "this is *your* beer"? It's frightening. I hope you teach the kids better grammar at your school.'

'Oh, I'm an art teacher. I don't teach grammar. Thank God.'

He looked at me, still leaning on one elbow. 'And how old are you, Katie?'

'I'm twenty-four.'

'Ah. So young.'

I felt defensive again. 'How old are you then?'

'Me? I'm ancient. Thirty-one. Over the hill.'

I smiled.

'What are you smiling about?'

'Well, you don't seem that old to me.'

'That's good to hear,' he said, voice soft.

Something inside me grew warm and my breath shortened. 'Why?' I whispered.

'Because I am going to marry you one day, Katie,' he said, and kissed me.

SATURDAY, 5 JULY
AFTERNOON

'Nice to meet you, Roger.'

Those rounded vowels.

I froze; tiptoed to the door. Sticking my head out, I smelled Chanel No. 5. Tammy, sans kids.

Bugger. No time to waste.

I ducked around the corner and crept up the staircase. Fortunately, the Harding house was the sort of place where floorboards didn't creak. Now I was in bedroom territory. My favourite place to search. I turned right, passing a second marble bathroom bigger than my bedroom, aiming for the back of the house where I'd find the master bedroom. The thick pile carpet underfoot made walking springy, taking me back to the bounciness of a gym floor beneath the balls of my fifteen-year-old feet.

Yes.

The master bedroom.

A king-sized bed had been made up with navy blue sheets topped with an apple-green bedspread, a multicoloured throw draped artfully across its lower half. The colour combination was exactly right in that way you couldn't imagine until you saw it. It would probably be the Next Big Thing I'd read about in a few months' time.

The rest of the furniture was pale wood and sleek white surfaces. No TV. No family photos. An artwork opposite the bed depicted a huge painted portrait of a budgerigar's head. I recognised it as the work of a famous Australian artist, one I'd long admired. I stood, lost in thought, until the muffled tinkling of laughter from downstairs made me start.

I had to hurry.

Padding over to the nearest bedside table, I slid the top drawer open. The owners had followed the real estate agent's twin maxims – *declutter* and *remove family photos* – because a framed family snapshot rested on a neat pile of flimsy female underwear in shades of black, pink and cream. No beige granny-pants here.

I picked up the photo. My legs wobbled. I sat heavily onto the perfect bed, staring at it.

Three people.

Three people rugged up for what must have been a skiing holiday in beanies and scarves. All of them grinning at the camera.

One of them I knew. One of them I didn't.

And one of them was my dead son.

* * *

I sucked in a breath, heart pounding in my chest with such force I feared I might be having a heart attack.

Sascha.

My gaze raked the image of the boy. I faltered.

Sascha?

I lifted the photo closer and touched the dark hair with a fingertip, remembering its glorious softness; the cowlick at the back I could never tame with a hairbrush. But the glass was cold and I pulled my finger away. My joy and fear fled.

It wasn't Sascha.

This wasn't my boy.

Stupid, stupid Kate.

Of course it wasn't Sascha. Sascha had died when he was five. I sat up and rubbed my eyes. There was no way it could be Sascha.

I really might be losing my mind.

It's just the timing, that's all. You've got him on your mind, even more than usual. Because of the date. The anniversary.

That's all.

Steeling myself, I examined the photo again. Standing beside the boy was a man with a pleasant face, despite a weak chin and receding hairline. Kind dark eyes and a five o'clock shadow. I supposed him to be Brett Harding, the owner of the house. On the boy's other side was a woman. A stunner. Assuming she was the boy's mother and the man was his father, she was well out of her husband's league. Black hair, vivid blue eyes and red lipstick, this was a woman used to being admired. Used to being adored. Used to having every single man in every single room she entered wanting to fuck her. I wasn't just hypothesising.

I knew this woman.

Pip Reeves.

Philippa Reeves. Or Philippa Harding now, I supposed.

We'd been at art school together. A lifetime ago. Both students at the Sydney College of the Arts. I'd majored in photography, while Pip was a talented painter. I shook my head, remembering. Pip Reeves; the golden girl. She'd seemed older than the rest of us. Curvy, poised, rich, she was an inventive artist with a reputation for being a bit wild. All the guys panted after her; tried to chat her up at the pub after class. Pip

Reeves, private-school educated, effortlessly cool – even when partaking in late-night karaoke or ridiculous toga nights. Yes, I wanted to hate Pip Reeves, but annoyingly she'd always been lovely to me. And now here she was. In my dream home, in a photo with a boy who could have been mine.

The boy.

Pip and Brett's boy, I presumed. He looked to be a couple of years older than Sascha had been when he died. In this photo, the boy's grin was reserved. Maybe he was a little shy, like my child. I smiled, remembering how Sascha used to hold onto my shorts with his chubby hands and hide behind me, how I'd pull him from between my legs and tell him it was OK, Mum was here and no one would hurt him.

My smile slipped.

This boy was dark-haired too, with the same blue eyes as his mother. In truth, they were nothing like Sascha's dark eyes.

A woman's voice raised in query came from the hall and jerked me back to the present. I jumped to my feet and thrust the photo back in the drawer, which slid shut silently, as expensive things so often did. I stepped back like a guilty child and smoothed the bed cover flat with my fingers.

I left the master bedroom, head full of the people in the photograph, and almost ran straight into Tammy in the hallway. Her perfume was now only just discernible.

'I'm so sorry,' I said, brushing past her before she remembered me.

I speed-walked down the stairs, slowing near the bottom where the staircase curved towards the front door to reveal Roger chatting with a well-coiffed older couple wearing matching Ralph Lauren polo shirts. Pink for her, baby blue for him. The Polo Shirts brayed with laughter at something Roger said then peered up at me in surprise before Polo Man asked him when the auction would be held.

'August ninth,' Roger replied, quite abruptly, turning as though to speak to me.

To bail me up over the whole pretending-to-be-Tammy-incident, no doubt.

I gave him what I hoped was an *I'm sorry* smile, flew down the last few steps and out the door before Roger could grab me, jogging inelegantly to my car while digging my keys out of my pocket. The beep of the car unlocking sounded tinny and cheap. Alongside Roger's Lexus was a deep-green Range Rover and a silver Mercedes. My little Hyundai couldn't have looked more out of place, the other cars dwarfing it like private-school bullies in the playground.

Driving through leafy Wahroonga I calmed a bit. By the time I'd negotiated the Saturday afternoon traffic and found a parking spot across the road from my apartment block in Artarmon I felt almost normal.

It wasn't Sascha, I told myself firmly, *just a boy with similar features, similar colouring. And a woman I once knew.*

Someone had left the security door ajar again. The lift reeked of Indian food. When I emerged on the fourth floor I dug around in my bag (thinking of the snazzy keypad at the Harding house) and unlocked the door. A stale alcohol and pizza funk hit me. I crossed the dining-cum-living-area and slid the balcony door open, shivering at the cold. I hardly noticed the constant buzz of cars from the highway, less than a block away. Or so I told myself. I left the door open and returned to the kitchen. Two open pizza boxes, dirty cutlery, crockery and glassware covered most of the bench, along with crumbs and some half-eaten pizza crusts.

The lead-up to the anniversary was always messy.

Until a couple of months ago I'd felt things were picking up, mental-health-wise. I'd caught up with Michelle – an old school friend who'd moved to the central coast with her three gorgeous children and firefighter husband – after two years of putting it off. That might not sound like much, but, for me, it was progress. I'd never had lots of friends; after marrying Peter I'd really only kept up with Michelle. And Jenna, from my teaching days. Then, after the incident, I saw them less and less, which was partly my fault and partly because – unlike me – they now had children and weekend sport and camping trips to keep them busy.

So when Michelle contacted me yet again and suggested a catch-up I'd been tentative but finally agreed and we arranged a time. And it had been … *OK*. We'd eaten Italian and I'd even laughed at her playgroup stories without racing home early or laughing too manically. Dr Evans would have approved of my sociability. We'd even made promises to do it again sometime soon. Not only that, but until recently I'd gone to the gym a bit, cooked a stir-fry once in a while and had a few nights where I'd stuck to a single glass of wine.

And then July fifth crept closer.

I rinsed a dirty wine glass under the hot tap for a while then let it drain. In the pantry was half a loaf of bread, an open cereal box, a few packets of two-minute noodles and a shiny silver bladder, like some futuristic half-deflated balloon. I picked it up, the sloshing of the wine inside igniting a spark of happiness. I grabbed the still-wet glass and spurted red liquid into it, ignoring the tiny voice inside my head reminding me of my earlier vow.

Not today. I couldn't be expected to abstain today. Not after the Harding house.

Not on the anniversary.

I sipped, the familiar tannin-y-bitterness seeping through my body, my shoulders relaxing in a Pavlovian response to the wine that would not disgust me until I remembered it the next day. For now, it was warm perfection in a fingerprint-smeared glass.

Tomorrow.

I'll have a day off drinking tomorrow.

Cradling the wine like I would a precious newborn, I headed to the bedroom. Which wasn't far, since my flat was as poky as it was unremarkable. Built in the early 2000s by cheap-arse developers, the place was already fraying at the edges. It wasn't a great buy, I knew that now, but at the time I'd just wanted to get out of my parents' house. It was the first apartment I'd seen after I sold our inner-city place. Now, it was all thin paint, shabby carpets and chipped tiles. A large mirror – a housewarming gift from my mother that came with all sorts of unsaid connotations – *You were pretty once, Katie, you just need to make more of an* effort, *darling* – dominated the hallway. But I didn't waste a glance that way, I was too intent on my wine – sipping while walking took more concentration than you might think. In the bedroom, I set the glass down next to the shoebox sitting on top of my chest of drawers. I pulled the white stone from my jeans pocket, lifted the lid from the shoebox and carefully added the stone to the contents. The box was almost full. I'd have to put this one in the wardrobe with the others and start a new one soon. As I replaced the lid I squeezed my eyes shut tight, my temples suddenly throbbing.

Fuck.

The Harding house.

I hadn't picked up anything there. The thought made my scalp prickle. It had been years since I'd left a house without collecting a souvenir. And the Harding house of all places.

It was special, I'd known that immediately. So *right* in every way. And that was before I saw the picture. My heart thudded in my ears, protesting my stupidity. I *needed* a memento. I needed to have a part of that house. To *be* a part of that house; for it to be a part of me. Just for a little while.

The Harding house wasn't mine, of course I knew that.

But for a moment it almost – *almost* – could have been.

I picked up the wine, took a large gulp and headed back to the living room. This time I glimpsed my bloated, pale face in the mirror. Two things struck me: the red wine that had already soaked into the furrows of my dry lips to leave rusty streaks, and the agitation in my bloodshot eyes.

It was time to do something I'd never done before. A break with tradition, if you will.

I'd have to go back to the Harding house.

Soon.

BEFORE

The dress clung like a second skin. I grabbed the hem, which finished far too high up my thighs for my liking and yanked it lower.

'You look amazing, Katie. Hot.' Peter's grinning reflection appeared in the mirror and I spun around, tugging the stretchy scarlet fabric self-consciously as I motioned him to close the curtains a little more. I didn't want people in the other change rooms seeing me.

'I don't know about that. I can hardly breathe. You could see my undies if I bent over.'

He laughed. 'Go on, get it. You can wear it out to dinner tonight.'

So I bought the dress. To make him happy, mostly. I loved it when he was like this.

As we left the store, Peter held my arm and steered me through the shopping centre towards another fashionable boutique.

'Oh, let's call it quits for today,' I pleaded.

Peter wasn't your typical male. He adored shopping. I guess I wasn't your usual female because I hated it. We'd been here for hours already and both carried several bags of new clothes.

'Surely it's time for lunch?'

'You and your stomach,' he chided, good-naturedly. 'If you're going to wear your new dress you'd better stick to salad.'

I felt myself redden.

He noticed and smiled. 'Oh, come on, Katie. I was joking. You're gorgeous. Get hot chips if you like.'

I smiled back but wasn't convinced. I looked ahead just in time to avoid bumping into two tall girls coming our way. Peter wasn't so lucky, his arm bumping the handbag of one of them. She spun around. No older than eighteen, she had long dark hair and way too much makeup but was quite lovely beneath it all. She tossed her hair and pouted.

'I'm sorry,' Peter said, giving her a concerned look, and she simpered – actually simpered – at him.

'Well, OK then,' she giggled and flung a look my way, one that clearly said, *Who are you to be with this dreamboat?*

As the girls flounced off, peering back at regular intervals, Peter grimaced at me. 'That's what I like about you, Katie. You don't go around throwing yourself at guys.' He took my arm again. 'You're just as hot as those two, you know, and you don't even realise it. And when you wear that red dress tonight, you'll be far hotter than them.'

Then he whispered into my ear, 'And you know something even better? You're mine. You belong to me.'

SUNDAY, 6 JULY
MORNING

The squeal of truck brakes jolted me awake.

Even after almost ten years the sound set my heart racing and I pictured – with an extreme lack of logic – a semi-trailer hurtling through my fourth-floor window. As the shrieking faded I slowly calmed, the only sound now the more restful *swooshing* of car tyres on asphalt as they chased one another along the highway. It was still dark but the flat yellow glare of the streetlights was enough to see by. I shivered, then realised I was lying on top of the bedcovers. A threadbare white singlet stretched tight over my middle and below that only undies, my pale legs exposed and cut into neat slices by the light shining through the open venetian blinds.

I moaned and rolled over to check the time. Instead I fell off the bed, expelling the last of my breath with a muted *ooof* as I hit the floor. Lying on a rug that smelled of unwashed socks, I squeezed my eyes shut. My mouth was a used dishcloth laced with cabernet shiraz, while the hammering in my head competed with the thudding of my heart. I decided it was a good idea to stay on the floor until the pounding subsided. Actually the rug was quite comfortable. I didn't know why I hadn't slept down there before. Then I must have passed out because that's when I had the Dream.

The Dream.

Not really a dream; a nightmare.

I thought of it as a recurring nightmare, although no matter how many times I had the Dream it was never the same. Not exactly. That night, it began peacefully enough. I was in a luxurious bathtub straight out of *Pretty Woman*, limbs languid and floating on scented water. I held my breath and drifted impossibly down, down, until I lay on the bottom of the tub, staring up at the marble and mirrors so far away. Slowly my lungs tightened. I tried to swim upwards, to the light and the air, but I was trapped – the water was topped with glass. Panicking, I kicked and screamed and thrashed, beating my hands against the glass until they were bruised. Finally, the fight ebbed out of me and my arms fell. Warm soapy bathwater filled my mouth and bubbled out of my nose and gurgled its way into my lungs until I felt I would burst.

The Dream ended with a gasp as I lurched to a sitting position on my bedroom floor, rasping noisily as the sun poked its bright fingers into my eyeballs. I shut my eyes and leaned against the bed, chest heaving, trembling with cold and the remnants of terror.

Despite the water-logged desperation of moments before, my mouth was bone-dry. I used the bed to lever myself up and stumbled out to the kitchen, filling a glass from the tap and drinking it in one long gulp. I stood in the kitchen, as buggered as if I'd run a marathon.

Ten seconds later the water came straight back up. Holding it inside my mouth with a cupped hand and bulging cheeks, I staggered for the toilet. Watery vomit sprayed the bowl, practically clear. I wiped my mouth and sat on the toilet seat, attempting to remember the previous evening.

I was pretty sure I'd only drunk red wine. I'd finished the last of the bladder before falling asleep. Red wine made me sleepy, which was mostly a good thing since it stopped me drinking more. I ran through my hangover checklist to determine how the morning would proceed.

One. I didn't vomit in the night, but couldn't keep water down this morning. *Good and bad.*

Two. I had a headache. *Bad.*

Three. The headache was average on the hangover register. *Could be worse.*

Four. Bacon, yay or nay? Yay. *Good.*

Result: not ideal, but better than the previous day.

My comprehensive knowledge of and ability to categorise my hangovers should have been shameful. But I had long ago done away with shame. For fuck's sake, I was sitting on an ice-cold toilet wearing an inside-out Bonds singlet with my stomach splayed out in a roll over the waistband of my undies. My opinion of myself could not have been lower.

Or so I thought at the time.

My phone buzzed nearby, vibrating on a hard surface.

Fuck.

It was on the toilet floor, bouncing near my left foot. How the fuck had it ended up there? I bent over to it, checked the screen.

Double-fuck.

My mother.

I considered letting her leave a message, but she'd keep calling all day until she got me. Might as well get it over with.

I tapped the screen.

'Hi Mum.' My whispery voice was gravelly and raw.

'Kate, darling, it's your mother.'

'Hi Mum,' I repeated, hanging my head between my knees and picking at a toenail.

'Kate, I'm coming over. I'll bring morning tea. Don't make anything, I'll buy a scroll at the bakery on the way. See you about ten.'

I held in a groan. 'What time is it now?'

'It is ... it's 8.47.' She paused. 'I'll get my bag and head off now. See you shortly.'

'OK, see you soon. Bye Mum.'

I allowed myself a moment to mope, sighing at the injustice of life and wondering why my mother continued to persist with the charade I'd whip something up for morning tea. I rarely made toast, let alone a tea cake.

I used the loo – might as well since I was already there – then began to tidy up. Though not without a great deal of swearing. I swore at my sore head when I stood up, swore at my pale-scarecrow reflection, and really let fly at the state of the kitchen. I scoffed two dodgy-looking Panadols found in the back of the bathroom cabinet (the foil was broken on the blister pack but they were alright, weren't they? Surely Panadol didn't go off?) and set to work. Pizza boxes, Chinese takeaway containers and empty Coke bottles to the garbage chute. Glasses and a week's worth of cutlery and crockery into the dishwasher. I opened the sliding glass door to my balcony – essential to remove the foul stench of body odour and fast food from my flat. The cold that whipped through was bracing but welcome.

Once the apartment was borderline-clean I showered and dressed. Jeans and a shirt. The shirt needed ironing, but so did everything I owned. I gathered piles of clothes from the bedroom floor and threw them into the washing machine, shutting the door on my unmade bed. I'd just started on the living room when the intercom buzzed.

I scrabbled for my phone.

9.42 am.

Typical bloody Mum.

* * *

'Katie – sorry – Kate!' Mum's ringing voice came from the hallway as she pushed the door open. 'Put this in the fridge, please,' she said, thrusting a recyclable bag my way and placing another two on the kitchen bench, before turning to me. After a long moment in which she took in my pallor, red eyes and wet hair, she went back to unpacking. 'So, how are you, darling?' she asked, speaking loudly and slowly, as if I were a toddler. Or a foreigner. Before I could answer, she continued. 'I bought milk, since last time I was here you didn't have any for tea. And some oranges. You sounded a bit throaty on the phone and I thought you might be coming down with something. Vitamin C is the best thing for that.' She pulled out groceries – teabags, sugar, something from the bakery in a brown paper bag – with what seemed to me excessive vigour, and spoke without turning to me, though I did catch her glance around the living room and the sniff that went with it.

I put the milk in the fridge and left the oranges on the benchtop.

'Oh, and teabags and whatnot. Just in case. And a bunch of flowers. Nothing flash. Just from the supermarket, but I thought they might brighten up the place. They'll be good in that lovely vase I got you for Christmas last year – is it still around here somewhere?'

Mum pulled out a limp bunch of tulips shrouded in clear plastic. A prominent 'Reduced' sticker told me why she'd bought them. I shuffled around behind her and found the glass vase on its side in the bottom of a cupboard, behind the juicer and the slow cooker and the food dehydrator. All presents from my parents, none used. I tipped the vase upside down over the sink and blew in it. Not too dusty, considering.

'Here,' I said, setting it on the benchtop.

Mum snatched it up and bustled past me to the sink carrying the flowers. Just a whiff of the fetid lushness of her familiar gardenia scent was enough to take me back to my childhood. I was suddenly twelve years old. My guts twisted at the memory of that girl. Determined to be a world-renowned photographer, to live in a loft in New York – to have it all, just like *Cosmo* magazine told me I could.

I burped red wine and smiled sourly.

Sure. Look at how far I've come. I should be proud.

Mum fussed with the tulips, trying to stand them upright. 'Oh well,' she said, shrugging, before setting the vase on the dining table. 'They'll still brighten the place up a bit.'

She turned back to the kettle and checked inside suspiciously before filling it with water and opening the packets of tea and sugar. I grew tired just watching her and sat down on a stool, a visitor in my own home.

As my mother moved purposefully around the kitchen I reflected that she never seemed to change. She was as robustly healthy as ever. A little heavier round the middle these past few years, maybe, but strong and tanned from twice-weekly golf, her short dark hair neatly styled with no visible greys, thanks to monthly visits to Lisa, her hairdresser. She wore stylish rectangular yellow reading glasses, navy pants and a blue button-up shirt. Her eyes were the same clear blue as her top. Deliberate, of course. Mum had always been proud of her vivid blue eyes.

Disapproval of me, my house and my life oozed from every pore.

Without asking she opened and shut cupboards, found mugs, gave them a quick rinse under the hot tap and added teabags. Half a teaspoon of sugar was measured into each.

'Three sugars for me, Mum, please.'

Her brow furrowed, but she did it.

As the tea brewed, Mum ripped open the paper bag and put a large apple and custard scroll on a questionably clean bread board, cutting it into pieces and setting a few of them – portion controlled as always – onto a small plate. The rest she covered in cling wrap and put in the freezer 'for unexpected visitors', shuffling aside ice, a three-quarters empty vodka bottle and frozen pizzas without a word.

Once we were seated on the lounge, things got worse.

'I saw these scrolls at the bakery this morning and remembered they used to be your favourite. Then while the man was ringing it up, I suddenly realised – that wasn't you, was it? They were your sister's favourites. Leah's. Not yours.' She shrugged. 'But you're not fussy about pastries, are you? You like breads. Carbs. You'll eat anything. Even back when you were a teenager, doing all that gymnastics and running, you liked your food. It was OK then, of course, because you were so active. You were a skinny thing then. You had a darling figure. You'd get around in such tiny denim shorts.'

She smiled dreamily, thinking about the young Katie. Pretty, quiet Katie. She preferred that Katie to the current one. Fat, boozing Kate.

Setting my cup on the coffee table, I lay back against the couch. Mum finally met my bloodshot eyes with her clear ones. Holding her gaze, I took the largest piece of scroll and put it into my mouth all at once. It was soft, doughy, and so sweet I almost gagged. I didn't much like sweet things, other than chocolate, and had never liked pastries. I chewed slowly.

Mum looked away. 'So,' she said, the words brisk, 'your father is playing golf again today. That's the third time this week. Not that I can talk, I played on Monday and Wednesday.' She paused before continuing more tentatively. 'How have you been, Kate?'

Before I could answer she turned back to look at me, half-frowning, then spoke in a rush. 'You know, darling, if you lost a bit of weight you'd really be quite pretty. It's not too late. You're only forty-four. I'm sure you could still meet a nice man.'

Not this again.

'Mum, we've been over this.'

'I know, Kate, but it needs to be said again. Obviously,' she added. Then she leaned in conspiratorially. 'I suspect I shouldn't say anything, but I had coffee with Vivian last week.'

Great. Talking about me with my boss again.

'Vivian said that with a bit more drive she'd consider trying you out as a real estate agent yourself, Kate.' Mum raised her eyebrows. 'She said you were too smart to be writing about houses and making those little brochures and advertisements forever. She said that if you tried harder to be nice to people – you need to be a people-person in sales, don't you? – and turned up on time every day, they'd help you get your realtor's licence. You'd even have a secretary of your own. Well, I think she said a group secretary. Or receptionist. But still. How about that?' she finished triumphantly, as though she was personally responsible. 'Kate? Wouldn't you like to be a real estate agent?

You inspect enough houses already. I thought it would be right up your alley.'.

Her voice was sharp with exasperation.

Real estate agent. Seriously?

Fuck, as if I'd go over to the dark side. How low did she think I'd sink?

'I don't mind my job.'

Her lips pursed and shoulders stiffened. 'Well, I'm sure you haven't forgotten your father and I got you that job. It would make us proud to see you get a promotion.'

'I'm sure it would, Mum,' I said, my voice flat.

Mum's mouth tightened even further. Little lines furrowed her top lip in a way I knew she would hate if she could see them. She sipped her tea, making a visible effort to relax her shoulders. When she spoke next it was as if she was trying to reason with a small child, her voice softer. 'Kate. I know what day it was yesterday.'

I froze. I had no desire to talk about this with my mother. I knew how the conversation would end.

'Last time you came round for dinner, when was that? Three months ago? Your father and I thought you seemed a bit ... better. But now ... Well, I realise this time of year is always hard for you. I do know that. *But*. It's been ten years, Kate. Your father and I think it's time you got over it.'

Got over it.

She cleared her throat. 'You remember my friend Margaret? Marge? Your father and I went to India with her and her husband, David, a few years back? Not the best holiday; we went in the wet season and it was so humid. Plus, well, all the beggars, you know? Anyway, Marge married David after her first husband died. He had cancer – lung cancer, I think. She met David and married him two years later and she's never been happier. And Marge told me she had five miscarriages in her first marriage, but she picked herself up and ended up with two lovely girls. They both live overseas now. Anyway, if Marge could cope after those separate, horrible incidents ... after something like that ... well, you know what I mean, don't you, Kate? It's been long enough.'

I had heard Marge's story before. Not told with such a clear get-over-yourself message though. Mum must be at her wits' end, as she liked to say.

'I know how long it's been, Mum,' I said, my voice tight.

'Yes, well. All I'm saying, Kate, is that there are so many people out there worse off than you. My friend Patty – her son is a meth addict. He steals from her! Now, that's hard. But you ... you have a home, a job, and your father and me and Leah, well, we're all here for you.'

I grunted.

'Kate. There's something else.'

'Yes?'

'I don't suppose you've seen Leah lately?'

I shook my head. To say I didn't see my younger sister very often was an understatement.

'I didn't think so. Leah has some news and I thought it might be better coming from me.'

Since Leah and I hadn't spoken for months I didn't think I was likely to hear any news from her any time soon, but, whatever. 'Sure, what is it now?'

'Your sister is pregnant.'

BEFORE

'You'll have my baby, one day, mark my words, Katie.'

Soda water sprayed from my mouth, splattering the linen tablecloth as I coughed, half-choking in surprise. I dabbed at my lips with the thick napkin, mortified by my culinary faux pas. And at Bennelong no less, the most expensive restaurant I'd ever been to.

Peter grinned and tut-tutted. 'Careful, Katie, this is a fancy place.'

I glanced from side to side, taking in the harbour views and the hushed diners around us, then grinned back at him as I put the napkin down. 'That was your fault. You can't spring something like that on a girl when we've only been together three months.'

He ran a hand through his hair and I admired his easy manner. Nothing fazed Peter. I looked around again, catching the lunching sixty-something socialites at the next table gawking at him like schoolgirls.

Bad luck, ladies, he's mine.

We'd been an item since the party. Peter had pursued me in a way I found incredibly exciting: flowers, meals out, texts that made me blush. Jenna complained she never saw me any more, but I think she was jealous someone as sexy as Peter fancied me.

Me.

Not her.

'I'm deadly serious, my love. We're going to have it all, Katie. Marriage, babies, lifestyle. The lot. You'll see.'

I believed him. Peter was the sort of man who got what he wanted.

I just couldn't believe he wanted me.

We'd been at the state art gallery all morning. I'd taken him to see my favourite photographers. My tastes weren't extreme – I particularly loved the black and white photos of Max Dupain and David Moore. Hard to dislike, I thought, so I'd been surprised when Peter said he wasn't keen on photography. It turned out he was a fan of dark and dramatic paintings by the Old Masters. Even the Impressionists were too modern – too light-hearted – for Peter. I'd jokingly poo-pooed him as an old man, but was secretly impressed by his steadfast views. I liked that he didn't pander to my tastes.

Afterwards, we'd strolled through the Botanic Gardens down to the Opera House where, unbeknown to me, Peter had booked a table at the ritziest place in town – right underneath the gleaming white sails. He ignored my pleas of being under-dressed as the waiter led us to a table overlooking a glittering Sydney Harbour on the most beautiful of summer days.

Now he reached across and took my hand in his. 'I can't wait to see you with an enormous belly,' he said, raising his eyebrows in the way that made my heart beat faster. 'You'll be the sexiest pregnant woman ever. And our children, well, they'll take after you, of course. They'll be beautiful, calm, kind.'

That's how he saw me?

I was flattered. I thought myself horribly shy, often flustered and never beautiful.

'They may, however, have a problem with spitting water all over the table in fancy restaurants.'

I slapped his hand lightly and gave a mock grimace. Peter's grin disappeared, replaced with a piercing stare. That stare of his made my stomach flutter in a way that was pleasurable, but sometimes a little uncomfortable too.

I wasn't used to such ... *intensity*.

'Katie Webb, my spluttering water-spitter, my love – will you marry me?'

I stared into the eyes of this gorgeous man. I couldn't believe my luck.

He was right, our lives were going to be perfect.

'Yes, of course, Peter. Of course I'll marry you.'

SUNDAY, 6 JULY
MORNING

I blinked, feeling my chest tighten. My mother watched me, sympathy in her eyes.

'That … that's great news. I didn't know they'd been trying,' I said, forcing out the words.

'No, well, I don't think they were really. She's only been with Ellis for a few months. A bit early, if you ask me. But there you go.'

'Well, that's great news,' I repeated.

We sat in silence for half a dozen heartbeats.

'Mum, I actually don't feel too well. I might go back to bed – try and get another couple of hours' sleep. Thanks for visiting, and for the morning tea and the flowers.' I leaped up, almost stumbling.

'Yes, of course,' Mum said, bustling to her feet. 'Bed is the best thing. Hopefully you'll be better for work tomorrow.'

'I'm sure it will pass. Probably the chicken stir-fry I cooked last night. Never trust deli chicken breasts on sale, right?' I tried a laugh, avoiding Mum's gaze.

'Look, Katie, I didn't want to tell you about Leah, what with the anniversary, but it's bound to be in the social pages soon. I couldn't have you finding out like that.' She sounded worried.

I swallowed and made an effort to keep my voice even. 'It's fine, Mum. I'm very happy for Leah. Give her – and Ellis – my congratulations.'

Before she could answer, I opened the front door.

Mum took the hint and put her half-finished mug of tea on the kitchen bench. 'Get some rest, darling,' she said once outside, concern in her voice. 'And come for dinner soon. I'll do a roast with extra potatoes for you.'

'Thanks Mum,' I said and shut the door before she saw the tears pricking my eyes.

From Mum, that was an apology.

I leaned against the door and on hearing the lift doors close I let the tears fall. Ugly, violent tears. To match my ugly, violent thoughts. I heaved myself upright and strode to the freezer for the vodka bottle. This was definitely a situation that called for vodka. The icy chill on my palm was momentarily satisfying, until the bottle's heft reminded me it was all but empty. I skolled through tears that became a hacking cough as heat ignited my throat.

Fuck.

Pregnant. My little sister. Well, not so little any more. Just over four years younger than me, so she was thirty-nine. Wow, she'd be forty in a couple of months.

Getting on a bit to be a mother, aren't you, Leah?

I drank again. And again. I tossed the bottle into the sink, a protest at both my mean-spiritedness and Leah's fecundity. The clatter was so loud I thought it had shattered. A second's relief when I realised it hadn't was immediately followed by rage.

I should *break the fucker. Smash it.*

No. No point in that. What I needed was more vodka. Vodka to celebrate my little sister's pregnancy.

Time to hit the bottle shop.

* * *

The need for alcohol – always my strongest incentive for, well, anything really – meant I was out the door in minutes.

The car was pleasantly warm, thanks to the sunshine.

Which bottle shop today, I pondered, tapping the steering wheel.

There were two in the main street of Artarmon, but I liked to mix up my patronage to lessen the pitying and/or downright rude looks from the mostly young male staff. I tried to keep the local bottle shops for emergencies, which came in one of two forms: either after work on my way home, knowing I'd run out of wine, or late at night and I'd drunk everything in the house. Today I could afford to go further afield.

I joined the Pacific Highway, heading north. Traffic was light. A great day for a drive, actually. Nice to get out of the house.

You're alone, Kate, no need to justify your sad little trip to buy grog.

Perhaps I should take another look at the Harding house? Make sure it was really as good as it seemed yesterday. I could get vodka up that way too.

Yep, I'd go to Wahroonga.

My willpower lasted almost twenty minutes, till Pymble. But, I reasoned, as I crossed the railway line and detoured down the main drag, I hadn't been to the bottle shop there in months.

This was my old stomping ground. We'd lived two blocks from here when I was a child. Ten lifetimes ago, it seemed. Despite that, I still half-expected to see people I once knew – and sometimes I did. Acquaintances of Mum and Dad's mostly or, worse, old school friends.

Luckily I didn't recognise anyone today while holding my brown-paper-bag-encased bottle like a bona fide alcoholic, all hunch-shouldered and trench-coated and twitchy and single-minded – which should have worried me more than it did. Instead, I felt quite proud of myself, as I'd only bought a 375 ml bottle. A victory, surely. If I was a real alcoholic I'd have bought the 700 ml.

I climbed back into my Hyundai and sipped the tepid liquid from the bottle, wincing at the harshness, waiting for the heat that started in my throat to flow through me, right to my fingertips and toes. When it did I closed my eyes and sank back into the seat.

Here's to you, Leah, to you and your rich husband and your unborn ba—.

I couldn't finish the toast. Fat tears dripped onto my boobs. I let the tears come for a full minute before wiping my face with the back of my hand, then starting the engine and making my way back out onto the highway.

I didn't drink again until I parked across the road from the Harding house.

Another win, Kate.

At that point I wasn't sure if I meant it or if I was being sarcastic.

The front gate was open and there was no one on the street. Homes in this area sat well back and I guessed the icy wind was keeping passers-by to a minimum. There was still no For Sale sign.

A mottled, rust-coloured plane-tree leaf floated down to land on the driveway near the open gate, somehow unaffected by the buffeting wind. I tapped the bottle with a finger thoughtfully. The gate was wide open.

Virtually a written invitation.

I had two more sips for courage, hid the bottle under the seat and climbed out of the car. The crisp winter air smelled appealingly of open fires. I lingered near the entrance and tried to appear nonchalant.

The paved driveway was visible for a dozen metres or so then curved and disappeared into foliage. A fluting bird call came from inside the property, as if coaxing me in. I strolled to the other side of the driveway. Now I could see the corner of the house. Could they be out? I needed to go in for a closer look. If they found me I'd say I was a Jehovah's Witness or something. My heart thudded.

I started down the driveway, trying to act as if I wasn't a crazy, drunken trespasser. By halfway, the turning circle was visible. I froze. A silver Mercedes was parked there, the driver's door open.

Oh God. They're home.

I couldn't move my feet. Then, from inside, a guffaw of muffled laughter.

Male laughter.

My legs moved before I had a conscious thought – lumbering towards the turning circle, not away from it.

Good one, Kate. Not exactly a great hiding spot.

Breathing heavily, I ducked into a crouch on the far side of the turning circle centrepiece. Through concentric circles of white roses and camellias, I could see the open front door. A figure moved inside.

Oh shit. What now?

Should I risk running back down the driveway to my car?

It seemed an impossible distance to the gate. I pictured the reassuring yellow of my Hyundai as my breath echoed loud in my ears.

A rumbling sound came from my left. Without thinking I pushed through a gap in the hedge and fell into the ring of white roses. I almost yelped as thorns from the nearest rose bush stabbed at my forehead. Automatically I reached out with my hands and sharp barbs speared the flesh of my palm. I fell backwards, managing to flop onto the dirt and release the rose branch. The rumbling grew louder. I kept my head down and held my breath, afraid to move, sandwiched by the camellia hedge. The noise came parallel, then continued past and I risked a glance through the foliage.

A woman walked down the centre of the driveway, dragging two wheelie bins, one in each hand, heading for the street.

Bin night.

I nearly laughed with relief. How banal.

The rumbling stopped. The woman spun and walked back towards me, quickly now without the heavy bins. I lay as still as possible, relieved my jacket was beige and I hadn't worn anything brightly coloured.

I saw the woman clearly through a narrow gap in the camellias. My breath caught in my throat.

Pip Reeves, no, Pip *Harding* now.

She looked incredible.

Dammit.

If anything, Pip was more beautiful than ever. Her wavy black hair was shorter than it had been at art school, shoulder length now, but as thick and bouncy as it had been back then. I remembered her sitting on a bar stool in the pub near campus, tucking her hair behind her ear, laughing throatily, her every move scrutinised by a scrum of first-years with their tongues hanging out. She was probably a few kilos heavier now; mind you, I couldn't even rejoice in that fact – it suited her. Wide mouth and full lips; yep, they were the same, still with her trademark red lipstick. No bulging tummy for Pip – she was narrow in the waist, ample cleavage visible beneath her white button-up shirt. Her jeans were tight enough to suggest she worked out regularly. Pip Reeves had evolved into Pip Harding, the epitome of a soccer mum, just conservative enough for straight-laced Wahroonga and no doubt envied by every woman in the suburb over forty.

My eyes followed Pip as she strode around the far side of the house and out of sight. I risked shuffling around in the dirt, wincing when I leaned on my injured hand to sit up, and worked up the courage to leave my hidey-hole.

Then it was too late.

Male voices came from the house before a clearly distinguishable 'Mum? Where are you? We're going.'

Two men appeared at the front door. Both wore jeans with football jerseys and maroon and white scarves. Off to a game, I supposed, being a Sunday.

The older one, in his late forties, was the man from the photo: Brett Harding. He now sported a neat beard flecked with grey. His face looked older and more jowly than it had in the photo. Black bags like bruises under his eyes gave him a sad air.

He paused at the top of the sandstone steps and idly glanced around. My heart stopped. I was sure he saw me.

'Forgot the beanies,' he said, heading back inside as the other man, no – a boy – emerged fully from the dim interior.

A boy, yes, still a boy.

But a boy who was almost a man.

Their child. The one from the photo. The one who looked so much like my Sascha.

The boy had grown up in the years since the photo was taken. No longer a child of seven or eight, he was now a teenager.

Fifteen? Sixteen? He took after his mother, mostly. Dark wavy hair, fashionably messy. A face beginning to sharpen from the softness of youth; he would become a very handsome man in the next few years. He was taller than both his parents, with a swimmer's wide shoulders and narrow waist. I knew from the photo I'd seen the day before that his eyes were blue like his mother's, but their shape was inherited from his dad. They had the same gentle look about them, with thick lashes and neat dark eyebrows. He'd be what my mother called a *heartbreaker* one day, if he wasn't already.

'Kingsley,' a woman's voice called out from inside the house. *Kingsley.*

Kingsley, not Sascha.

I bit my lip.

Never Sascha.

BEFORE

'Sascha.'

Peter watched me expectantly.

'Yeah, that's a good name,' I said, trying hard to load my voice with enthusiasm.

'You hate it,' Peter said flatly, his jaw tightening.

'No, I don't hate it. I like it. I'd just had some different names in mind. That's all.'

Peter turned to unlock the door. We stood on the rubbish-strewn footpath of Oxford Street in inner Sydney. A homeless man watched from a nearby doorway, his matted beard studded with crumbs. I tried not to wrinkle my nose at the smell of him. The door in front of us was nondescript. On one side was a sex shop, on the other a dirty neon sign read 'Mirage Kebabs'. It was nine on a Tuesday morning and both shops were closed.

'What are we doing here, Peter?'

Peter spun around to face me again, the door now open. I could see a small, modern space and a steep set of timber stairs.

'I've got something to show you,' he said, and smiled at me almost slyly.

He motioned me in, locking the door behind him. I followed Peter up the stairs, puffing and holding my rounded stomach. I'd entered the sixth month of pregnancy and was starting to feel it. Cankles, heartburn, back pain. You name it, I had it. Nothing major, thankfully, but it seemed all annoying pregnancy side effects had mobilised to attack and torment me over the past couple of weeks.

It had taken two long years and three early miscarriages for me to get pregnant. I'd started to think it would never happen. We'd done all the tests; they'd found nothing. So when I saw those two blue lines for the fourth time I'd felt all the emotions.

Joy. Relief.

Fear.

In the meantime, our lives had continued. Not long after we met, I'd snagged a position in a school in the inner west, where the demographic was wealthier than at Green Hills High and the commute not so trying. After the wedding we'd moved in together, renting a cute cottage midway between my school and Peter's job in the city. Peter had been working on a novel for a long time and put everything he had into it – writing early in the morning then late into the evening. When it was published, I'd been so proud of him but never expected it to take off like it did. The novel – a noir thriller set in inner Melbourne – hit a collective nerve around the country, becoming a bestseller, sales growing exponentially via word of mouth. Three months ago he'd given up his day job and convinced me to do the same, telling me I could focus on my photography again while I was pregnant. So now we spent all our time together, which, if I was honest, wasn't as fabulous as I had hoped.

Not with his writer's block.

Peter's publishers were waiting on his follow-up, but he'd been struck by a crippling case of writer's block. I'd thought being at home full time might kick-start his creativity, but it hadn't happened. Not-writing made my husband grumpy and it appeared misery really did like company. I had pulled out my camera, venturing to locations that fed my creativity – the bush, remote beaches – but Peter wanted me to stay close, to look after my health, petrified of more miscarriages, treating me with kid gloves. It was a surprise he hadn't tried to carry me up these stairs.

At the top he halted. 'Welcome, darling Katie, to our new home.'

I reached the stair-summit and stood breathing noisily through my mouth, then realised what he'd said. 'New home?'

'Yes, it has everything we need,' he said, beaming with excitement. He seemed to have forgotten our argument. 'Three bedrooms. One for us, one for Sascha and one I can use as an office. We'll put a spare bed in there for your parents when they visit; I'm sure we'll want them to babysit sometimes. Look at it! All the mod cons. Just renovated. Isn't it perfect?'

I blinked. Still fuzzy-headed. 'An apartment, Peter? On *Oxford Street*? I thought we'd decided we needed a house. A garden.'

The words were out of my mouth before I could think them through. I could see by his clenched jaw this wasn't the reaction Peter had hoped for.

'There *are* parks around here, Katie. And so much culture. Right on our doorstep. We'll be able to take him to the theatre, the Opera House. Shit, the art gallery is just down the road. You'll love it.'

'This isn't what we talked about, Peter,' I said gently, choosing my words with care. 'Have you already signed the contract?'

His face darkened. 'Yes. It is my money, Katie. Rosemarie urged me to buy something with the royalties. She saw this place in the paper and brought me along for a look last week.'

I bet she did.

Peter's agent had never liked me. And when his book hit the bestseller lists she had become his bosom buddy.

In the kitchen, he gestured to the island bench. 'We can eat our meals here. We'll get a highchair for the baby and we can sit together, like a family. You'll be so happy, Katie.'

So much for my dream.

The house in the suburbs. The front porch. A big back yard with a trampoline for our child; our children. This place didn't even seem to have any windows. Not that I was keen to look out at the homeless man and the syringes on the pavement. Or at the stream of buses passing at all hours; the punters queueing for nightclubs.

I tried for a smile, my throat tight.

Peter moved closer. He sighed then spoke. 'Sascha — Alexander — was my grandfather's name. He died in a concentration camp in World War Two. I wanted to honour him.'

I melted. 'Oh, Peter. Why didn't you tell me?'

He shrugged, not speaking, still put out.

'Sascha is the perfect name,' I said. 'Our son will be perfect.' I blinked away tears. 'And so will this apartment.'

SUNDAY, 6 JULY
AFTERNOON

Kingsley turned back to the front door and the day grew a little gloomier. A little colder.

I shivered.

Pip emerged wearing an indulgent smile, arms wide, silently demanding a hug. Her son stepped forward into her embrace.

My heart sat small and shrivelled in my chest as I watched from my seat in the dirt.

They parted as Brett reappeared, this time wearing a beanie that matched his scarf. He held an identical one for his son. 'We'd better go if we want to catch reserve grade.'

Kingsley took the beanie, facing both parents so the three of them stood in a triangle. One side of his collar stuck up and I fought an urge to get up and smooth it into place. Why didn't Pip reach out and fix it?

Brett smiled at his wife. 'You're sure you don't want to come?'

Pip laughed again and I was instantly twenty-five years younger, a skinny geeky girl waiting outside the sculpture studio for class to begin. Before Peter. Before Sascha.

'You know how much I love footy, darling,' she said, sticking out her tongue. 'I'd prefer to stay home and clean. And you know how much I love cleaning!'

'Oh, come on, Mum,' Kingsley protested. 'You cheered louder than anyone last time you came. Half the crowd was watching you not the game.' Such a teenager, despite a voice that was already a man's. Charismatic and confident. I bet he was a school prefect.

I wondered if Sascha would have been a leader. He'd been a quiet little boy but I believed he'd have come out of his shell eventually. I smiled, imagining Sascha and Kingsley as friends. If things had been different maybe our two families would have headed off to watch the football together. Then I remembered Peter's ambivalence about sports. And my own. Maybe not.

'That was a great day – we beat the Roosters by more than twenty, didn't we?' Pip victory-punched the air. 'I need to stay home, though, sorry. Roger's coming over to get our advertising signed off. We have to get it sorted today to make the paper's deadline in the morning.'

Both adults glanced at Kingsley, but he didn't speak.

'It's better I stay and do it,' Pip continued. 'You guys enjoy the football. Go the Sea Eagles!'

Brett shook his head and rolled his eyes at Kingsley before responding. 'Do you want us to get takeaway on the way home?'

'No, you may as well make a night of it. I'll have leftovers. Go and get pasta or something. I know you've both been missing carbs since I went all paleo on you.'

'Italian sounds good, Dad,' Kingsley said with obvious interest.

'OK, if you're sure?' Brett said, frowning a little at Pip.
She nodded.

Brett took his eyes off his wife almost reluctantly. 'Boys' night out then, hey, Kings?'

'Sounds like a plan.'

They looked at one another.

'Well, I'd better get started,' Pip said, interrupting the slight pause. 'Roger's due in ten minutes.'

Brett and Kingsley climbed into the Mercedes, and Pip closed the front door behind her. I flattened myself among the rose bushes, but they drove around the turning circle without noticing me as Roger's blue Lexus came into sight. Brett's car slowed to an idle and he waved Roger forward. Roger lifted a hand in greeting, all teeth with his insincere real estate agent's grin.

Shit.

I'd be buggered if they all got out to chat.

The Lexus pulled up where the Mercedes had been parked and the Mercedes rolled on. I sighed with relief.

Roger watched them leave then took the steps to the house two at a time. I craned my neck to see him better. He wore semi-professional clothes — dark jeans and a navy-blue suit jacket, with leather shoes. He straightened his jacket and lifted a fist to knock just as the door swung open. Pip Harding faced him, one hand on her hip, freshly painted red lips glistening. She said something, her words too soft for me to hear. I leaned forward, two hands in the dirt now, bleeding forgotten.

Pip lifted a hand to the nape of Roger's neck and pulled his head to hers. They kissed, bodies melding together as Pip stepped backwards, drawing him with her, over the threshold and into the house. The heavy door closed behind them on its expensive hinges without a sound.

I was left alone in the garden, my blood leaching into the dirt, feeling unclean. Like a grimy voyeur.

MONDAY, 7 JULY
MORNING

The worst thing about getting the train from Artarmon to North Sydney at 8.45 in the morning was that it was always packed.

I never got a seat; sometimes I was lucky to make it onto a carriage at all. I was often forced to stand, pressed up against the door, beneath some tall man's armpit or holding my breath under an Eternity-for-Men-drenched chin. I mostly did it with a hangover, which didn't help matters.

Today, it was 8.55 when I elbowed my way inside and staked out a few centimetres next to the door. I'd be about fifteen minutes late to work if I stopped for coffee. Which I would. And, by my way of thinking, fifteen minutes late was a win on a Monday morning after the weekend I'd had.

After the shock of seeing Pip with Roger, I'd raced from the Harding house as though they'd set the dogs on me. I defrosted the rest of Mum's apple and custard scroll (*none left for visitors, sorry Mum*) and shovelled it into my mouth in front of a blaring TV cooking show as I polished off the vodka – and, yes, I was aware of the irony. I must have passed out around 7.30. I woke to ab-crunchers and husky voices reciting 1800-hotlines and dragged myself down the hall to bed. Somehow I slept off the worst of it, waking without an alarm and with only a headache and dry mouth. It was almost as if I hadn't had a drink at all. Practically sober. Bright-eyed and bushy-tailed, if you will. After a Berocca and a couple of glasses of water I left my flat feeling the best I had in weeks.

And all this despite the anniversary.

I wanted to believe I'd turned a corner and tried to forget about Pip and Roger. What was it to me if they were having an affair? I didn't even know them.

I rested my face against the smeared glass of the train door, trying not to think about when it had last been cleaned. Winter seemed unable to penetrate Sydney trains, and humidity made the air of the carriage thick. The smooth coolness of the glass helped me breathe. I'd had enough sense between drinks the previous night to rinse the dirt from the rose-bush wounds and plaster them in band-aids. Most of the thorn injuries were just scratches, except for one deeper gouge on my left hand near the thumb. It hurt like hell, but I'd live.

The weekend was over. The anniversary had passed.

Ten years.

Maybe Mum was right. Maybe it was time to move on. Just the thought made my heart thud louder, as if in denial. I brushed my fingers against the band-aids on my palm, remembering how I used to buy Wiggles plasters for Sascha; I'd sing 'Big Red Car' to him as I pressed one onto a grazed knee. He'd stop crying long enough to listen.

And now Leah was going to have a baby.

I ground my teeth together so my jaw ached. Leah, who'd never wanted kids.

My fingers pressed harder against the band-aids, until I had to bite my lip against the pain.

I should call her; congratulate them.

The train slowed for St Leonards Station and people started jostling. With a tortured squeal it halted and the door hissed open. I hunkered back as commuters spewed out to the freedom of the platform. Space suddenly opened, fresh air wafting in. Only briefly though. People started shoving their way onboard before passengers finished disembarking, and we were pressed even more closely together as the train shuddered off again.

The tunnel fell away and apartment buildings materialised, their balconies laden with barbecues and dusty outdoor chairs, their owners' belongings on display as if they were exhibits in a museum for bored commuters to peer at. Like voyeurs.

Closing my eyes, I saw again Pip's hands on Roger's neck. An affair. So tawdry. So unbefitting for people living in a house like the Harding house. And so unfair to poor schmuck, average-looking Brett with the kind eyes. The Hardings seemed like the perfect family. Brett and Kingsley in their matching scarves. Their little footy jokes. How they teased Pip.

How could she do this to them?

Pip Reeves. The darling of art school.

Pip had an easy manner that was hard to dislike, no matter how much I'd wanted to hate someone so gorgeous and talented. She'd been glamorous, though not stuck-up. I hadn't thought she'd been a cheater, but what would I know? Pip certainly never seemed to have a serious boyfriend, no matter how many guys – from the confident third-years with upcoming exhibitions to the more sensitive types – chased her.

And what about Kingsley? Her beautiful boy.

How could Pip risk her family for a fling?

And with a smarmy real estate agent, no less.

I opened my eyes, tracing a scratch in the window with a finger. Anyway, why should I care?

I should forget all about the Hardings.

And the Harding house.

I sighed.

So many shoulds.

A loud beeping preceded the hiss of opening carriage doors and I joined the throng of people disembarking. We moved along the platform, up the escalators and outside in a well-practised manoeuvre.

A sudden memory came. Of how, after we'd both quit our jobs, Peter would watch the traffic report on the evening news. How he'd laugh at people caught behind a three-vehicle pile-up, or stuck in trains delayed by signal failure or the all-too-common 'person on the track'.

'We're better than that, Katie,' he'd say, chardonnay in hand. 'We're special, you know. We aren't sheep, like the rest of them.'

I emerged from the station into the sunlight.

I guess Peter was right. I had been special.

He had made me special.

Just not in a way I had ever expected, or wanted.

* * *

Ten minutes later I pushed open the door to Imperial Real Estate.

The use of 'Imperial' in the name suggested that Vivian, my boss, had once had high hopes for the future of her business. Now it seemed ironic. We didn't have much in common with agents like Roger Bailey, or McQuilty Real Estate. Vivian would kill to have just one Harding house on her books. Our properties were mostly older apartments in the Chatswood area, smaller commercial properties and the odd run-down house ready to be detonated and turned into a duplex.

Imperial Real Estate sat beneath a skinny high-rise on a main road in North Sydney. The glass-fronted space consisted of a lounge-room-sized shop front with a reception counter, plus three offices out the back. Not to forget the tiny kitchenette where a toaster and kettle lived on a permanently crumb-covered bench, or the unisex toilet that ran constantly. Vivian owned the place and had talked about renovating it ever since I started – nine years ago.

I nodded to the receptionist, Tahlia, who acknowledged me frostily as she spoke to the air, the ever-present headset perched on her up-styled hair. Tahlia had been with Imperial Real Estate for a year. Round-faced, very young and capable, not to mention confident, she'd been super friendly at first. She used to make a sad face at me, one that told me she knew about the incident. However, once she figured out the incident didn't make me interesting or clever or worthy she didn't waste her time. Tahlia physically itched to quit Imperial. She wriggled in her swivel chair with an impatience to move somewhere better. I gave her another two months, at most.

Tahlia ended her call and sang out to me as I reached the door to the back offices. 'Vivian was asking about you. I told her I'd send you in when you got here.'

My stomach fluttered, but I said OK and kept going. I was holding a cardboard coffee holder carefully in my right hand. Two coffees: one for me, one for Vivian. Never once in nine years had I bought a coffee for Vivian, and I had no idea why I had decided to do so now.

I entered the first room – my office-slash-cupboard. Much of the floorspace was taken up by piles of brochures, and one entire wall was shelves, stacked with a motley assortment of stationery. At least it was mine. Vivian had the largest room and the other was shared by three part-time agents. As often as not they were out with clients so most days the office was quite peaceful. I dumped my handbag on my cluttered desk, then balanced the cardboard tray on a stack of flyers, removing the cups and went down the hall to my boss's office.

Vivian sat behind her desk, engrossed in something on her computer monitor. I knocked on her open door with an elbow. She glanced up and smiled.

'Sorry I'm late, Vivian. I got you a coffee; it's from that new place on the corner.'

Vivian tilted her head, a frown creasing her smooth forehead. 'Oh, thank you, that's very thoughtful, but I don't drink coffee. I'm a tea person, I'm afraid.'

Fuck.

'Really? I'm sorry. I should have known that, shouldn't I?'

Vivian's expression softened into the extra-sympathetic one she reserved for me. It really gave me the shits – she was such a lovely person. 'Don't worry about it, Kate. I'm sure Tahlia would love it. I know she's a coffee drinker. Anyway, come in. Please, sit down.'

Vivian wasn't your typical real estate agent. Tall and graceful, she was an attractive woman with a softly spoken manner, a neat grey bob and pearls. Vivian was the sort of person who usually got her own way, with an infuriating knack of making it seem that her way was what you'd wanted all along. As such, she was a great salesperson. She didn't have the smarmy way of so many agents; though I still didn't quite trust her when she was in full-on sales mode. But Vivian was one of the good guys. I had to admit, albeit grudgingly, there were *some* good guys among the real estate agents I'd met over the years.

Vivian's smile morphed into a look of concern. 'How are you? I know what day Saturday was.' Trust Vivian to remember the date; the woman remembered everything. 'I wanted to check you're alright. This time of year can't be easy for you.'

'I'm OK, thanks.'

'Well, if you need anything just ask.' She waited a beat, then added, 'I spoke to your mother last night. She told me about Leah.'

Wonderful.

Sometimes – most times – it wasn't a good thing for your mother to be friends with your boss. They'd met playing competition golf; Mum was the better golfer, though Vivian was ten years her junior. After Sascha died and I'd spent months at home in pyjamas with a bottle in my hand, Mum had asked Vivian if she had anything I could do, then bullied me into taking the job. I laid out ads for the weekend papers, wrote copy for flyers and organised printing. After nine years I could do it in my sleep.

I didn't have any particular interest in open houses. Not at first. Back then, I did my nine to five, saw Dr Evans once a fortnight and spent the rest of the time alternating between drinking and trying to quit drinking. It was only after I'd been at Imperial for several years that Vivian called me on a Saturday morning and asked me to ferry a stack of newly minted brochures from the printers to the house she was showing at Turramurra – and I discovered the power of an open house.

I'd rocked up, hungover and grumpy at the disruption to my busy weekend of doing fuck-all, and found the house she was showing was exactly what I'd once dreamed of for Peter and Sascha and me. Not as fancy as the Harding house, of course, but a lovely family home, with a perfect climbing tree in the back yard and a fireplace and a big timber dining table.

Entering that house, I'd experienced an actual burst of real happiness for the first time since Sascha died. There was something about it that was so open and welcoming I immediately pictured what it might have been like to live there. What my life might have been; the three of us sitting round the table, helping ourselves to lasagne or roast lamb, laughing at an anecdote from Sascha's school day. Or watching a stupid American sitcom on TV, all squished up together on the lounge. I'd put the dishwasher on and Peter and Sascha would play borderline-too-violent video games while I pretended not to notice. I'd leave them and go down to the cellar I'd converted to a darkroom, working on my first solo exhibition.

It had all been so clear to me.

So right.

After that, I started attending other opens – not often, just when something special came up. They were modest family homes that I could picture Sascha growing up in. A different life.

An alternate reality, if you will.

It wasn't until later that it became an addiction.

My eyes slid away from Vivian's, my face warm. 'Yes, it's great news for Leah, isn't it?'

Vivian's brow furrowed but she said nothing.

'She'll be a great mother,' I added.

More silence.

I gripped the cups tighter, ignoring the throbbing of my hands. 'I'd better get to work,' I said then waved the spare coffee, 'and give this to Tahlia before it gets cold.'

Back in my office I plonked onto my squeaky chair. Vivian had left information about two new properties we needed flyers for, and I also needed to prepare the weekend newspaper advertising for the Saturday lift-out, which was due surprisingly early in the week. I settled into my chair and started up my computer.

Though I knew this stuff back to front and inside out, it was slow going today. Thoughts of the Hardings kept me distracted. I spent my lunch hour on the internet, beginning with my ritual real estate website search. When my open house addiction had really taken off, I'd saved all my regular search criteria: House/3+bedrooms/2+bathrooms/2+car spaces/Wahroonga, Pymble, Turramurra, And Surrounding Suburbs. All I needed to do was click an icon in the top right corner of the screen and up popped the listings.

And there it was: the Harding house.

The first house on the list. The Featured Property. Identified by a small green label as NEW.

I clicked on *Highfields – For Auction – Price Guide on Request* and was taken to the listing for the house. It wasn't hard to make a property like the Harding house look good, but I could tell this photographer was way more expensive than the guy who took our brochure shots. Sometimes I thought our guy used his phone – and as someone who knew her way around a camera, I found this highly offensive. I couldn't say anything, though – a few years back, after one too many complaints about a clothesline being left in shot, an exasperated Vivian had offered me the job and I'd turned it down. I'd always seen myself as an 'artiste', not a hack real estate photographer. Besides, photography – all creative endeavours, really – were part of my past now.

As for the future, well, I never let myself think about that.

I examined the dozen or so images of the Harding house, went back to the start and looked again. Then again. The kitchen, the master bedroom, another bedroom, the pool area from two angles, library, lounge, gardens, dining area and one of the bathrooms. Plus a couple of arty photos. One from the kitchen looking out the window to the garden and pool, the other a close-up showing masses of spectacular gardenias in bloom. A couple of the rooms – a bathroom and a bedroom – I hadn't seen, having left in such a hurry. I leaned closer to my screen, taking in every detail.

In the master bedroom, I again envied Pip's knack for colour matching. In the kitchen, I admired anew the apple-green mixer I would never in a million years use. The arty kitchen shot was designed to allow me to imagine whipping up something fabulous on a warm summer's evening, while the out-of-focus pool and garden invited me for a swim after dinner. On the windowsill sat a magazine-worthy vignette: the cactus in its terracotta pot, a designer-made white candle in a glass jar and cheerful red flowers in a vintage Coke bottle. The effect was almost homely in the multi-million-dollar mansion; a nice touch.

I scrolled back to the top of the page.

The next inspection was at 1 pm on Saturday. I bit my lip. I'd never returned to a house for a second open. Never been to an auction of a house I'd been through either; though of course I'd often followed up to see what they sold for.

Should I go back? I did still need to get my memento.

I rubbed my face with both hands as I thought about it.

What was so special about Highfields? Was it the anniversary? The house itself? The family?

Images flickered in my mind. Sascha. Peter. The photo of the smiling Harding family. The cactus. The perfect house, with the boy who could have been mine.

I skidded away from the question, preferring not to figure it out. I just knew one thing.

I'd be there.

BEFORE

Peter kissed me on the neck. I made an automatic moaning sound but couldn't relax.

Does he really want to do this now?

Sascha had finally fallen into a deep sleep after two solid hours of crying. Peter had been at me to give controlled crying a try, but the absolute horror that coursed through me as I watched my distraught baby from the doorway or heard his blood-curdling screams over a crackling monitor was too much to bear. After half an hour I'd been traumatised, racing in to scoop Sascha up and hug him as Peter watched from outside the room, stony-faced. After that, my husband spent the evening nursing a bottle of red wine, watching TV and ignoring me each time I crept from the room to soothe our baby.

At last Sascha fell into an exhausted slumber in my arms and I leaned over his cot, inch-by-freaking-inch, gradually setting him down, my back aching. At nine months, my boy was getting too heavy to rock to sleep yet what else could I do?

He needed me.

And afterwards, when I'd poured myself my usual small glass of Thank-God-Sascha-Is-Asleep wine and flopped down next to Peter on the lounge with a muffled sigh, he'd turned the TV to low and reached a hand across to rub my neck.

Fuck.

I knew what that meant.

Sex would mean no zoning out to an old sitcom on TV, but, on the bright side, if we got it over with soon, I'd get a couple of hours sleep before tending to Sascha again. I reached forward to put my glass on the coffee table and in the process knocked over the bottle of red. Fortunately it was all but empty, and only a dribble splashed across his folded newspaper.

'Shit, Katie,' Peter said, pulling away from me, 'did you do that on purpose?' He jumped up and walked over to the kitchen, yelling over his shoulder. 'You have zero interest in this any more, don't you?'

I wanted to shush him. To hiss, *Don't wake the baby*. I didn't dare. Peter stomped back with a tea towel. He bent over and jabbed at the wine.

'This?' I asked, keeping my voice expressionless.

'Us. Sex. With me.' He threw the red-smeared tea towel to the floor and stood up, wobbling slightly after drinking almost a bottle of wine. His hooded eyes demanded a response.

'Peter, I'm sorry. I'm tired, that's all.'

'You're always tired. If you did as I said and let Sascha cry, he'd be asleep in twenty minutes and we'd all get some rest. But what do I know? I'm just the father.'

I opened my mouth, then closed it.

Peter grabbed his keys and headed for the stairs. 'Don't wait up,' he called over his shoulder as he clomped down the steps.

The door slammed and I exhaled. Perhaps I should have been upset. Or jealous. Instead, the only emotions I felt were annoyance that he might wake Sascha, and relief I'd now have control of the remote.

I grabbed my drink, taking a big sip. I picked up the remote and changed to the entertainment channel. A rerun of an 80s movie was on and I watched it half-heartedly, wondering why

I cared so little Peter had walked out. And who he might be with. Although I could take a pretty good guess at that last one.

Rosemarie. His agent. Who lived barely three blocks away. I'd always suspected that's why she was keen for Peter to buy this apartment in the first place.

We'd last caught up with Rosemarie just a week earlier, at a dinner party Peter insisted we host. His publisher came, along with two other authors and their highbrow partners. I'd slaved all day making chicken liver pate and beef bourguignon only to have two of the guests – Rosemarie was one – announce they were vegetarian. None of them was my kind of people. Wankers, I thought. They clearly didn't think much of me either: an ex–school teacher, now stay-at-home mother.

Nothing of interest there.

Peter was on a deadline and he'd still written nothing. Nada. That night his publisher had made a couple of pointed comments about it, but Rosemarie defended her client like a pit bull. She was ten years older than Peter, attractive for her age. The way she watched him – like she wanted to devour him whole – clashed with her boho outfits and too-cool manner. Me, she ignored. Or else spoke to me as if I was Sascha's age.

I drank the last of my wine then jumped up and strode into the kitchen, plucking a chilled bottle of white wine from the fridge. I hesitated, then put it on the bench and opened the freezer, grabbing one of the bottles of breastmilk I kept for emergencies. Sascha wouldn't be breastfeeding tonight. I turned on the hot tap and put the bottle in the sink to defrost, then took the wine back to the living area. I poured a big glass and sat back.

An hour later I opened another one.

People said wine dulled the pain.

Fuck that. Wine made the pain go away. Wine made me happy.

How had I never realised this before?

PART II

SECOND
OPEN HOUSE

SATURDAY, 12 JULY
MORNING

I woke on Saturday feeling sick but despite that my mood was strangely light.

I'd had a dream – nothing like the Dream, though, thank fuck – about the Harding house. Even as I woke, sleepy and peaceful, the details began to slip away from me, as they always do in the very best dreams. Sascha had been there; I closed my eyes again to better recall his face. He'd been sitting at Highfields' sunlit kitchen bench. Everyone – my parents, the Hardings, even Peter – was there, gathered around as if they were all great friends. Pip had poured batter from the mixer to a cake tin and had passed the chocolatey beaters to Kingsley and Sascha who licked them gleefully; Kingsley acting like a little boy despite being a teenager. They'd all looked at me as I entered the kitchen, Sascha's face lighting up as he called out, 'Mum!'

That's where it ended.

I tried to hold on to the warmth of it, to hug the feeling to me.

But it faded and nausea intruded, rousing me from my bed. I fussed around having coffee and getting ready, all the while feeling like shit. I somehow got myself together enough to leave the house at ten, which felt like an achievement. A drunk's achievement, but an achievement all the same. I took with me a bottle of Coke and a list of houses and times. The same as every Saturday. But today I had the second Harding open house at 1 pm, and I felt a fluttery excitement I hadn't felt since the early days of Peter's courtship.

And look how that had ended.

The thought brought Sascha to mind and my enthusiasm plummeted.

My list contained four other opens before the Harding house. By the third – a pleasant three-bedder near the highway – I had pocketed a crumpled shopping list, a small piece of red Lego and a tan-coloured button with some similarly hued thread still knotted through the holes. My heart wasn't in it, though. I felt dirty, like I was somehow cheating on the Harding house. I didn't bother with the fourth house. Instead, I drove to Wahroonga and sat in the car outside the Hardings' front gate – which was closed today – drinking a slushie and eating a pie bought from a nearby servo.

I stared at the For Sale sign. The three photos on it were from the house's website listing: the façade, the pool area and the kitchen. All good choices. Probably decided upon by Pip and Roger in between fucks the previous Sunday. I idly critiqued the real estate-ese on the sign. Apparently the Harding house was a 'sophisticated, graceful entertainer' offering a 'celebration of luminous natural light' and a 'sumptuous retreat for parents'. Despite the sign's turgid overkill, my desire to go back into the house was strong. I wanted to see the rooms I'd missed. I needed to find a memento. And I hadn't seen Kingsley's room yet. Now was my chance to find out more about him – what sort of kid he was, if he really had anything in common with my Sascha.

I bet he did.

They would have been friends, for sure. Kingsley would have been the more outgoing one, but Sascha would have been his voice of reason – the one who gave the best advice about girls and reminded him to do his maths homework. They'd swap sandwiches at lunchtime and catch the bus to the beach together on Friday afternoons and do bomb after bomb in the Harding house pool on weekends, so that Pip would have to tell them to stop before all the water was gone.

I closed my eyes and lingered over the pleasant daydreams, starting at the sound of a voice. 'Ah, Tammy, isn't it? Oh wait, no, that's right. You aren't Tammy and the phone number you gave me was a fake.'

Roger's aftershave filled the car. I held back a sneeze.

'Hi Roger,' I managed, brushing pastry off my chest. 'I owe you an apology.' I climbed out of the car and smiled tentatively. He, quite rightly, stared at me in a rather hostile fashion. 'My name is Kate Webb. I'm very sorry about last week. It was a spur of the moment thing, you know? I heard Renee telling Tammy about this place and it sounded so great I just had to come and have a look.' I grimaced at him in a rueful kind of way. 'I've been to a few of Renee's opens, though she's never been a big fan of me. She didn't want me to come. I'm sorry. I should have told you the truth.'

Roger was silent for a long moment. I held my breath.

'Well, Renee can be a bit of a bitch, can't she, Kate?' He smiled. 'It's an amazing property, isn't it?'

'It's incredible. I just had to come back again. I hope you don't mind.'

'Of course not.'

He turned around and stared at the Harding house, apparently captivated. I didn't blame him but at the same time

I didn't like his smug expression. It was too possessive. Roger turned back to me and pulled a business card from his jacket pocket. A post-it note fluttered to the ground and I bent over and picked it up, trying to look helpful.

'Oh, I need that,' Roger said.

I passed the note towards him, noting the four digits followed by a hash symbol. With a jolt I realised it was the year Sascha was born. I had been right, Kingsley was the same age as my boy.

Roger smiled as he took the post-it, his expression so candid I knew he didn't know about my past. I could always tell.

'It's such a perfect home for a family. Do you have children, Kate?' He looked around as though expecting them to appear from behind a bush. I was saved from answering as the Hardings' gate smoothly began to open. 'Ah,' Roger said, and checked his watch. '12.55. Mrs Harding is a very organised woman. I'm not surprised she's ready.' He put a hand on my shoulder and I fought the urge to pull away. 'If you'll excuse me, I'd better go and set up.'

Roger crossed the road and pulled a flag and a small suitcase from his Lexus. He waved as he walked back towards the driveway, then paused to slot the flag into a tube running down one side of the For Sale sign. 'Open for Inspection' blew lightly in the breeze. People started to arrive immediately, as though the flag had some sort of voodoo powers.

I reached into my car to grab my bag then turned back to the house – and there, walking up the driveway towards me, was Pip Reeves. Pip *Harding*.

She wore full-length Lycra leggings and a green, long-sleeved zip-up top that showed off her curves. Neither Kingsley nor Brett was with her. I twisted back to my car, fiddling with my keys and hoping she hadn't recognised me. I needn't have worried. Pip walked straight past, striding off with the tidy, purposeful walk of a seasoned exerciser. I watched her go, wondering at her energy and her body. I looked down at my bulges and unfashionable clothes.

When had my body become *this*?

I made my way down the driveway to where Roger was standing just outside the front door. He asked, with a raised eyebrow, for my true phone number, which I gave him. This time there were brochures on the kitchen bench and photocopied piles of contracts and pest and building reports. I took one of everything, shoving them into my bag.

First thing this time was to see the pool and back garden. I wandered the manicured lawns, noting the well-chosen trees – currently leafless but which in summer would offer shade.

I imagined fairy lights strung up through the trees for Kingsley's fifth birthday party. Kids would have run wild with sticky faces and there'd have been balloons and cake, with champagne for the parents. Peter and I would have stayed late, laughing with Pip and Brett as the boys worked together building a Lego pirate ship or castle. His fifteenth would have been a pool party where they played Marco Polo and the boys showed off for the girls while Pip and Brett supervised unobtrusively.

I opened the pool gate and wandered in. The rectangular pool was long enough to swim laps in, with deep-blue tiles. The paved area around it had been set with lounges and an outdoor table. I pictured alfresco lunches laid out on a white linen tablecloth.

Back inside the house, many more people had arrived. I climbed the sweeping staircase to the first floor but this time at the top I turned left instead of right and approached the door on the left. As soon as I entered the room I realised it was Kingsley's.

This room hadn't been in the real estate pictures, perhaps to protect Kingsley's privacy. It was neat for a teenager's bedroom. The colour scheme was as interesting as in the master bedroom. Not your ordinary 'blue for boys'. Perhaps Pip had decorated it, or maybe Kingsley had inherited his mother's eye for design. All walls except one were painted a cool white and most of the décor was monochrome. On the floor was a huge black and white chequered rug. A soft grey doona lay across the bottom half of the double bed. A round stool made from pale wood served as a bedside table, a stack of art books piled on top. No novels, as far as I could see. A white desk had been positioned with a view out the window to the front garden and the driveway. Except for a notepad, a lamp and a container holding a few pens, the desk was bare; a black metal stool slotted neatly underneath. The only touch of colour in the decor was an orange 70s-style rounded plastic desk lamp.

But it was the wall behind his bed that grabbed my attention.

Painted like a blackboard, every inch of it had been covered with coloured chalk.

I moved closer, fascinated. The chalk scribbles were hugely varied. Everything from simple lists and reminders, due dates for assignments, upcoming parties and birthdays, right through to intricate drawings and patterns. His handwriting veered from an almost illegible scrawl to funky typography, some of which had been painstakingly rendered. A row of heads spaced along the top of the blackboard included a Frankenstein's monster, an owl, a lion, a chimpanzee and a beautiful girl. They looked like trophies; like severed heads on spikes. I moved nearer, trying to see some of the smaller drawings. A mouse, sitting on top of a sleeping cat's back. A young girl, tears running down her face. A skull and crossbones, lightning bolts, the solar system. This wall was Kingsley's mind laid bare in art form; I just needed to decipher it.

Then, down in the bottom corner near one side of the bed, I noticed a sketch that sucked the breath from my body.

A car, an ordinary sedan, captured mid-air, its front wheels falling towards what was obviously water.

No.

No. No. No.

The car about to sink into its dark depths.

Suddenly nauseous, I raced out of the room, almost colliding with a man who had to step aside as I barrelled past.

Oh God, please, please don't let me throw up in the Harding house.

I stumbled down the hall, ignoring the looks from people as I glanced into rooms, trying to remember which was the bathroom. I couldn't make my brain work. I came across two more bedrooms on the left. On the right, finally, was the marble bathroom. Beside it, a toilet. I entered, shut the door and sat on the closed toilet seat.

Don't be sick. Don't be sick.

I hung my head between my legs and took deep breaths.

Kingsley had drawn a car sinking into water. Into Sydney Harbour?

Did he know about the worst day of my life? Why was it depicted in chalk on his bedroom wall?

Kingsley wouldn't know. He's just a child.

He couldn't know.

Within a minute I was calmer.

But I had to go back in there and have another look.

BEFORE

'Ruff! Ruff!'

The children finished their song about doggies in the window with gusto and parents clapped loudly. We perched on too-small plastic seats, latecomers leaning against side walls in the main room of the Three Bears Preschool. Sascha was hardly visible in the cluster of children gathered at the front. To be fair it was difficult to tell the kids apart anyway, as most of them were dressed as dogs and their costumes largely consisted of 'brown clothes'. Staff members had painted each child's nose black and pencilled whiskers across their round cheeks. Some kids had lolling red tongues painted on their chins while others sported black spots over one eye. I could identify Sascha from the pointy ears he wore. I'd cut them out from a cardboard box late the night before and attached them to one of my old headbands.

As the clapping died away, the preschool's owner – her face made comical with her own eyepatch and whiskers – disentangled herself from the little girls on her lap and addressed the parents. She spoke about the kids' hard work and the dedication of the staff to help prepare this year's show then directed us all to the tea and coffee.

Sascha had moved to the other side of the room and stood on his own, cardboard ears in his hands now, scanning the crowd. I waved at him and his big eyes lit up with relief and happiness. He looked for a way to approach me through the crush of adults and children. I excused myself as I made my way along the row in his direction and, when I'd finally pushed my way free, he jumped into my arms.

'Mummy! Did you see me?'

'Yes, sweetheart. What a great show! You were the best doggy up there.'

The makeup covering Sascha's nose had smudged and he'd smeared some across one cheek. His red puppy tongue had mostly worn off, so it looked like he had a rash on his chin. He grinned, the happiest I'd seen him since rehearsals for the play began. He'd been so nervous about getting up there in front of everyone, and I was pleased he'd managed it.

Sascha stroked the collar of my shirt with one hand, the other twisting locks of my hair – both unconscious habits of his.

'Is Daddy here?'

My smile faded. 'Ah, well, I know he was hoping to make it, sweetheart, but he had to see his publisher this morning. Maybe they lost track of time ...'

It had been almost seven years since Peter's book was released. He was now back working as a sub-editor three days a week, as writer's block didn't pay the mortgage. Actually, neither did editing. Several years earlier we'd been forced to borrow some money from my parents to tide us over. Peter's publishers had dropped him long ago, but he occasionally set up a meeting – also attended by his agent, of course – to pitch them a new idea. They usually loved it, gave him a chance and then ... waited. Peter's charm went a long way, but eventually the lack of an actual, physical book for them to publish became a problem.

I sensed someone at my shoulder, and Sascha's face lit up.

'Daddy!' Sascha reached his arms out to his father.

My heart raced. Now Peter was here I realised part of me had hoped he might not come. Then I could put off what I knew I had to say. But, on the other hand, I needed to do it here and now, in a place where he wouldn't make a scene.

I took a deep breath and turned around.

'Sasch, mate,' Peter said, 'that was awesome! How good were you, buddy?'

I handed Sascha to his father. Peter towered over most of the other dads. Nearing forty, his Germanic bone structure meant his looks had improved with age. He'd kept all his hair too, wearing it a little shorter now than when we'd first met. His smile at Sascha was wide and proud. I hoped it meant things had gone well with the publishers. When he turned to me the smile congealed a little. Not so an observer would notice, but obvious to me. I swallowed, wondering if I could go through with my plan. 'Let's go outside, Peter,' I said. 'It's so noisy in here.'

He nodded and spun around, still carrying Sascha. I followed them, Sascha chatting the entire time. I nodded to some parents I'd met at drop-offs and pick-ups over the past eighteen months, but didn't stop to say hi. I didn't have close friends here, just acquaintances.

No one spoke to Peter. They just stared, or tried not to. There was something really compelling about him. You wanted him to notice you; to give you his attention.

We filed out the door. Sydney's winter air was clear and clean, the kind of brilliant weather where everything appeared to be in high definition. But the sun lacked the warmth to heat me up and I shivered. Peter wandered to a far corner of the playground.

'Dad. Dad. Watch me on the bikes?' Sascha asked, already scrambling to be put down.

'Sure. Show me how fast you can go.'

I watched my husband as he watched our son racing off. It was adoration, pure and simple. He was a father in love with his child. Was there anything more beautiful? A lump solidified in my throat.

Was what I was about to do the right thing for my boy?

Sascha found a helmet and put it on, even managing to fasten the buckle with his small fingers. Now, a frown on his serious face, he stood in front of the half dozen or so bikes propped haphazardly in the corner of the yard. His favourite colour was green and I knew he was searching for the 'greenest' bike.

'How was the meeting?' I ventured to Peter.

'Fine.'

Not good then.

I wasn't surprised, though I wished it had gone better, for the sake of what I had to tell him. I took a deep breath and dived in. 'Peter,' I said, keeping my eyes on Sascha, 'I need to talk to you about something.' My voice was more timid than I would have liked. I'd always hated confrontation. 'I want to move out.'

He didn't say anything, so I looked up at him to see if he'd heard me. He'd tilted his head to face me, wearing a half-smile. Was it directed at me or was he still thinking of his son?

I cleared my throat. 'I want a trial separation.'

Peter's smile faded and he turned back to Sascha, giving him a nod of encouragement as he struggled to pull the chosen bike out from behind another.

'I'm not saying I want a divorce. I just need some space. Some time to think things through, you know? To be on my own for a while.' My words had spilled out in a rush and now I paused, my stomach curdling as I watched my husband's impassive profile. 'Well, not on my own, exactly; I'll take Sascha with me. That way you can work on your book and I can keep things as normal as possible for Sasch. We'll go and stay with my parents. Sascha will think it's a little holiday. I spoke to Mum about it this morning. She said we can come, but she's not happy.' A small snort escaped me. 'You know how much Mum loves you – she thinks we should make it work.'

Peter continued to watch Sascha.

'And maybe we will. Make it work, I mean. But I need some time. Without you. You can see Sascha whenever you want, of course. He's still your son. And it won't be forever. Just till we work things out.'

Still nothing.

'Peter?' My voice cracked on the word.

He finally turned back to me. I almost recoiled at the hard set of his face, his eyes ice-blue and far away. But then his expression seemed to soften and I wondered if I had imagined it. When he spoke next it was with a mild voice. Not placating, almost unconcerned. Indifferent. 'That's really what you want, Katie?'

I swallowed.

Was it?

'Yes,' I said, trying to sound decisive.

Peter held my gaze with the intensity I knew so well. I remembered how it used to feel when he looked at me like that. Like I was the only girl in the world.

Now it just made me scared.

Scared for me, and for my boy. I fought the need to look away as my heart thudded.

Finally I couldn't stand it any more. I turned to Sascha. He was pedalling furiously along the bike track, grinning at us, his little legs pumping on a green bike with the largest training wheels I'd ever seen.

How could I take Sascha away from his dad?

But I couldn't go on living with Peter. Things had worsened over the past couple of years. When we first met I'd been flattered he was so interested in my life. Because he was older, and so much more confident than me, I'd trusted his advice. Jenna was *a bit tarty*, teaching was a job *for people who couldn't hack the real world*. We'd exchanged passwords, because we were closer than *ordinary couples*. It was us against the world.

So romantic. Or so it had seemed at first.

But more and more it began to feel claustrophobic. Peter kept me close. He checked my mail, my Facebook account, my emails. I'd caught him reading my text messages once and he hadn't even flinched. Didn't bother to give me some lame excuse. Just walked away.

I needed to get out of the house. I loved my son, but I itched for the company of other adults and dreamed of finding a part-time job. Not photography. I needed creative space for photography, and there was no space in my current life. I'd take any job – even just photocopying for a publishing or auction house.

A couple of months earlier I'd sent my CV to a major art gallery asking about work or internships for the following year. When I plucked up the courage to tell Peter I'd been offered an interview, he'd accused me of not caring about our son.

Of betrayal.

I steeled myself, turned back to Peter who was still watching me. The look in his eyes now was the same as it had been then. 'I need space, Peter.'

His eyes became opaque, but then he smiled as Sascha ran over and jumped into his arms. Peter pulled him in for a tight hug, then looked at me and spoke in a quiet voice. 'Be careful what you wish for, Katie.'

SATURDAY, 12 JULY
AFTERNOON

As I emerged from the toilet, there was no one in sight. Thank God for small miracles.

I headed back to Kingsley's room on legs weak with foreboding. A child appeared in the doorway and my heart thudded. He bolted past, eyeing me with stranger-danger suspicion.

Back in the room I zeroed in on the drawing, tiptoeing closer.

My shoulders slumped with relief.

He'd drawn a car, that was true. But I had the rest of it wrong. The car wasn't mid-fall, and it wasn't going *into* the water. It was mid-*jump*. To the left of the car was a ramp, curving up like an egg cup cut in half. On the right was its mirror image – the landing ramp. The car was leaping *over* water, not falling *in*. I sighed, yanking the stool out from under the desk and falling onto it. He'd drawn a typical teenage boy car-fantasy picture. It wasn't a comment on my life.

I put a hand to my temple. I really was losing it.

What was it about the Hardings that made me so crazy?

Something about these people – this house – really got under my skin.

At least part of it was Kingsley, I knew that. His beauty, his youth; his likeness to Sascha. I ran a finger over his desk, thinking now of my boy. Sascha had never grown old enough to need a desk. He hadn't even started kindergarten. He'd just played on the living room rug with his Lego and plastic dinosaurs as I made us Vegemite sandwiches for lunch.

I swallowed.

Voices came from the hall. I stood up and shoved the stool under the desk, trying to act normal.

Normal.

I almost snorted. I didn't know what normal was any more.

A man entered. I stared hard at him until he looked away, glancing around the room before leaving. Good. I wasn't finished yet.

I spent several more minutes in Kingsley's room. Belatedly, I realised it had an ensuite. It was a small, pleasant space, with a black and white tiled shower and clean toilet. The vanity drawer contained little of interest, just the usual toothbrush, toothpaste and deodorant. There were no stray hairs or spilled tubes. I went back to the bedroom and, keeping a careful ear out for incoming visitors, riffled through the desk drawer. Nothing unusual there either. Just assorted pens and a notepad with what appeared to be biology notes on it. No photos or personal letters.

A family of five entered and lingered, so I wandered back down the hall, peering into the other two bedrooms. Guest rooms. I'd assumed Pip and Brett had no other children, and the lack of personal belongings in those rooms seemed to confirm it. One had an enormous, earthy-coloured Aboriginal artwork on the wall and an indigo and white handmade quilt on the bed. The other was completely different, with an Andy Warhol-esque series of prints on two walls and a polka-dot doona in citrus shades on the bed. Both somehow worked. As a regular attendee of open houses and someone employed in the industry, I was impressed by the interior design. Most houses were so over-styled now you could hardly remember anything to differentiate them. Pip and Brett had far more class than that. Highfields would appeal to people across the board, despite individuality generally being considered a no-no in real estate parlance.

When I finally returned to Kingsley's room I stood at his bedroom window, enjoying the lovely view; leafy and green, with glimpses of neighbouring houses. I wandered around the far side of his bed, keen to get on my hands and knees, to search under the bed, needing to find out everything about him. But there were still too many people. Instead I stared at the chalk drawings a little longer. Part of me was tempted to find some chalk and leave him a message of my own.

Your mother is having an affair with your real estate agent.

Pip and Roger's affair was wrong. Lying to Brett and Kingsley was wrong. Surely if they found out, Pip would have to end it.

Then they could go back to being a happy family.

A perfect family.

In their perfect home.

I sighed.

Kingsley needed to know the truth, I believed that. But I couldn't do it that way.

I'd have to tell him in person.

I'd be compassionate and gentle. He'd be upset and angry at first but after he calmed down he'd be thankful someone had finally told him the truth. We would become friends. I could be like a second mother; if not that, then a trusted aunt.

I shook my head, annoyed at my selfishness. And confused by it. Kingsley wasn't my son. I hadn't been anyone's mother for ten years.

He's not Sascha.

No one could take Sascha's place, I told myself with some guilt. And, anyway, it was far better for Kingsley to remain with his parents. If Pip and Brett divorced it would affect his grades, not to mention his mental health. He'd feel abandoned. Unloved. I couldn't stand the thought of Kingsley – still just a boy – feeling so lost and alone.

Better to force Pip and Roger to end their affair. I just had to work out how.

My gaze wandered over the heads along the top of the wall. They were beautifully drawn. Pip had always had a talent for charcoal sketching. Kingsley took after her. Must have been genetic.

I wondered if Sascha would have been artistic like me or a writer like his father. Or something else completely. His own person.

I would never know.

My jaw ached with the effort of holding back tears.

No, Kate, don't go there. Not now. Not here.

I closed my eyes for a moment and when I blinked them open I saw it.

On the floor, just poking out from behind the leg of the stool, lying on its side.

A small plastic dinosaur.

I glanced at the door; at last, I was alone. I reached down and plucked it from the floor, immediately straightening up as if nothing had happened. I turned to the window, my back to the door, and examined the dinosaur.

It was a parasaurolophus. A duck-billed dinosaur. I knew this because the same unprepossessing dinosaur had been Sascha's favourite. He'd been obsessed by dinosaurs for the last year of his life, but he loved the parasaurolophus the best. God only knew why. It resembled a small T-Rex, with a comb on the crown of its head that gave it a comical bird-like appearance. This one was khaki, with dirty yellow stripes across its back. Through my watery eyes I smiled. It was perfect.

I'd found my memento.

I closed my hand around the little dinosaur, its sharp plastic digging into my palm.

It was time to go.

BEFORE

Fun Fact Number 8: The crest on the head of a parasaurolophus was a resonating device – it probably sounded a bit like a trumpet. Scientists believe the dinosaur used it to communicate with family members.

'Wow,' I exclaimed to Sascha, for once genuinely interested in a dinosaur fact. 'I did not know that. How cool is that, baby?'

Sascha was tucked up in bed in his brand-new dinosaur pyjamas. The little T-Rex and stegosaurus silhouettes littering the fabric were cute, but he'd searched for a parasaurolophus, unable to understand why his favourite dinosaur wasn't featured. It was impossible to explain the duck-billed dinosaur he so loved wasn't popular enough to sell pyjamas. The book we were reading, imaginatively titled *101 Fun Dinosaur Facts for Kids*, was also new.

Both were blatant bribes. It had been a week since Sascha and I had moved back to my parents' house.

When he didn't answer my over-enthusiastic question I glanced across at him, thinking he might be asleep. He wasn't. He stared at me with those big serious eyes, so like his father's.

'Did you hear that one, Sasch? They think the parasaurolophus could make a really loud noise in his crest. A bit like a trumpet. You could be right over one side of the park and let out a woot-woot and I'd come running. That's if we were parasaurolophuses, I mean.'

I grinned at him, trying to raise a smile. If my mood had lightened with the absence of Peter, the same hadn't proved true for Sascha. While he was having a whale of a time in some respects — Mum slipped him lollies whenever she thought I wasn't looking and Dad had taken him for a spin round the golf course in his buggy — he obviously picked up on the tension between Peter and me, no matter how hard I'd tried to hide it. He missed his father.

'Mum?' Sascha wriggled under the covers and twisted the top of the sheet with his newly slender hands. I ached just looking at them, remembering how chubby they once were.

'Mmm?' I held back a yawn. I'd be in bed not long after Sascha at this rate. I hadn't been sleeping well. It wasn't just the horrible spare bed; the central heating in the house made it too hot to sleep comfortably.

'When are we going home?'

I froze.

Sascha had stopped wriggling and was staring at me, hope and fear warring for control of his expression.

'Oh, I don't know, honey.'

'But I want my *own* bed. And I want Daddy to read me a story.'

Ouch.

His bottom lip quivered.

'Look, how about when we talk to Daddy tomorrow night on the phone, we ask him to read you a story? Would that be good?'

He nodded but didn't smile.

I stood up and tucked him in. 'Nighty-night, Sasch.'

He closed his eyes obediently, screwing them up tight. Before I'd even left the room he rolled over to one side. I couldn't believe it was normal, how Sascha slept. He wound himself up in the sheets, doona, blankets – whatever bedding I gave him – like a caterpillar in a cocoon. Before I went to bed I'd lift one side of his bedding and pull, and he'd tumble over and over before popping out the side, sweaty and overheated, but without waking up. I'd straighten his bedding, tuck him in again. And by morning he'd be back in his cocoon.

He needed to be tightly wrapped, sheltered from the outside world, my boy did.

To feel safe under the covers.

But the covers weren't enough to protect him.

SATURDAY, 12 JULY
AFTERNOON

I nodded to Roger as I left.

He saw me and smiled as he continued to chat with a middle-aged man. Outside there were five or six cars crammed around the turning circle. I stood for a moment, looking up at Kingsley's window, imagining him standing there, then dragged myself away as people continued to come and go. I flopped into my car, sitting the plastic dinosaur upright in the centre console. Looking at it reminded me of Sascha, but instead of making me sad, my heart seemed somehow lighter with it nearby. I drove just half a block before parking behind a large dual cab ute. From here I could still see Roger's car on the opposite side of the road to the house, but I didn't think my yellow car would be too visible.

I righted the dinosaur, which had tipped onto its side, and wished I'd brought something to drink. Nothing too heavy, just a cider or beer or something.

No matter. I would be out of here soon, and I could stop at the pub on the way home. It was a Saturday afternoon, after all. That's what people did on weekends, didn't they? It was a perfectly acceptable weekend activity.

I kept my eye on Roger's Lexus. I don't know what I hoped to see; I just knew I didn't want to go back to my own life just yet, not even via the pub.

People continued emerging in dribs and drabs, climbing into cars around me and driving off. Finally, half an hour after the end of the advertised viewing time, Roger appeared. He crossed the road and loaded his suitcase and flag into the boot of his car then pulled out his phone. He leaned against the driver's door, scrolling and texting. After a few minutes, he looked up and down the street. For a second I thought he'd spotted me, but then he turned the other way and waved. Pip walked down the footpath towards him. It all looked very professional. Above board. Roger showed Pip the clipboard, at one point flipping over to a second page. They chatted. Nothing untoward. Nothing sexual. Nothing hidden. Pip and Roger acted as if they were exactly what they were supposed to be: a real estate agent and his client.

Maybe I'd been wrong?

I closed my eyes hard, rubbing them with my knuckles. God knows I'd been wrong often enough lately. First, I'd mistaken the photo of Kingsley for my beautiful Sascha. Then – only an hour or so ago – I'd mistaken Kingsley's innocent drawing of a car for a comment on my own history. So maybe I'd imagined their kiss too. A horrible thought grew in my guts.

Maybe I'd hallucinated the entire incident last weekend.

Was that even possible?

I opened my eyes. Roger said something to Pip then climbed into the driver's seat. I expected her to wave goodbye but she didn't. She opened the passenger door and got in.

I sat up straighter. Was he taking her somewhere? My fingers edged over to the keys dangling from the ignition and I prepared to follow them – no doubt a stupid idea considering my car was a distinctive yellow that Roger had seen on two separate occasions now. I didn't care. I had to know where they were going.

It was difficult to see through the glare on his windscreen. Then they leaned towards each other.

And kissed.

My heart leaped in relief. I wasn't crazy. They *were* having an affair. But any elation was swiftly replaced by anger. What if Pip's neighbours saw her? They would surely tell Brett and then the Hardings' marriage would be over. A family destroyed.

How dare she be so reckless?

A person on a bicycle appeared at the end of the block, riding along the footpath.

With a feeling of dread, I recognised him. Something in the line of his jaw; in the set of his head. Even from a distance, it was unmistakable.

Kingsley.

He didn't have a helmet and his hair had been ruffled by the wind. Wearing jeans and a grey hoodie, he rode at a leisurely pace.

Slow down, Kingsley, go back!

I looked at Pip and Roger, but they were engrossed in one another, as entwined as two people could be across the centre console of a Lexus. Kingsley's childhood of privilege and happiness was about to end. I worried at a fingernail with my teeth. How could I have thought it would be good for him to find out his mother was having an affair? He was still a child. It would devastate him.

Roger and Pip pulled apart. One of them must have glanced in the rear-view mirror and seen Kingsley because Pip suddenly ducked down out of sight.

Roger got out of the car. He waved to Kingsley, then walked across the road towards him. The boy climbed off his bike and faced the real estate agent, not sparing a glance at the car with his adulterer mother in it. Roger smiled his big fake smile. He said something, then gestured down the street. In response Kingsley pulled a set of keys from his jeans pocket and jangled them in the air. He waved goodbye then pushed his bike through the open gates and down the driveway.

Roger walked back across the road to the Lexus and stood on the footpath near the passenger door, his eyes on the Harding house. Pip was still hidden. His lips moved, but he continued to stare across the road. Pip popped up and in one smooth movement she opened the door and emerged from the vehicle. They conversed briefly.

My heart thudded. They were going to get away with it.

Pip looked at the house, smiled then kissed Roger hard and fast on the mouth. He hadn't time to respond before Pip twisted away from him, flicking her hair as she crossed the road.

The anger in me hardened into a rock that sat heavy and cold in my belly.

Pip didn't care about her family.

Maybe she didn't deserve one.

BEFORE

'Marriage is a *two-way street*, Katie.'

Mum spoke out of the side of her mouth as Sascha ate his sausages and chips, delighted both at the lack of green vegetables on his plate and the bowl of tomato sauce Mum had given him. He dunked each piece of sausage thoroughly and sat up at the dining table way past his bedtime like a little prince.

Mum and Dad were sure Peter and I could make it work. According to Mum, divorce would *scar Sascha for life*. Did I not care about *the sanctity of marriage*? Peter and I just needed to *talk it through*.

Mum's face was pinched with disapproval. I knew what she was thinking.

What would she tell the ladies at the golf club? They'd always been in awe of her celebrity son-in-law. 'Why would your daughter break up with Peter Bauer the author?' they'd ask. 'The man is so clever, and a dreamboat to boot. His book was a bestseller!' Mum knew they'd been surprised when her shy Katie had caught herself a man – a clever and attractive man, no less – who then became a celebrity (*I'd expect it from Leah, of course, but not Katie*, I'd heard her tell a friend over the phone). It, in turn, made her mother a celebrity. At the golf club, at least. What was wrong with Katie that she would even consider leaving him?

'Our street's been one-way for a long time, Mum,' I replied wearily. 'Dead-end even.'

She cast me a sharp look but refrained from comment.

* * *

Despite my resolve, her lectures took their toll. So when, a week later, Peter called and – with exaggerated and excessive politeness – asked if he could have Sascha the next weekend, I was all for it. Sascha had been asking for his father every day. Now I could tell him he'd see him soon. Peter told me he'd book a hotel and take Sascha to the zoo; I was welcome to spend the night in our apartment.

'It'll give you a chance to get away from your mum and dad for a bit,' he said, and I almost responded to the smile in his voice.

I couldn't believe my luck. Peter was being so reasonable. Plus a night to wander round my own house in my undies, eat food I wanted, not watch *A Current Affair*. It sounded like heaven.

He arranged for a pick-up early on Saturday morning, said he'd return Sascha to our apartment on Sunday night. The grin on my boy's face when I told him he'd get to spend some time with his dad made me doubt my decision to leave Peter all over again.

How could I separate such a loving father and son?

What kind of a monster was I?

MONDAY, 14 JULY
AFTERNOON

I glanced away from my computer and yawned. It was smack bang in the middle of that afternoon slump where time slowed and it seemed five o'clock would never come. Kingsley's dinosaur stared at me from beside my keyboard with its blank painted-on eyes.

I'd meant to put it away in my box of mementoes on Saturday night, but when I had arrived home from the pub, unsteady and maudlin, I'd found I couldn't do it. The thought of entombing it there in the dark with the rest of my collection was unbearable. So I'd kept the dinosaur with me, like a lucky charm, running my fingers over its rough spine from time to time. When I'd arrived at work that morning I pulled it from my pocket and propped it up near my computer keyboard. That's where it was now, leaning forward as if in a parody of drunken me, thanks to a bent front leg that meant it couldn't stand up straight.

Did little-boy Kingsley bend the leg, playing too hard with his plastic friend one day? Or had it been inadvertently crushed by a table leg or a shoe?

I continued typing a spiel about a renovate-or-detonate cottage in Lane Cove, the words automatic after so many years of practice, but my mind was on the Hardings. I couldn't stop thinking about them. A family on the cusp of being torn apart.

Why were they so important to me? The cactus on their kitchen windowsill popped into my head. The one like Peter's. I coveted the house, sure, but it was more than that. The family was special. They needed to stay together. Kingsley needed both his parents – and Pip and Brett needed to be together, even if they didn't know it.

I knew it.

I knew what could happen if you didn't keep your family together. And I couldn't let it happen to another family.

Something within me hardened, like Sascha's playdough left out of its tub too long.

I had to break up Pip and Roger.

But how?

I completed the listing and saved it, then opened Imperial Real Estate's Facebook page, ready to update our upcoming open houses.

Facebook.

Of course. I could do some research. Social media would allow me to spy on the Hardings. Roger too. Information was power, wasn't that the saying?

The search icon at the top of the page beckoned. I glanced around as though expecting Vivian or Tahlia to burst into the office and say 'Gotcha!' – which was, of course, highly unlikely. My fingers hovered over the keys, and for a moment I felt a twinge of guilt. This is what Peter used to do. Checking up on me, searching for secrets.

My jaw clenched.

Maybe I should have been sneakier back then. Done some checking up of my own. Perhaps it would have helped me guess what he would do. What he was capable of.

No, Kate, don't think about it. Don't go down that rabbit hole.

I shook my head, forcing my thoughts back to the task at hand. I pictured the smiling Hardings from that skiing photo I'd found. They could be that happy again, I knew it. Perhaps this was a tiny bit morally improper, but, really, what choice did I have?

None.

Roger Bailey was a common name on Facebook, but he had a business listing that appeared near the top of the search results. Most of his posts listed houses he was selling, with details of inspection times. The first post was about the Harding house. I clicked on the image and a pop-up screen displayed a larger photo: 308 likes, 84 comments, mostly people tagging others. I clicked on the like symbol and a list of names with attached thumbnail photos appeared. I'd hardly scrolled down at all when I saw a face I recognised. A close-up photo, black and white. An arty shot but not overdone. Pip. She was so beautiful it made my chest tighten.

I scrolled further down his feed but it was all pretty standard stuff, mostly homes for sale interspersed with the odd funny dog meme or video. Most people were pretty Facebook savvy nowadays, so perhaps I wouldn't find this as useful as I'd hoped. I clicked on Roger's profile details. Status: *single*. Old profile pictures showed him with two girls, presumably his daughters. Albums from a couple of years earlier showed a happy family: a sharp-featured but attractive blonde wife, a toddler and a baby. I remembered the strained phone conversation I'd overheard him having with his wife at the Harding house. He'd said they were in the process of separating. What was her name? Susan? No, Steph. Stephanie.

A quick search showed me they were no longer Facebook friends but I found her easily – she hadn't given up her married name, but she too listed her status as *single*.

Stephanie Bailey.

Aged forty. A lawyer. Little Meg and Hannah were aged three and six. Stephanie's most regular memes were about useless husbands, plus there were several espousing the value of strong discipline for children to stop them becoming 'little arseholes'. Smacking and the like.

I returned to Roger's page. His latest profile picture was a professional shot. His white teeth and tanned face made him look like something from a child's glow-in-the-dark nightmare.

OK. So much for Roger. Not a lot to work with there.

I scrolled back up and clicked on Pip Harding's thumbnail image. In the larger photo Pip looked even better. The background image for her page was an abstract painting in the vein of Jackson Pollock. I didn't recognise it, but I had no doubt it was beyond cool and worth a fortune. I clicked straight through to her profile details. The first thing I saw was her workplace.

Zero Seven White Gallery (ZSW).

Fucking perfect.

Pip worked at the most cutting-edge art gallery in Sydney. Make that Australia. I slumped back in my chair. It didn't say what she did there, not that it mattered. Any job at ZSW would be amazing. Cleaning toilets there would be awesome.

I rubbed my face and looked around, taking in my grey desk and flimsy black swivel chair. Even the carpet was the cheap fit-together-square type that sometimes lifted up at the edges and threatened (OH&S scandal!) to trip me over. My computer was out of date, the keys sticky from lunches eaten at my desk.

ZSW, by contrast, was a sprawling modern building squeezed onto a block in inner-city Redfern. I'd been there a few times, after Sascha died. Dr Evans said it would be good to do some of the things I used to love. That I should try to remember who I'd been before Peter.

Before Sascha.

It didn't help. I gave up art galleries again. They made me sad for everything I wasn't any more. For everything I didn't have.

I guess I took up open houses instead.

I clicked angrily back onto Pip's timeline. She hadn't posted much. A few shared articles about up-and-coming artists, some family holiday snaps – including the one of the three of them I'd seen in her bedroom, dressed for the snow. She'd captioned it: *Best holiday ever – black diamond experts, Niseko.* There was a shot of the three of them at the Statue of Liberty, and one where a young Kingsley was pretending to hold up the Leaning Tower of Pisa.

I soon located Brett's profile photo among Pip's friends; it must have been a shot from long ago given that he still had a full head of hair. He held a baby in his arms, probably Kingsley. I clicked on his page.

Investment Banker at Morris and West.

Well, that explained the holidays. The Hardings were rolling in it.

Brett's page was corporate not personal. I didn't realise investment bankers used Facebook as part of their job, but I guess that was the nature of modern life. He'd posted about mergers and alliances and he'd tagged other bankers, who commented about what a terrific bloke he was and how he'd made them heaps of money. There were social posts too, Christmas parties and fundraising galas, occasionally featuring photos of Pip in glamorous ball gowns.

I sat back again.

So far I'd found nothing to help me decide what to do about Roger and Pip.

I bit my lip.

Did Kingsley have a page?

I found him in Brett's friends list. Kingsley's profile picture was a line drawing of a snarling leopard leaping towards unseen prey. Intricate and lifelike, it was the same style as the blackboard drawings on his bedroom wall.

I clicked on the leopard.

Kingsley's posts were few and far between. His timeline was made up mostly of photos he'd been tagged in by someone else. He'd usually liked those posts, sometimes commenting, but he rarely posted anything of his own. Other than that single drawing, there was little useful information. Perhaps he kept his privacy settings tight. But then I found a post he had added himself about three months earlier, a photo of him and his father at a Test match in Melbourne. In the next photo he was with two other boys, all in grey and navy school uniforms, complete with ties and blazers. I enlarged the photo, squinted at it. Reading Grammar, according to the crest on his breast pocket. One of the most expensive private schools in Sydney.

A cheerful 'goodbye' alerted me to Vivian's departure as she passed my office, and I waved absently in response, surprised it was home time already. I hadn't even thought about having a drink yet. Perhaps amateur sleuthing suited me. Something like euphoria – or at least hearty self-congratulation – swept over me. Maybe I should celebrate. I could go see a movie on the way home.

I shut down the computer and grabbed my things. The little parasaurolophus peered over my keyboard.

'I've done some useful research, wouldn't you agree?' I whispered to it.

Its blank, black gaze appeared approving. I scooped it up and put it gently in a side pocket of my handbag, then headed out to reception feeling happier than I had in a while.

I said goodnight to Tahlia, who was shutting down her computer. She appeared surprised by my chipper farewell.

Out on the street, my stomach growled and I remembered I hadn't eaten since scoffing a Mars bar not long after lunch.

By the time I reached the train station I had concluded my good mood and new-found strength of character deserved a celebration. Nothing crazy, just one drink with dinner before the movie.

Just one drink.

BEFORE

Peter arrived at Mum's at eight on Saturday morning, looking better than ever. Somehow he was tanned, despite it being the middle of winter. Plus, he'd shaved and worn the blue and green checked shirt he knew I loved because it highlighted his blue eyes.

Time away from me did not appear to have been a hardship for him.

In stark contrast, I had bags under my eyes from sleeping – or, rather, *not* sleeping – on the rock-hard, sloping sofa bed. I'd put on my favourite knitted jumper and jeans, even applied foundation and lipstick for the first time in a week, but I still felt like a washed-out mess beside my husband. Sascha leaped into Peter's arms like they'd been separated for months not ten days. And Peter – no matter how often I recalled that moment and analysed every part of it – appeared overjoyed to be reunited with his son. Mum and Dad all but disowned me and adopted him on the spot. As I filled Sascha's water bottle from the kitchen tap, I saw Mum cup Peter's elbow and whisper something up at him then turn towards me, shaking her head.

So much for family loyalty, Mum.

Sascha was no better. After Peter kissed him and swung him to the ground, he raced outside and straight to the rear door of the car, climbed into his child seat and buckled himself in. He held an old coin purse of mine chock-full with several of his favourite plastic dinosaurs. I walked over and leaned in, trying not to mind he hadn't said goodbye.

'See you, Sasch. I'll miss you. Have fun with your dad, OK?'

He grinned up at me. 'Bye-bye Mummy. I will. See you tomorrow.'

His eyes were bright and I saw him as a stranger might. Not a baby any more, but a shy, gorgeous child kicking his legs with excitement.

'Pat some dinosaurs at the zoo for me.'

'There's no dinosaurs at the zoo, Mummy! They're all dead. Ex-tint, remember?'

I smacked a hand to my forehead. 'Yes, of course, I remember now. Silly Mummy,' I said, shaking a rueful head.

'Don't worry, Mummy, I'll pat a lion for you. RAH!'

I laughed, closing the door as he continued to roar, his hands forming claws that he raked at the window.

Peter said his farewells to my parents. He strolled back to the car, nodded at me and climbed in. 'Who wants to go to the ZOO!?' he asked, turning to the back seat and mugging a monkey face at Sascha.

'Me! Me! Me!'

And with that my boy was gone.

WEDNESDAY, 16 JULY
2.33 AM

I drifted awake.

I'd been dreaming of the Harding house again. This time we'd been around the pool. A toddler-aged Sascha sat on teenager Kingsley's shoulders in the water, shrieking with glee. Me on a sun lounger, sun-warmed and drowsy with a chilled margarita in my hand. In this dream, it was just us three. No Pip or Brett or Roger. No Peter. No Mum and Dad.

Cicadas called. A light breeze lulling me almost into a doze.

It had been perfect.

I closed my eyes and tried to drift back to sleep before the dream disappeared completely.

It didn't work.

I dozed on and off and then slept, the dream lost.

THURSDAY, 17 JULY
EVENING

By Thursday I'd scrolled through the Facebook pages of Roger, Pip, Brett and Kingsley at least a dozen times. I clicked through to their friends' pages and their friends' friends' pages. I kept Facebook open as a tab on my work computer, checking it regularly – a new secret shame.

That night, I took my laptop home after work and parked myself on the lounge with a pizza and a bottle of wine. I'd just settled in, a slice of oozy pepperoni in hand, a chilled glass of white wine on the coffee table and Facebook open on the screen, when my mobile rang.

Leah.

I couldn't handle talking to my sister right now. The ringing stopped and seconds later the phone buzzed to tell me I had a new voicemail. I picked up the wine and took such a big mouthful its bitterness made me wince. Then I took another sip, just to show it who was boss.

Leah.

It wasn't that we didn't get on, not really – we just had nothing in common. Leah had always been the golden child. A chubby-cheeked angel compared to gawky, shy me. She was an extrovert who got away with murder. She hadn't studied at school. Friends had let her copy assignments with a laugh and a 'that's Leah' shrug. Instead of going to uni she'd travelled the world, somehow landing amazing jobs everywhere from London to Santiago. She'd met celebrities, had wild adventures, did whatever she wanted. She'd been gone so long Leah didn't meet Peter until we'd been together two years. She even missed our wedding. I think she was living in Hong Kong – or maybe it was Singapore – at the time. And she'd seen Sascha at most half a dozen times before his death. She came home for the funeral, but I wasn't in a state to care.

Leah had been married to Ellis for six months and she'd only known him for two months longer than that. He was a rich American. Some sort of retail magnate. They'd met on a plane to Australia when Leah snuck in to first class. And the rest, as they say, was history. Society wedding, social pages. And now, to top it all off, a baby.

I picked up another piece of pizza. The thick layer of oil on top made me feel queasy but I chewed on. My phone rang again.

Leah. Again.

Filled with sudden rage, I snapped my laptop shut and barked a hello into the phone.

'Katie?' The word emerged timidly.

'I prefer Kate now,' I said, words falling like stones from my mouth.

'Yes, of course,' she said. 'Kate. How are you? It's been a while. Too long.'

I let the silence hang before answering. 'I'm fine.'

'That's good.'

'Congratulations on the baby. Mum told me.'

'Ah yes, thanks, Katie – Kate. Look, I know this must be hard for you —'

'No, no,' I interrupted her, my brusque tone belying my words. 'Don't be silly. I'm very happy for you and Ellis.'

'I know it was the anniversary the other day. The timing of it ... it's not what I wanted, of course. I was thinking of Sasch—'

'No, really, it's fine, Leah. Great news.'

'Yes, well. It's just that it's going to be in the *Herald* this weekend. Rumours about the pregnancy somehow leaked to the press and they've been hassling us. In the end Ellis told them the truth. He's just so happy, I couldn't make him keep a lid on it any longer. He set up an interview for us both tomorrow.' Leah tried to keep her tone flat but the inflection crept higher and higher as she spoke, betraying her excitement. Whether it was about the pregnancy or the interview I couldn't tell. Probably both.

Suddenly I was tired. Leah was what she was. Why did I expect her to change?

I opened up my laptop again. 'OK. I'll look out for it,' I said, my anger gone.

I typed in Pip's name, scanning her page for something I could possibly have missed. Her latest post, from 2.19 am the previous night – so she was a night owl – linked to an announcement of an upcoming Cezanne exhibition.

Leah was babbling on about the interview. How she didn't look pregnant yet, so she'd just have to put a hand on her belly for the photo, but what should she wear – something mumsy or would that be too much, she didn't want to look tarty ... 'I'd love to catch up sometime,' she said, jolting me back to our conversation. 'You could give me some advice on the whole pregnancy thing? What to buy? Prams and stuff? We could compare notes on how many times a night we had to get up to do a wee! Having been through it, you know? I'd love that.'

I didn't say anything.

'I mean, we wouldn't have to talk about that, we could just talk about … well, anything really …'

Her words petered out to an uncomfortable silence and I was too tired to make an effort for her. I clicked through to Kingsley's page and then sat up straighter. He'd posted something. An hour ago.

'Leah, I've got to go,' I said.

'Oh, OK, Ka—'

I pressed the button to end the call, turning my full attention to the computer.

Kingsley had posted a photo of a couple of tickets sitting on a white background – his desk, maybe. The caption said: 'Boys night out.' He'd tagged his father.

I clicked on the photo. The tickets were to a Monday night NRL game. Manly versus Parramatta. My thoughts raced. Maybe I could follow him and Brett? Talk to them? The thought was exhilarating but terrifying. What could I say? How would I explain why I was involved in their lives?

The post had fifteen likes. Roger was one of them. Why had he liked it?

Just then, a comment popped up below the picture. Pip. My heart beat faster and I leaned in to read it. 'Shame I can't come too. Damn computer course on Monday night! And on my day off. Why did I sign up for that again? Oh well, I'm sure you'll have fun without me!'

I picked up another slice of now cooling pizza, feeling antsy. It *was* possible Pip was going to attend a computer course. But

I couldn't help thinking how convenient it would be for her and Roger if she wasn't.

Another comment. This one from Kingsley: 'Shame. More carbs for us though.'

I dropped a piece of pepperoni onto the keyboard. I picked it up and put it in my mouth, then wiped tomato gunk from the keys with my fingers. Licked them clean.

The comment was quickly liked by three people. One was a friend of Kingsley's I'd spied on yesterday, one was Pip.

The other was Roger.

I kept an eye on the post for a while longer but no one else of interest commented on it. In any case, I'd had enough. Something was off. I just didn't know what.

But I would be there on Monday to find out.

PART III

THIRD
OPEN HOUSE

SATURDAY, 19 JULY
MORNING

I woke on Saturday with a headache, but feeling virtuous.

I'd obsessed over the Hardings all day Friday, going so far as to search – unsuccessfully – for nearby computer courses on Monday nights, and had polished off a bottle of wine by about eight-thirty that night. Practically nothing, really. I'd debated with myself for a good ten minutes over whether it was worth leaving the warmth of my flat to buy another, but the thought of the next morning's open house had convinced me to be good.

Such self-control.

It did cross my mind as I lay in my cosy bed that, for most people, drinking a bottle of wine in one sitting while watching a rerun of *Lethal Weapon 2* wouldn't be considered a win. Well, fuck them. As Roger Murtaugh might say, 'I'm too old for this shit.'

I'd take what small wins I could.

I spent a lazy morning at home, as I'd decided not to see any other houses. Somehow it would have felt like a betrayal. I ducked out to buy a bacon and egg roll, a coffee and the *Herald*, which I left on the benchtop, eyeing it as though it might leap up and attack me. After a second coffee – instant this time – I plucked up my courage and flicked through the pages until I came to the article about Leah and Ellis.

The story took up two-thirds of the social spread at the back. In the photo of the happy couple, Ellis stood behind Leah and she leaned back into him. His arms were around her, their hands clasped together over her flat stomach.

I hadn't seen Leah in a while. She looked good. Slim but strong. Her smile was wide and easy and her hair was shorter than I'd ever seen it, sitting just above the shoulder. It had obviously been straightened, as dark, wavy hair was one of the few things we shared.

Ellis was fifteen years older than my sister. A tall, athletic man with flowing grey hair. A typical American over-achiever. The type who attended ten-thousand-dollar-a-plate fundraisers. Ran marathons for charity. Who – in his spare time, mind you – read books to children in hospital. Ellis dabbled in car racing, an expensive pastime, but one I guessed you could try your hand at when you were worth $450 million.

I skimmed the article, which gushed about how wonderful they were, how in love, how excited to be parents, etcetera, etcetera. Then towards the bottom I saw my name.

Leah, of course, has been through tragedy of her own. Ten years ago, almost to the day, Leah's sister, Katie Bauer, lost her son, Sascha, in the worst possible way. Leah told us how she still misses her young nephew, who would have turned fifteen earlier this year. Those of you with long memories might remember the horrible event that shocked the nation all those years ago, when Katie's husband, bestselling author Peter —

I scrunched the paper into a ball and shoved the lot in the bin, my face hot but my insides icy.

How could she talk to them about me? About Peter?

About *Sascha*?

With barely contained fury, I grabbed my coat, handbag and keys and left the apartment, desperately in need of fresh air.

It was five degrees colder in the lobby, thanks to the door being stuck open again. I shoved it, surprised when the wind took it, whipping it back open to slam against the building. The glass shuddered but held firm. A wallop of air hit me, fresher than I'd expected. Frigid even.

Outside, the iron-coloured sky seemed oppressively low and glacial gusts of air probed my outfit as if searching for a weak spot.

Heading north on the Pacific Highway, traffic was light, as though everyone had decided to stay indoors by the fire. I drove erratically, heater blasting, my thoughts swirling and snaking their way back to Leah and that article. Rage simmered inside of me.

How dare she use my tragedy, my son's *death*, to get sympathy in what was nothing more than a vapid froth-piece of journalism?

Leah and Pip were peas in a pod. Selfish. Oblivious to the pain of others. They sailed through life without a care in the world. Everything came easily to them. Money. Success. Men.

And neither of them knew a thing about what it was like to lose someone you loved.

I yanked the steering wheel to the left and pulled into a suburban side street, jerking the car to a halt near the kerb. I turned the radio up and screamed, my hands clenched on the steering wheel, my feet kicking against the carpeted interior of the footwell. A few sobs escaped me as I slumped over the wheel. My toes throbbed. My rage vanished and I raised my head, staring vacantly out the window for several minutes while a rapper sang without obvious emotion about his shorty. Then I started the car and turned back onto the highway.

I headed for the Harding house and parked across the road a couple of houses away, switching the engine off and wrapping my coat around me more tightly. Soon Roger came with his signage paraphernalia and began setting it out. He'd almost finished when Pip came up the driveway. She spoke to Roger casually, not at all intimately, and for a moment I was thrown. Then Kingsley appeared and I understood. They chatted a little more before Pip and Kingsley climbed into a black sporty SUV, parked on the street. Pip's car, I presumed. Then they were gone.

Roger walked down the drive, wheeling his bag along behind him. I sat in the car until two other cars arrived. Heading for the house, my excitement rose and I hardly noticed the cold.

Roger stood inside the front door, grinning his big fake grin in welcome. Then he saw me. Something in the set of his shoulders, the way he held himself – how his grin faltered for just a split second – told me he now knew about the incident.

My heart sank. Had Renee told him? Maybe he'd just seen the paper this morning, read Leah's drivel, and put two and two together.

I considered walking past him with a wave and a smile, but for some reason I didn't. I waited for him to finish talking to the couple. At last they wandered off towards the kitchen and Roger stood for a moment as if steeling himself then approached me, clipboard in hand, his smile even broader and faker than normal but with an undercurrent of nervousness. He reached out his other hand for mine, shaking it firmly, not quite meeting my eyes. 'Kate. Back again. It's good to see you.'

So he wasn't going to say anything. I wasn't sure if I admired or despised him for that.

'Hi Roger. Yes, I hope that's OK?'

'Of course. I have your details already,' he said, tapping the clipboard as if to corroborate that fact, 'so feel free to look around.'

A family entered as he finished the sentence and he made a beeline for them, grin set back to full beam. I took the chance to escape, heading upstairs to Kingsley's bedroom where I examined his drawings again, more enthralled by his talent than ever. This time I thought to pull out my smartphone and take some photos I could examine at my leisure later. I knew this was a disturbing thing to do, but I quashed the thought.

You are just documenting the house. That's all. It's a perfectly normal thing for a prospective buyer to do.

But you aren't a prospective buyer, Kate.

The voice didn't stop me.

As the end of the inspection time neared, I went back downstairs, passing Tammy, the stylish vowel-strangler from the Turramurra open house. She was back for another look too. The thought of Tammy, her rich husband and their silent children living in the Harding house was not one that pleased me. The Harding house wasn't for just anyone.

It was special.

The children again followed at Tammy's heels, though this time she was also accompanied by an older man who I took to be her husband. He was as well dressed as his wife, but seriously overweight, his shirt buttons threatening to pop where they strained over his belly, his face purple-red. He too was silent. As I passed Tammy she caught my eye then averted her gaze. I recognised that look.

At the front door Roger farewelled someone then turned and saw me. A gain the normal expression slid from his face, replaced by the one I'd just seen Tammy sporting.

Pity.

'Kate, how did you go?' His voice was different too, the syllables drawn out. Almost condescending.

'Oh good, yes.'

Roger looked like he might say something then – something *real* – but he didn't.

Anger bubbled up inside me and my words came out quite forcefully for a change. 'This is such a great family home, isn't it? You have children, don't you?'

Beneath his orange tan he blanched. 'I … um, yes, I have two daughters,' he said apologetically, and he spoke the next words as if they were a peace offering, 'although I'm separated from my wife.'

He'd forgotten he'd told me already.

'I'm sorry to hear that,' I said, speaking flatly. I could hear his mind whirring as he tried to decide what to say. He couldn't very well ask me about my own family, could he?

He cleared his throat. 'We only separated about six months ago. We are trying to get on, though Stephanie's not making it easy for me, I have to say. I worry about … No, never mind. But I do miss seeing my girls every day.'

As soon as the words were out he seemed to realise what he'd said. His orange face darkened to red and he fiddled with his clipboard.

'Do you think you'll get back together with your wife?'

A look flashed across his face. Another one I was familiar with.

Fear.

Fear of me? Or of his wife?

'What do you know about Stephanie? What have you heard?' he asked, then quickly waved the words away as if he shouldn't have said anything. 'I mean, no, I don't think so.'

I thought about letting him off the hook, but the words spilled from me before I could reconsider. 'I'd try and make it work if I was you,' I said, my voice harsh. 'Separations can end badly. You remember what happened to me, don't you?'

I walked out the door, leaving him open-mouthed.

MONDAY, 21 JULY
AFTERNOON

It was still light when I arrived at the Harding house. I coasted past. The front gate was open, apparently the norm for the Hardings. I pulled into a spot across the road from the house with a line of sight to the front gate, but not close enough to draw attention to me. Or so I hoped. My yellow car wasn't great for discreet surveillance but I figured none of the Hardings were familiar with it, only Roger. Hopefully the darkness and his infatuation with Pip would prevent him from noticing it tonight.

If he showed up.

An SUV was parked near the front gate. Possibly Pip's. I couldn't see Roger's Lexus.

I shut off my engine. It was just after 4.30 pm and the skies were already darkening. I'd feigned a migraine at work after lunch, worried if I came too late Pip and Roger would be gone, doing – well, whatever it was they had planned – without me there to witness it. Since Saturday I'd pored over the Facebook posts again and again, looking for more clues. There'd been no further comments added to Kingsley's original post, so I had to use what little information I already had. Pip had said the course was Monday *night*. She hadn't said *afternoon* – plus she had the day off. These facts, I hoped, added up to her currently being at home.

Now I just had to wait.

I'd picked up some essential victuals on the way: a family-sized bag of cheese Twisties and a packet of Tim Tams. And, of course, a little heart starter: a bottle of Russia's finest crystal-clear vodka. Well, there was just an inch left in a bottle I'd discovered that morning in, of all places, my infrequently used gym bag. I'd decided it was better than nothing, convincing myself alcohol was necessary to keep me warm – and given how cold it was already, I was pleased with that decision. No point being frozen and unable to complete the task at hand.

It was basically a necessity.

The next question was: were Brett and Kingsley still home?

The Parramatta versus Manly game was scheduled for kick-off at seven. They'd have to allow at least half an hour's travel time, longer in peak-hour traffic. Maybe they were having dinner somewhere before the game, in which case Brett would have left work early and they'd already have been long gone.

I couldn't leave my car running so it didn't take long till I was shivering. I tucked the rug I'd thought to bring over my knees with a self-congratulatory smile. Neighbourhood watch was my biggest worry. People in fancy suburbs like this one tended to get nervous if they saw a person loitering outside their house in a car. With a bit of luck the coming darkness would be enough to protect me.

The sky was clear but the shadows were lengthening and the sun sat low on the horizon. I grabbed the bottle of vodka from the seat beside me.

This was the moment.

I could do the right thing: set the bottle down, put my fingers to the ignition key, turn it and leave. I could stop right now, go home, switch on a heater and the TV and forget all about Pip and Brett and Kingsley and Roger. Pour a wine and flop onto the lounge. Not go down this path.

Even I could see this path was crazy.

I could choose to walk – or, in this case, drive – away.

Right now.

Breathing deeply, I held the bottle cap between my thumb and index finger for a long moment before twisting it off and chucking it onto the passenger seat.

I lifted the bottle to my lips. The liquid, at first cold, soon seared my throat. It tasted unbelievably good and I knew all at once I was doing the right thing.

I needed to stay. For Kingsley.

The warmth of the alcohol worked its way down to my icy toes as darkness slowly descended. No movement at the Harding house.

I wrapped the rug tighter around my thighs and opened the packet of Twisties, at first choosing one at a time, forcing myself to savour their cheesy, salty goodness. But soon I was grabbing them by the handful, my fingers orange and powdery.

I waited.

By six it was fully dark. The exposed silver insides of the Twisties bag winked at me from under the streetlights and I shoved it onto the floor, ripping open the Tim Tams to spite it.

Something outside caught my eye. A woman's legs disappeared into the SUV, barely visible under the dim streetlights. The door slammed. The car's headlights flashed on as she started the engine.

Shit.

Shit. Shit. Shit.

She sped off as I flung the blanket from my knees and tried to turn the ignition key with frigid fingers.

By the time I reached the T-intersection at the end of the street I was wide awake and worried I'd lost her. I peered in both directions and only saw one set of taillights, so I followed them, heart in my mouth. At the next set of traffic lights I was relieved to discover it was indeed Pip's black SUV.

The light changed and she drove off smoothly, then increased her speed. My Hyundai lurched after her car, following like a devoted dog trailing its owner. The road emptied out as we drove through an area dark and quiet with bushland. Pip picked up her pace. My car whined unhappily but I forced it to stay within a car or two. We continued like that through suburban streets that occasionally transformed into well-lit shopping strips.

I concentrated hard on not losing Pip, who was a bit of a speed demon. Finally – almost forty minutes later – we arrived in Manly. The harbour glinted darkly under a string of streetlights as we neared the ferry terminal. Pip turned down a dark street and pulled into a car space. I followed, counting my lucky stars to find a tiny spot less than half a block away. I climbed out and scurried after her. She'd crossed the street, heading in the direction of the pedestrian mall. With relief, I slowed to a more casual walk, trying to quiet my breathing.

Pip looked amazing, as usual.

She wore a black wrap dress, a denim jacket and long black boots with a very high heel, her hair hanging loose in dark waves. In comparison I felt like a frump, but I was pleased at least I hadn't changed clothes after work. My black pants suit, blue shirt and flat pumps was about as presentable as I got. The warmth from the vodka had long worn off and I shivered as a sudden draught lifted the back of my jacket. The air smelled strongly of the sea, but it wasn't a fresh ocean breeze, more like rotting seaweed. I wrinkled my nose and put my hands in my jacket pockets, hugging it to me as I trailed Pip.

The wind was stronger in the mall. Whirlpools of rubbish threw themselves against the dirty windows of a series of closed-up bargain shops and discount chemists. I followed her past several dimly lit restaurants and bars, their doors sealed tight against the wind.

The pavement was speckled with oyster-grey patches of chewing gum and other unidentified flattened substances. I stepped to one side to avoid dog shit that must have come from an animal of a size I would not want to meet in a dark alley then lifted my gaze just in time to see Pip pulling open the heavy wooden door of a bar about twenty feet ahead. I came to an abrupt halt, watching the door as it slowly closed behind her.

What now?

I roused myself and continued on, sauntering towards the place she had entered. As I drew level I risked a glance. The bar's name – *Bar Petit* – was written in an old-fashioned looping typeface across the glass frontage, but any view inside the window was obscured by a heavy crimson velvet curtain.

Shit.

A few shops on, I stopped and pretended to send a text, trying to decide my next move.

Should I risk going inside?

What if I walked in and everyone – including Pip or, even worse, Roger – turned to stare at me? Pip might not remember me from art school. In fact she probably wouldn't. Roger, on the other hand, certainly would.

I chewed on a nail, ripped it off with my teeth then spat it onto the bitumen.

I had no choice.

I trudged back to the bar, pushed the door open and walked into the warm air.

Straight into Pip Harding.

* * *

She stood three paces in front of me, leaning on the bar. As I stared at her hair, Pip spoke to the barman, not even turning around at the gust of arctic wind I'd brought in with me. Pip laughed loudly, throwing her head back.

Roger wasn't with her.

Fuck, I need to get out of here before she turns around.

'Good evening and welcome to Bar Petit. Can I help you?'

I nearly jumped out of my skin. A man in his mid-twenties had materialised beside me. He had an ironic twisty moustache, a nose stud and wore a hot-pink vest and black jeans.

'I, uh,' I stammered, my eyes darting to Pip then around the room.

The bar was cosy, with a loose theatre theme. Crimson velvet curtains ran not only along the front windows but all the way around the space, which actually was quite petite. Mismatched ornate lounges and chairs, upholstered in deep shades of velvet – emerald green, maroon, hot pink and teal – peppered the room. Semi-circular booths lined the curtained walls. Slow jazz played in the background. A few groups laughed and chatted but the soft furnishings muffled the noise and it was surprisingly quiet. On weekends this place was probably packed. However, on a blustery Monday night in the middle of winter clientele was harder to come by, which was making me rather nervous.

Oh God, what if Roger walked in right now?

The hipster waiter smiled at me in that patronising way young people reserve for the dowdy middle aged.

'I … I wanted to have a glass of wine, if that's OK?'

'Certainly, madam. Would you like to sit at the bar or —'

'No,' I said, butting in, desperate to be less conspicuous, 'one of the booths would be good if I can?'

He gestured to the nearest one. I darted over, pulling off my jacket and sliding across the smooth, cool leather into the corner of the booth. It was lit by a dangling chandelier, dimmed to a very low setting.

Perfect.

The Hipster presented me with a leather folder that announced the superiority of the wines listed within and wandered back to polish glasses behind the bar. In the booth directly across from me a group of four women in their late-twenties chatted in a surprisingly sedate manner.

I pretended to read the wine list as I watched Pip and the bartender. He was burly and a little scruffy, with three-day growth and a black t-shirt – more like a sexy lumberjack than someone who mixed drinks for a living. He was at least ten years her junior. As I watched, he leaned towards Pip, a half-smile on his face as she whispered to him, her eyebrow raised.

Ease up, Pip, you've already got one piece on the side.

She finished her story and he laughed. Then she peered around the room. I almost ducked but forced myself to remain still. She turned back to the barman, said a few words and pointed at the last empty booth, two along from the group of women. Perfect from my point of view. I could see the entire booth while remaining mostly hidden if I sat to one side.

I studied her as she slid into her seat. She wore her usual red lipstick but tonight also had on smoky eye makeup. Pip didn't look slutty, though, just classy. I had to admit it – she was as beautiful as she'd been at twenty-two.

My handbag (black, faux-leather, Kmart) sat on the booth beside me. It was full of useful items that had saved my hungover bacon many a time. Mints, eye drops, dry shampoo. Sunnies for the worst days. Foundation and concealer. I opened it and scrabbled around until I found an ancient lipstick. A sort of a beige nothing-colour. I smeared some on my lips.

It didn't make me feel any better.

The sexy lumberjack barman carried a drink over to Pip on a silver tray. Whisky. Neat. Or something that resembled it. 'On the house,' I heard him say, and Pip replied, 'Ky,' – or maybe Ty? – 'you shouldn't have,' and blew him a kiss.

'Have you decided what you'd like, madam?' The Hipster asked me. I bet he wouldn't call Pip madam like she was an old lady.

I flicked through the heavy card pages. The cheapest glass of white was fourteen dollars. I ordered it.

As The Hipster left my booth, I saw Roger standing just inside the door. He looked around, running a hand through his wind-ruffled hair. I shrank back against the leather, but he had eyes only for Pip. He saw her and smiled broadly.

I still didn't get the attraction. He was good-looking enough, yes, but the man was all teeth.

Roger strode across the room and slid in beside Pip. For a moment it looked like he was going to lean in for a kiss but then he pulled back, as if realising where they were.

Back at the bar, The Hipster said something to Sexy Lumberjack and he looked over at Pip and Roger and shrugged.

You agree with me, don't you. She's out of his league.

Sexy Lumberjack set a glass on the same silver tray Pip's drink had been on. The Hipster picked it up and turned my way.

'The Bibina sauvignon blanc, madam.'

He set the enormous glass down and I sighed inwardly. It barely contained a dribble. I drank more wine than that walking from my kitchen to the lounge.

Fourteen dollars.

I switched my focus back to Pip and Roger, who – to the casual observer at least – looked to be colleagues enjoying a drink together.

I wasn't buying it.

The Hipster made his way over to Pip and Roger. Roger spoke to him briefly and turned back to Pip.

'Another wine, madam?' The Hipster asked me, almost keeping the distaste from his voice. Almost, but not quite. I looked down. I'd finished my glass without realising I'd even started.

'Yes, that was lovely, thanks. I'll have a bottle of the same, please.'

'Of course. Just one glass?'

'Yes. One glass. For now,' I added, fooling no one but feeling compelled to do it anyway.

As he left, I returned my attention to Roger, who now sipped from a stemless glass of red wine, and Pip. What if they ran into someone they knew? Pip was supposed to be off computering somewhere. I watched her red lips as she looked at Roger with a half-smile on her face.

That smile. Pip seemed … excited.

She was enjoying this, I realised. My face grew hot with anger.

The possibility of being discovered must thrill her. I clenched my fists, digging fingernails into my palms. Pip laughed, throwing her head back so her white neck was exposed. Rage flashed in my brain and I had a sudden desire to slash at her throat, to see her scarlet blood mingle with Roger's red wine, flowing in waves as fluid as the Dracula-cloak curtains behind her.

Didn't she know what she had at home? Didn't she value her family? Her husband?

Her *child*?

The Hipster returned with a silver ice bucket, the neck of a bottle of wine extending from it like a swan's. Like Pip's. I shook off my bloody visions, disturbed by how vividly I'd conjured them. 'Your wine, madam,' he said, placing a glass before me and setting the ice bucket in the centre of the table.

'Thank you,' I managed, forcing my face into an expression less likely to scare the staff.

He nodded and went back to the bar, without pouring my wine. I did it myself, trebling the quantity he had poured earlier, before returning the bottle to the ice bucket.

I looked back in Pip's direction and froze.

She'd moved one hand from where it had been resting on her lap, below the level of the table, and was extending it towards Roger, first touching his knee, then running her fingers along his jeans, moving higher up his thigh slowly, taking her time. My face flamed again. Roger was doing his best to let nothing show in his expression but he seemed a little pink under his tan.

I forced myself to look away, finishing my glass of wine and pouring another before glancing back. Pip's hand was now resting on Roger's crotch and she was speaking to him as if nothing at all was amiss. He looked like he wasn't sure if he was happy or terrified.

Pip was better at this than him.

She took pity on Roger and removed her hand. She glanced at Sexy Lumberjack, who was wiping the counter idly, and he scampered over to her in a manner I found a little unbecoming.

He took her order and two more drinks were delivered, along with a cheese plate. Maybe it was complimentary, maybe they'd ordered it. Either way, Pip barely touched it and Roger ate little more.

What are you doing, Kate?

Watching them. Taking notes. I wasn't a private detective. I was just a voyeur. Again. I poured the last of the wine into my glass. What was I going to do? Confront them? Threaten them?

I could.

I supposed I could do that. Not here, though.

I swirled the wine around in my mouth. Maybe when they went outside. I could put a stop to it.

To help Kingsley.

I could follow them; threaten to tell Brett and Kingsley everything if they didn't end it right then. Roger was separating from his wife so there wasn't the same opportunity there – though she *was* a lawyer. Perhaps she'd stop him seeing his children if she knew about him and Pip? I winced. A step too far. But I could imply I'd tell McQuilty he was having an affair with a client. His bosses would frown on that, surely.

I swallowed the rest of the wine in one mouthful, suddenly ready to do it. Ready to confront them. I looked around a little fuzzily and realised the women in the opposite booth had left.

If Pip and Roger hadn't finished up in the next ten minutes I would get another glass. Nine minutes later they called for the bill. I did the same.

Sexy Lumberjack took a small folder over to Pip and Roger almost straightaway. My bill took a little longer to arrive. I tried not to baulk at the price, rooting around in my wallet for something close to the amount plus a couple of extra dollars for a tip. As Pip and Roger left I scrabbled to stand, shoving my arms into my jacket as I took the bill to the bar. I muttered my thanks and pulled open the door.

Then I took two steps into the icy wind and fell over.

* * *

I fell on my arse, thankfully. Not my face.

My head was spinning and I thrust out a hand, trying to move sideways to lean on the bar window, but I didn't make it. My feet weren't obeying my brain and I stumbled forward and then fell backwards, landing with a thud on my tailbone.

A sharp pain screamed up my spine and I crumpled onto my back, right across the entrance to the bar. I blinked in shock at the sky, at the darkness lightened with the glow of the city.

I pushed myself up onto an elbow, feeling blurry. But I'd been blurry many a time. I was used to that; it didn't matter. What mattered was Pip and Roger and where they were. I sat up. The mall was empty, save for several slouching teenage boys a few shops away. They watched me, making no move to approach.

Too bad if I was actually injured, I grouched, though in fact I was relieved they stayed away.

I got to my feet and squinted in both directions. Panic set in. I couldn't see Pip and Roger. Maybe they'd ducked down an alley to an even cooler, more-difficult-to-find bar. If they had, I was stuffed. I limped towards the centre of the rubbish-strewn paved area, desolate this wintry evening. Staring in the direction of the ferry terminal, I couldn't see anyone apart from the teenagers, who must have decided I was unworthy of any further interest and were skateboarding desultorily away. I spun in the other direction, ignoring the sharp twinge of pain shooting up my spine.

There.

Two figures disappearing into a large building down near the beach. I hitched my handbag up onto my shoulder, shook the fog from my brain and strode towards the distant goal, eyes fixed on the last place I'd seen them. I knew where they were going. It was the kind of place I knew well.

A pub.

Not just any pub, more an institution. The Northern Lights was infamous. A super-pub. *Northies*, in the local vernacular. Set over three levels, with five restaurants and God-only-knew how many bars, Northies was a temple to alcohol. My kind of place.

I pushed open the door and heat poured out, so humid it was almost visible. Inside, heavy bass thumped but the large room was virtually empty. The rainbow strobe lights seemed extra sleazy on a Monday evening. Most of the hotel had been updated, but this room had been passed over. Its walls were marked, wooden floors grubby and scuffed. A bar along the right-hand side was manned by a gum-chewing young woman with a ponytail busy pouring a draught beer. A very drunk, grey-haired man in skinny black jeans and a white singlet lurched around near the small stage at the far end of the room in an approximation of dancing. A middle-aged couple sat at a table near the door drinking matching blue cocktails with umbrellas, staring at one another like love-struck teenagers.

And then there was Pip and Roger.

They stood about halfway along the bar, apparently waiting for drinks. I stepped inside, the floor pulling at my shoes with a tacky grip, and walked towards them. Roger had his back to me. Pip stood on his other side, with her body tilted towards him not the bar.

Music thudded in my ears with a doof-doof beat that made me feel old and gave me a headache, which in turn made me feel even older. I slowed my advance. Maybe this was a bad idea. I could go outside and wait for them to finish, and confront them there. But it was freezing outside, and what if they left via a different door?

As I vacillated, Pip looked over Roger's shoulder, straight at me. Her gaze immediately moved on, without any suggestion she knew me. She leaned close to Roger and whispered in his ear, then laughed. He paid for their drinks and they headed for a door in the back corner that led further into the building.

I moved fast, almost without thinking.

'Hi Roger,' I yelled over the music. 'I thought it was you.'

Roger turned and paled under his tan. He smiled at me, but I noted with malicious glee his eyes gave him away. 'Kate. How nice to see you. Are you here on your own?'

'Yes,' I yelled again, then looked at Pip. She smiled at me, and I wondered if she'd recognised me yet. I gestured at her but spoke to Roger. 'And your friend?'

Roger opened his mouth to say something but no words were forthcoming.

It was Pip who spoke. 'Grace,' she said, not even flinching at the lie.

'Hi Grace. It's nice to meet you.' I smiled at Roger, who looked like he might be sick. But then I stumbled to one side, which kind of ruined the moment. Pip frowned at me then gathered herself and took Roger's arm.

'It's nice to meet you – ah, Kate, was it?' she asked. 'We were just going to sit somewhere quieter. Enjoy your night.' She turned away, dismissing me.

Roger touched my arm and for a moment I thought he was worried about me.

Don't concern yourself with me, I wanted to yell in his face, *you're the one in trouble. You're a liar. An adulterer. This is about you and Pip.*

And Kingsley. The innocent boy whose life you are both about to ruin.

Instead I just smiled in a way that I hoped was enigmatic and watched them walk away. I ordered a double vodka from the bored bartender. It turned out 7.39 on a Monday night was somehow Happy Hour. That explained the drunken dancing guy, who spun and twirled as though he was alone in the world. I envied him; he was past caring about anything. I propped my elbows on the bar and drank my vodka. Partway through, the waitress approached me. Happy Hour was finishing in five minutes, did I want another?

I did.

I definitely did.

I drank it greedily. Had Roger told Pip who I was by now? Would she remember me?

Did she have her hand on his crotch again?

As the vodka warmed me further, I started to wish I'd said more. Properly confronted them. Told Pip off for destroying her marriage. Yelled at Roger for breaking up a loving family.

My gaze followed the strobing lights back to the dance floor. The drunk guy had succumbed to lethargy. He sat on the lone chair on the far side of the room and slept, chin on his chest. He looked smaller. Sad and alone.

I stood up, the bar stool tipping up on two legs before settling back on all four. I skolled the rest of the vodka and set the glass down with exaggerated care. I swayed, grabbing the edge of the bar. The bartender looked at me without curiosity. I smiled at her anyway.

'Thanks for the drinks,' I slurred.

Okay, where were they again?

Ah yes, through the door, off kissing or groping somewhere. I strode towards it, placing one foot precisely after the other with intense concentration. Even so, I fell onto the door and threw it open with such force I went flying into the other room. I managed to get my hands onto a table and stopped short of hitting the floor. I tried to focus.

Pip and Roger sat at a table for two in a far corner, the only people present. Thankfully the tables were close together and I leaned on them as I stumbled towards my destination. Even drunk, I realised Pip and Roger must have chosen this place because no one they knew would come here.

Or so they thought.

They watched my approach. Roger's expression sat somewhere on the scale between concern and nausea. Pip's look was pitying now instead of dismissive, and if I'd been more sober I'd have realised just what that meant.

I yelled at them again, but this time, in the quiet dining room, the words were extremely loud. 'Hello, again!'

Neither Pip nor Roger said anything.

I stopped and squinted hard at them, trying to keep everything in focus. 'I want to talk to you two. Lovebirds. Roger and ... what was your name again?' I paused for effect. '*Grace*, did you say?' I waved my hand triumphantly. 'Or is it perhaps Philippa, or even Pip, by any chance?' I attempted to put my hand on a nearby chair, missed and almost tumbled over. 'It's Pip Harding, isn't it? I know you. We went to art school together. You were Pip Reeves back then. Pip the beautiful. Pip the perfect.'

Pip regarded me, her expression composed.

'You don't remember me, do you?' I asked.

She carefully placed her knife and fork on her rocket-filled plate before smiling at me with scarlet lips. A smile that didn't show her teeth. 'Of course I remember you. It was Katie then, though, wasn't it? We had a lot of the same first-year classes. Still Life, I think, and Sculpting with dreadful Professor Fordham. Old letch.' She made a face. 'You never said much. But of course I *remember* you.' Pip gave a little laugh. 'I didn't at first,' she continued. 'I can't be expected to remember everyone from art school. But once Roger told me your name it all came back to me. I mean, we've all … *changed*, haven't we?'

'I got fat, you mean.'

Roger stood up, his knife and fork clattering onto his plate as his chair scraped back. 'Kate, I think you've had a bit too much to drink. Do you want me to call you a taxi? Or get you some water or —'

'I don't want water. I want to talk to you two.' I waved my hand at them, then dropped my voice to an exaggerated whisper. 'I know what you're doing.'

Roger looked at Pip but her expression gave nothing away.

'You're good, Pip Harding,' I went on, 'but you can't fool me. I've seen you. I've seen you together. I want you to stop it. You have to stop it. Finish it. Don't hurt Kingsley and Brett.'

Roger started. 'Kate, how do you know Kingsley and Brett?'

'I just do, alright?' I yelled, waving my hands again. 'It doesn't matter how. You need to finish this, this … *thing* you're doing. It's not fair. It's not *right*.' I lowered my voice, filled it with righteousness, trying to make them believe it too. 'Family is everything, you know? You have to think about your family. Don't destroy what you've got.'

Pip stood up, her face a mask of pity.

Fucking pity.

'Katie — Kate, I know it must be hard for you, considering what happened to your son …'

I felt cold. 'What?' I replied quietly.

Pip glanced at Roger and they both gave me the look again.

'I heard about it on the news,' she said. 'I remembered you from art school and it really hit home. It was truly terrible, what your husband did. I'm so sorry.'

I stared at her, suddenly sober.

'I'm sorry about your boy,' she said. 'About … Sascha, I think his name was?'

'Don't say his name.'

Now she looked confused.

'Don't either of you … *adulterers* … say my son's name. Ever.'

Roger and Pip were destroying the Harding family. Pip was destroying her marriage, tearing Kingsley's life apart, for what? For an *affair*? I didn't want her saying my son's name. It felt like a blasphemy. And though I'd sobered at her mention of him, I was still drunk enough to act on my anger.

I took a step towards them. 'Stop looking at me like that!'

'Kate, we aren't looking like anything,' Roger said. He spoke as if I were a skittish horse.

'I'm not crazy!'

'We don't think you're crazy. Of course we don't,' he said, his tone conveying exactly the opposite.

Then Pip stepped forward, her smile still infuriatingly pitying. 'Kate, no one is suggesting you're crazy. I really do remember you. You were always the good girl, the one who did the right thing. I *know* you. You wouldn't harm a fly.'

She knew me?

Pip Harding thought she *knew* me?

I stared at those red lips, the lips with which she kissed a man other than her husband. And did who knew what else. I wanted to hurt Pip for what she was doing to tear her family apart. I wanted to punish her, as I'd been punished. The red filled my vision, blurred before my eyes and I lashed out, or tried to. I lunged forward then stumbled.

Roger loomed like a creature from a nightmare, his hands grasping at me. He missed and I fell, arms flailing, banging hard against the table, clattering the plates and cutlery. I closed my eyes and scrabbled for a table, instead felt something softer and warmer – human – under my hand and then it was gone.

I heard a groan, wondered for a moment if it was me.

No. Not me.

I tried to sit up but exhaustion and a familiar biliousness overtook me. I opened my eyes and attempted to focus, finding myself a child in a forest of table and chair legs.

'Pip, are you alright?' Roger sounded worried.

The groaning started again, louder this time.

Oh God. What have I done?

I pushed up, my tailbone throbbing, and sat back against a table leg. I needed my bed. I needed to sleep this off.

'My wrist. I think it's broken.' Pip's voice was a whisper.

Her words finally penetrated the fog of my brain. She sat on a dining chair clutching her arm, Roger by her side. I whimpered, trying to summon an apology. The room spun and I shut my eyes.

'There. That's her,' said a woman's voice.

'OK, we'll take it from here.'

This one a man.

'Are you alright?' he said, but I kept my eyes closed against the nausea and the shame.

I could hear Roger explaining my behaviour from his point of view, but in a nice way I didn't deserve.

Then a different man spoke. 'Doug, can you stay with this couple and organise a paramedic to check them out, please? I'll take the lady here outside. It might help her sober up.' His non-judgemental tone made me feel worse.

Two cool hands gripped under my arms and stood me up. I gasped as a sharp pain shot up my spine.

'Are you OK?' the man asked.

I nodded, and he looped my arm around his shoulder then started to half-drag, half-walk me away. I tried to open my eyes, but vertigo threatened and I closed them again.

'Watch the step,' he said, and I leaned further into him as we stumbled down some stairs.

Cold air washed over me, so good – more welcome even than vodka. The man must have found a door leading directly outside. Down two more steps and a dozen paces and we stopped again.

'Let's find you a seat,' he said.

The cold air had revived me enough to open my eyes and breathe in and out deeply. My arm was still draped around his neck, and when I looked down I saw his navy pants, the holstered gun, his shiny black boots.

A policeman.

Panic set in. I stood up and tried to pull away, to get away, but it was too late.

I bent over and vomited all over his boots.

BE CAREFUL WHAT
YOU WISH FOR

Be careful what you wish for.

Be careful what you wish for.

Wish for.

Be careful.

What did Peter mean? I'd spent hours – days – going over those words. At the time, I assumed he meant little more than that I would miss him, that I'd regret leaving him because I'd be lonely. That I would miss 'us' – the three of us, the family unit he so worshipped. That I would come crawling back to him. That I couldn't live without him.

I couldn't have known what Peter really meant.

Could I?

There'd been nothing to alert me to his intention.

Had there?

What about two weeks later when he'd picked up Sascha from Mum's, raised a hand in farewell and driven off with my baby in the back seat?

No.

Not a look. Not a gesture, not a hesitation, not a flicker of a suggestion of what he would do a little over twenty-four hours later.

But I knew what people thought; what they said behind my back.

How could she not have known?

I'd read up on similar cases later – obsessed over them – and talked it over with Dr Evans too. In most cases there were warning signs. An escalation in domestic violence. Palpable anger from the aggrieved husband. Threats. But with Peter I had truly had no clue. Just that one phrase.

Be careful what you wish for.

I'd been over it in my brain a million times.

Maybe it wasn't something Peter had planned. Maybe he didn't mean anything when he'd said it that day in the preschool playground, and I've since read too much into it.

I'll never know now, of course.

It's too late for that.

BEFORE

Two police officers on my doorstep.

The sun almost at the horizon, silhouetting them with an unearthly glow. One male, one female. Both wearing navy pants and light-blue shirts, their distinctive peaked caps in their hands. Guns in holsters, thick black belts and boots polished to a brilliant shine. The male officer was older, maybe fifty, with a salt and pepper moustache and a paunch. The woman was young, not long out of the police academy by the looks of her. Neither wore a jacket.

My first thought was *you must be really cold*.

Later I would wonder at that. At my naivety. My stupidity. Why I wasn't more concerned – why it didn't even cross my mind to wonder what they were doing on my doorstep at 5.15 on a Sunday afternoon, the first really cold day of that winter. Why I didn't notice the resolute set of their jaws, the extreme neatness of their uniforms, their hands clasped awkwardly over their hats in front of their bodies, as if trying to protect themselves from me. From what they were about to tell me.

Until then, I'd had a great day.

I'd been shopping all morning, had lunch at a café, watched a movie, then gone for a run around the Botanic Gardens. I'd just returned and was still in my old muscle-shirt and joggers, my hair pulled back from my reddened face. I'd done five kays and had well and truly warmed up, but the weak winter sun had by then practically vanished. I shivered. Peter was due to bring Sascha home at 6 pm then I'd head back to Mum's. In one hand I grasped a glass of half-drunk tap water, the other rested on the door frame.

The male officer did the talking. I don't remember the words. I know he asked if I was Katie Bauer and if they could come inside. I took them upstairs and into the kitchen. He told me – gently – *you might like to sit* but I remember saying *no, what is it, tell me*, suddenly terrified. The woman frowned, watching me as if expecting me to attack or scream, or harm myself. In hindsight, any of those reactions would have been understandable to her.

I don't remember everything they said after that.

I do remember dropping the glass, hearing it smash on the tiled floor. I do remember looking at the puddle of water as if it were a puzzle I couldn't solve. I do remember the female officer finding a dustpan and brush and ineffectually dabbing at it while the male officer kept on talking. I remember thinking, half-numb, how even in the police force the woman was expected to do the chores. I remember his words went on and on. So many, most of them, I didn't hear.

But I heard some of them. I heard *your husband and son* and *involved in an accident*.

Accident.

Except it wasn't, the police already knew that. And when I looked into the eyes of the male officer, I knew it too.

I heard *so sorry* and I heard *dead*.

Dead.

Then it was dark and the police officers were gone. I buried myself under the doona. I remember my mother perched on the edge of my bed, staring at the wall with unseeing blue eyes.

I don't remember crying. I remember curling up, silent and empty, my hands wrapped around my stomach.

A husk.

A shell.

They told me the details later.

Details.

Like I needed to know the details.

MONDAY, 21 JULY
EVENING

I stood up straight, my throat burning as I apologised over and over again.

'Don't worry about it,' the policeman said.

He ignored the vomit splashed over his boots and led me further away from the hotel until we stood by a park bench in the centre of the mall. I lowered myself onto the seat, dropping my head between my knees. He stood in front of me and I stared at his vomit-covered boots.

'Had a few too many tonight, did you?' he asked, apparently unconcerned by the mess all over him, not to mention the stench.

I groaned, and then the nausea really hit. I stood up and looked around wildly. Just behind the bench was a stunted tree in a dusty patch of earth. I stumbled around the bench and threw up again onto the dirt. Then a hand materialised before my eyes, the clean white tissues it held the best things I'd seen all night.

'Thanks,' I said, wiping and then spitting foul-tasting saliva onto them before balling them up in my sticky palm. 'You're game, putting your hands in front of my mouth.'

I was surprised to hear the man laugh lightly.

I lifted my head and peered up at him. He looked to be in his late thirties, and was tanned with a round face and wide cheekbones. His head was shaved – perhaps to camouflage a receding hairline, I couldn't tell. He was Asian, maybe Japanese, with striking, intense eyes: dark and piercing. But despite the severity of his face he appeared kind. He was a little taller than me and looked stocky, although that could have been because he was weighted down with a full patrolman's uniform. I couldn't help but flinch at the sight of it. Not that I had anything against the police. I even believed they deserved to arrest me for what I'd done to Pip. But they'd been there on the worst day of my life. And although they had been gentle that day and in all my dealings with them in the weeks following, just seeing an officer in uniform now made me feel ill.

'What's your name?' the policeman asked.

I told him in a small voice, still facing the scraggly plant.

'Kate Webb, did you say?' he asked and I nodded without turning around. He paused for a moment, no doubt writing my name on a charge sheet to use when he took me to the police station. 'Did you drive here tonight, Ms Webb?'

I nodded.

'Well, you won't be driving home,' he said in a wry voice I didn't expect from an officer of the law. 'Where do you live?'

'Artarmon.'

'Look, my shift ends in a minute. The station's just around the corner so Doug can walk back without me. How about I take you home? You can get a taxi to your vehicle tomorrow.'

I turned to face him, then looked down to stem the nausea the movement caused. 'I'm not being arrested?'

'No. Well, I don't think so. I'll go and check with Doug and the people you were … talking to, but I'm sure we can sort something out.'

Relief washed through me.

'Sit tight. When I come back I'll need to get some details from you. Just phone number and address, that sort of thing. I'll have to write this up.' He handed me another wad of tissues and led me back around to sit on the bench. 'Don't move, OK?'

I managed to look into his eyes. He seemed concerned and something lightened inside me. He paused then appeared to decide something and he walked away.

After a minute or so I glanced in the direction he'd gone in. Pip and Roger were standing near the hotel, talking to the two policemen. Pip's wrist was bandaged but there was no sign of a paramedic. As if on cue, they turned towards me. They were too far away for me to hear them, but I could see Pip speaking emphatically before shaking her head and my heart sank. That was it then, I was going to be arrested. I tried to look as pitiful as possible, which wasn't hard since I was bedraggled and spattered with vomit. Roger pulled out his wallet and for a moment I was horrified. He was *paying* them? What for? Then I realised he was giving them his business card, probably for an address. Then Roger spoke to the kind policeman with the intense eyes and they both glanced my way. The policeman nodded his goodbyes and walked back to me.

'Well, it's your lucky day,' he said. 'The woman was pretty pissed off – she was all for pressing charges, but the man convinced her not to.'

'Really? Roger did that?'

I might have misjudged him. Underneath all that tan maybe he was a big softie.

'Yep. Like I said, it's your lucky day. But don't get too excited. They'll be going in to the station tomorrow for a restraining order.'

'Oh.'

A restraining order.

Hot shame washed over me. What was I becoming? First stalking, and now a restraining order. I was lucky the stalking hadn't been discovered, or I'd really be in the shit.

'What does that mean?' I asked, looking up at him.

'It means you'll have to stay far away from the both of them.'

I looked down at his boots.

Stay away from Pip and Roger.

Oh God. The Harding house.

That meant I couldn't go back there.

The policeman cleared his throat. 'Look, I don't normally pass on messages like this, but the man specifically requested you stay away from the rest of the family as well.'

I was quiet.

'Does that mean something to you? Did you threaten their families?'

'What?' I replied, looking up at him in shock. 'God no. Just the opposite.'

He raised an eyebrow, waiting.

'They – those two, they're having an affair.'

He didn't seem shocked. I guessed he'd seen it all before.

'I was trying to break them up,' I continued reluctantly. 'Pip … the woman … Her husband and son – I didn't want them to get hurt. I thought I could … fix things, I guess …'

'Why do you care about them? Are they friends of yours?'

'No. Not really. They don't even know me.'

'Then why?'

I thought for a moment, at a loss to explain it. I pictured the photo of the three of them in the snow. The perfect family. How kind Brett's eyes were, how Kingsley was still just a child really, one who didn't deserve to have his world torn apart by divorce. How horrible it was, what Pip and Roger were doing to the Harding family.

The Hardings were different. Special. They were supposed to be together.

But Pip and Roger were ruining it.

'It's just … wrong,' was all that came out.

'Well, it might be wrong – I'm no supporter of adultery – but it's no longer your concern, OK?'

'OK.'

He stared at me for a moment and I sat uncomfortably under his scrutiny, feeling he could see too much. 'Come on then, Kate Webb. I'll take you home.'

'Thank you, officer. I appreciate it.'

I stood up, looping my handbag over a shoulder as I watched Roger put an arm around Pip. She cradled her bandaged wrist in one hand. A simultaneous wave of anger and shame swept over me. Anger at their closeness; shame at myself for hurting someone like that.

Then another thought hit me.

Pip would have some explaining to do to Brett and Kingsley – about how she sprained her wrist at a computer course. I couldn't help the smile that broke across my face.

Let's see her tell them about that.

Just then Roger and Pip both turned to look at me. Pip's eyes widened as she saw my grin. Roger frowned. I lowered my head and bit my lip.

What was wrong with me? Hadn't I done enough damage?

The policeman was right. I needed to stay away from the Hardings. And Roger.

I gave them a final glance and saw Roger lift a hand to cup Pip's cheek. He stared into her eyes and told her it would all be

OK – at least that's what it looked like – and I felt the rise of the righteous anger yet again.

It certainly will be alright, Roger, though not for you and Pip.

I'll make sure of that.

I'd keep an eye on Pip Harding and at the first sign that she was hurting her child I'd act. I didn't yet know what I'd do, but as I remembered her long white throat and my vision of the curtain of blood I hoped – for her sake – she didn't destroy her perfect family.

As the policeman led me towards his cruiser I was already plotting my next move.

* * *

The heated car was warm and comfortable and the policeman had turned down the static hiss of the two-way to a low murmur. I rested my head against the window, still feeling sick but with my insides empty. Heat from a side vent wafted across my face. Soon I was lulled into a doze.

When I woke, the officer was pulling into my street. Drowsily, I pointed out my building and he pulled up right out the front (in a no-parking zone as if to celebrate the benefits of being a policeman) and cut the engine. We sat in silence for a moment, lit only by the lights from the lobby of the building, then he turned to face me, his gaze so open he suddenly appeared much younger. 'OK then, here we are. Are you feeling any better?'

To my surprise, I was. Perhaps it was the nap, but my nausea was gone and I felt virtually human again.

'Yes, actually,' I said. 'Thanks for bringing me home. I feel terrible about what happened earlier. I don't know what came over me.'

That was only partly true, though I thought I should say it anyway. I thought I might have seen a flash of the policeman's teeth – *a smile?* – I couldn't be sure. He leaned closer and his face came further into the light. His eyes were flecked with blue and green. I had the feeling this man saw more than I was comfortable revealing to him.

Or anyone.

'Well, as an officer of the law I advise you to keep your distance from those two. I'll be in touch if they press charges but a restraining order is more likely. Just don't go near them, OK?' He waited for my nod. 'Here. Take these, and this,' he said, passing me my keys then reaching into the centre console to rip a lined page from a notepad, scribbling on it with a pen he found in the same place. 'This is my number. If you need anything, call me, alright? Don't go doing anything stupid.' He smiled to take the sting out of his words.

'Ah, OK, thanks,' I replied, not sure of his motivation. 'And thanks again for the ride home. I do appreciate it.'

'No problem. Will you be alright to pick up your car tomorrow?'

'Sure. I'll get it on my way to work.'

'Do you have to go out of your way?'

'Yeah, Manly is definitely not on the way to North Sydney,' I said with a laugh. 'But I'll survive. And it's not too much of a problem if I'm late – Imperial Real Estate will cope without me for an hour or so.'

Unusually for me, conversation came easily.

I climbed out of the car, putting the notepaper into my handbag as I straightened up. Just before I shut the door something occurred to me and I bent down and looked back at the policeman. 'I never asked you your name.'

'Are you asking me now?'

'Yes.'

'Senior Constable Rik McBride. Call me Rik.'

'OK, Rik. It was nice to meet you, despite the circumstances.'

He grinned, and dimples flashed. He looked younger still, and I blushed like a teenager before smiling back, the shameful events of the night falling away from me like a discarded overcoat on a warm day. I breathed in the night air and walked towards my building, shaking my head at the strangely light sensation in my chest. I turned and waved from the door and Rik pulled away from the kerb.

Maybe getting stinking drunk, stalking an old acquaintance and her real estate agent-slash-lover, almost being arrested and vomiting on a policeman suited me.

Who would have guessed?

TUESDAY, 22 JULY
MORNING

My good mood had deserted me when I woke at 2.37 am after the Dream.

This time it had me on the silty bottom of a murky lake, seaweed tickling my face. I swam for the surface but the dim light of the sun never grew closer. I woke screaming, my head pounding, thinking how much I preferred my recent Harding house dreams to this recurring nightmare. After that I slept fitfully before rising early to catch a taxi to Manly before parking fees kicked in.

I skulked into the office just before ten. I tried hard to concentrate on my work, more to keep the memories of the previous night at bay than out of any sense of duty.

I didn't want to think about what I'd done and what it said about me.

So I didn't.

Avoidance. Evasion. Call it what you want. Years of practice had made me an expert at it.

Just before twelve, my musings about whether I'd have a Thai red curry or a burger and chips for lunch were interrupted by my phone ringing. *No Caller ID*. Usually I wouldn't answer such a call, but today wasn't a normal day. Today I might find myself the subject of a restraining order. Or worse.

Dry-mouthed, I picked it up. 'Hello?' I said softly, almost a whisper.

'Kate Webb?' asked a male voice.

'Yes.'

'It's Rik McBride here. The policeman from last night,' he explained, as if I might have forgotten the whole episode in my alcoholic fugue. Rik sounded official, although not going-to-jail official. What did that mean?

'Hello,' I repeated, for want of something else to say. I spun my chair to face the back wall of my office, bending over to put my elbows on my knees and feeling my lower back twinge.

'Look, Kate, this is an official call, but it is good news,' he said quickly, sensing my fear.

'Yes?' I spoke to the floor, my voice muffled.

'So the couple involved in your altercation last night – that is, um,' and here he must have checked his paperwork, 'Mrs Harding and Mr Bailey – did approach a lawyer about the possibility of obtaining a restraining order, an AVO, against you.'

I swallowed, but didn't speak. This was good news?

'However,' he added, and I exhaled, 'once they discovered they would both have to appear in court to obtain the AVO, they changed their minds.' I could almost hear him smiling. 'It seems they weren't keen on disclosing their relationship in such a public fashion.'

'So what does this mean?' I managed, my voice croaky.

'It means you're off the hook, Ms Webb.'

I took a deep breath and sat up, totally unprepared for his next question.

'So, how would you like to have lunch with me? To celebrate, you know, not being arrested?'

TUESDAY, 22 JULY
LUNCHTIME

I grinned at Tahlia as I passed reception.

She raised an eyebrow as if she knew where I was going, and with whom, which of course she couldn't. Must have been my guilty conscience again.

I'd stammered an *OK* to Rik's question. He'd explained he'd just met with lawyers about another matter in North Sydney and had time for a quick bite before heading back to the station. He'd named a café I knew and as I walked the two blocks there I tried to work out if I was excited to see him or just straight-out terrified.

Rik sat by the open window. He saw me coming and waved. He was wearing his uniform again, his hat perched on the end of the table. He smiled and passed me a menu as I sat down. 'Kate. You look better this afternoon.'

'Thanks,' I said, squirming with embarrassment.

I shouldn't have come.

Why did I think it would be a good idea to have lunch with the policeman who nearly arrested me for drunk and disorderly behaviour?

'Don't worry about last night,' he continued as if reading my mind. 'It happens to the best of us every now and then.'

'Well, I must be the best of the best then.'

The words popped out before I could stop them.

Rik grinned again. 'I admire your honesty. So, what are you having?'

'Oh God, it has to be a bacon and egg roll. They're excellent here.'

'Let's make it two. My shout.'

Before I could argue he walked over to the counter to order. He pointed at drinks and I mouthed *Diet Coke*, which he somehow understood.

We chatted about Sydney traffic and my boring job, which he pretended to find interesting. Soon the rolls came and as always they were amazing. Rik did a convincing impression of a foul-mouthed drug dealer he'd arrested a few weeks back and I asked him if he took that guy out for lunch as well, or did he only eat with people he didn't end up arresting? Then I told him how I'd finally bought coffee for my boss of nine years, not realising she'd never been a coffee drinker. 'And she's best friends with my mother!'

'Ouch. That must be fun for you,' he said, shaking his head. 'My parents live in Japan so at least I'm spared their interfering.'

We chatted about his last trip to Sapporo, where his Japanese mother and Australian-born father now lived. It was an easy conversation, with no mention of the Hardings or Roger. It was enough just to enjoy the company of a funny, pleasant man. I'd forgotten what that was like.

'Don't forget what I said on the phone, Kate,' Rik said as we left the café. 'Stay away from those two, OK? In my experience these situations never end well. Not unless you keep your distance.'

I remained silent.

'You might feel you're in the right,' he said more softly, 'but as far as the law goes, you need to back off.'

Of course he was right. Still, an image of the Harding house popped into my head. That perfect house. And Kingsley. The perfect son. I wasn't sure I could do what Rik advised. I knew I needed to do *something*. I cleared my throat. 'Of course, Rik. I won't bother them again, you can count on that.'

TUESDAY, 22 JULY
EVENING

As soon as I hit send I knew it was a stupid thing to have done.

Really stupid.

Rik's face popped into my head and his expression was …
disappointed. I bit at my lip, tasting the red wine.

I shouldn't have done it.

Too late now, Kate.

I closed the laptop and lay back on the lounge.

It was Rik's fault, though, really. He'd told me to stay away
from Pip and Roger. So I was staying away. I was doing what
he asked.

Wasn't I?

Best not to poke that anthill with a sharp stick, Kate.

It had started after I returned to my office. I'd begun laying
out a brochure for a unit in Artarmon, just around the corner
from my own place, trying to push all thoughts aside. I just
needed to get through the rest of the workday without thinking
about my lunch with Rik, the Hardings, Pip's injured wrist or
how I'd vomited all over a police officer. I read the blurb about
the Artarmon place. It looked good on paper. New kitchen and
bathroom. Two bedrooms with new built-ins. But I knew they'd
have trouble getting the price they wanted, as it overlooked the
highway. The owners would need to drop a hundred thousand

off at least. Also, I tutted, it had feature walls. Both bedrooms. *Everyone* was over feature walls. Especially feature walls like these with paint that looked smeared on. Distressed, I think it was called. They should definitely have painted the bedrooms a crisp white.

Shaking my head, I moved on to a 70s-style home in Chatswood, finding the best pictures out of a pretty poor bunch and inserting them into our template.

The text came just after three.

I was photoshopping an ugly rococo-style vase out of the Chatswood place – why the photographer hadn't removed it I had no idea – when my phone buzzed. I flipped it over and my heart skipped a beat. It was a message from Roger Bailey.

Kate, I appreciate you have problems of your own. However, I need to tell you that you may no longer attend any open houses held by McQuilty Real Estate. This includes the Highfields house. If you show up to any future inspections the agent in charge will call the police. I'm sorry. Look after yourself. Roger Bailey.

Heat rushed through me. And embarrassment that Roger might bring my name up at some McQuilty monthly meeting. Or maybe he'd email my photo to his colleagues with the word BANNED splashed across it. Vivian might hear about it through the real estate agent grapevine. If there was one.

At least he wouldn't be able to tell them why I'd been banned. He couldn't very well tell his colleagues about his affair with Pip.

For a moment I was tempted to text Roger back and do some threatening of my own – the thought of Rik and his disapproval stopped me.

For the time being.

And then Roger's words truly sank in. He had banned me from McQuilty open houses. And, more importantly, from the Harding house.

I tried to get back to work but my focus had vanished. I ruminated about my situation. Banned from the Harding house. Warned by a policeman to keep my distance from the Hardings and Roger. It didn't leave me many options.

But there were a few things left I could do.

Online.

Technically, I would be keeping my distance. And not breaking my promise to Rik. Keeping an eye on Pip and Roger online surely didn't count. It just offered me a way of peering into their lives without hurting them.

What harm could it do?

I went back to Facebook, Instagram and LinkedIn and trawled again through their Facebook friends, Kingsley's school website and e-newsletters, the McQuilty website, Pip's funky art gallery site and Brett's corporate website and profile.

But as usual online stickybeaking wasn't much of a release after all. So I went one step further. I set up a fake Facebook profile and sent Brett a private message. Nothing too detailed, just a one-line sentence.

Your wife and your real estate agent are having an affair.

THURSDAY, 24 JULY
EVENING

I dragged myself through the lobby of my building. It had been a long couple of days.

After I had messaged Brett on Tuesday he'd contacted me to find out more. Not immediately. Two hours after I sent it I saw he'd read it, but he didn't reply. I spent a sleepless night, getting up to check my laptop every couple of hours. I was a mess at work on Wednesday. Still nothing. I couldn't work out why. Perhaps he'd laughed the message off, thought it was a stupid prank or something. Or maybe he thought it was a jealous friend or colleague of his or Pip's or even Roger's.

When I woke on Thursday morning, dry-mouthed and headachy, and stumbled out to check Facebook it was there. A reply. It too was a simple one-line message.

Who are you? What are you talking about?

Simple enough questions. Straightforward. Yet behind the words I thought I detected something else.

Panic.

Did he already suspect Pip?

I wasn't sure if I should answer. I'd given him all the information he needed. If he paid attention to Pip he would see for himself. It was up to him now. To watch her face when she answered, to see if her eyes slid from his when she said, *No, what are you talking about, darling*, with a light laugh that was just a little too high-pitched.

Still, all day at work I tried to decide if I should reply.

And if so, what should I say?

Back at home I poured a glass of wine and took it out to my balcony, thinking the fresh air might give me inspiration. Car after car whooshed down the highway somewhere out of sight, like an old record needle had jammed on the noise. Lights were on in the apartments across the road. Cradling my glass, still with my coat on, I sat down on the rusty old wrought-iron chair – a hand-me-down from my parents – and watched the familiar blue of televisions flickering, some in synchronicity. Directly across from me, a young couple argued as they did their dishes under a fluorescent glare. In the apartment below them an old lady sat motionless in a leather armchair, her head on her chest.

I wondered what the Hardings were looking at right now.

Perhaps they were enjoying an aperitif by the pool. I bet they had those gas heaters to keep them warm. Or maybe they were around the dining table, laughing about their day as they ate a quinoa salad that Pip had whipped up. Perhaps Brett had barbecued steaks.

Did he watch Pip for signs of betrayal? Or had he dismissed my message as ridiculous?

My eyes flicked across to the couple's glowing kitchen. The woman was now alone, shoulders slumped as she cried into the dirty dishwater.

I stood up and walked back inside and sent Brett another one-line message.

I'm a friend. You need to talk to your wife.

This time it took only ten minutes before he replied.

I will.

I exhaled and bit my lip.

Had I done the right thing?

FRIDAY, 25 JULY
EVENING

The next train to Hornsby would be arriving in nine minutes. After battling the after-work crowd for three vodka and tonics at Finnegan's Irish Pub I was ready to go home.

I rummaged about in my bag for change and squinted at the buttons on a vending machine, ending up with salt and vinegar chips when I wanted cheese and onion. Oh well. I sat on an ice-cold seat at the end of a row and devoured them. I licked the salt off my fingers and shoved the empty packet into my handbag. There were a couple of dozen people on the platform. With a minute to go, I stood and moved further along to where I knew the train would be the least crowded. The sad wisdom of the commuter.

Air rushed into the underground station, the shoosh and pinging metal sounds of an approaching train grew louder and then burst from the dark tunnel.

The doors hissed open. No one alighted from the carriage nearest me. I stepped inside, not bothering to find a seat. I only had four stops. On the platform a group of teenagers strolled past, shoving one another and laughing. The girls were dressed in a matching uniform of tight denim shorts and t-shirts (goose bumps too) and the boys in denim jeans and checked shirts. Despite their casual outfits, they were obviously wealthy children used to a life of privilege and opportunity.

One girl laughed so hard she snorted. The others jeered good-naturedly, hooting with mirth. Beside the snorter stood a boy. A tall boy, his dark hair familiar. It couldn't be, could it? There. With her. I tried to focus.

It was, wasn't it?

'Stand clear of the closing doors,' said the robot voice, followed by a double beep as the doors started to close.

I stepped off the train back onto the platform.

Kingsley.

I followed them up the escalator.

* * *

I stared at the back of Kingsley's head in the Macca's queue, noting the way his hair curled at the nape of his neck, just like Sascha's used to.

'Hey, Taj my man, get me a Big Mac, will ya?' asked one of the boys, his face splotchy with angry red acne. He lounged against the wall, his arm around a short blonde girl – actually all four girls were short blondes – who leaned into him.

'Get your own, ya scab,' the boy in front of Kingsley replied. He turned, shaking his head at Kingsley in a *get a load of this guy* way.

'Kings, mate. You'll get me one, won't ya?'

Kingsley turned to the pimply boy. I stared at his profile. His skin was shockingly clear for a teenager, but I was close enough to see a light fuzz on his chin. He looked so young. 'Yeah, sure, Gus. You owe me, though.'

'Legend, bro. I owe you for sure.'

'Caitlin – what about you?'

'Oh thanks, Kings,' said the blonde with the pimply boy, her smile revealing a large gap between her front two teeth. 'Yeah, maybe a few nuggets.'

'Sure.'

The kid in front shook his head and said, 'You are a total sucker, man.'

Kingsley shrugged.

The queue cleared and they were both ordering at once. I couldn't take my eyes off Kingsley. The first boy finished and moved off. A loud *next please* jolted me back into movement. I approached the counter, now standing beside Kingsley. Without really being aware of it, I ordered something, aware only of Kingsley moving away from the counter to wait with his friends. I glanced at his face as he walked past me. He noticed and frowned. I dropped my gaze and stood a few feet behind them while waiting for my food, listening to their banter. Kingsley was more reserved than his friends, not joining in when they started to argue about where to go next. The boys wanted to go to a party at Donno's. The girls preferred to go back to Caitlin's house because her parents were away. Then Kingsley turned towards me. I averted my eyes.

'Do I know you?' He had moved in front of me, his words softly spoken. He was taller than I thought; I had to look up at him. And those eyes! A lighter blue than his mother's, they would turn heads wherever he went.

'I … What?'

'Are you watching me?'

'I'm … No,' I said, not knowing what else to say.

'Are you a friend of Mum and Dad's?'

'I … no. I mean yes, sort of.'

He smiled, looking appropriately confused, and a little piece of my heart seemed to break off and make its way through my body to lodge in my throat. The sheer beauty of him. The beauty of youth. So invincible. He didn't think anything I said could possibly affect him. Could possibly harm him. 'Which is it then? Yes or no?'

He looked at me, his eyebrows drawing closer in consternation but not real concern. Perhaps he'd never had a reason to be concerned about anything before.

'So, what do you want? Why are you watching me?'

'I … like you said, I knew your mother.'

'So why didn't you just come up and say hello?'

'I … I'm shy.'

How did I manage to sound so stupid?

'No, that's a stupid thing to say,' I continued, my words rushing out of me. 'It's not that at all. I do know your mother from years ago, that's true. But there's something else.' The uneasiness that appeared in his eyes was too much for me. He'd seemed self-assured in front of his friends, but perhaps it was all an act. A mask worn by a teenage boy who was more vulnerable than he'd seemed. I'd gone too far. I couldn't do it to him. 'Actually, it's not my business.'

A bit too late for that, Kate.

'Look, talk to your father,' I continued in a small voice. 'There's something he needs to tell you.'

'I thought you knew my mother,' he said, with wariness – and something else I couldn't decipher – flashing across his face. 'But now you say I need to talk to my father. Do you know him too?'

'No, I mean ... No. You just need to talk to him, alright?'
Panic set in as I realised what I was doing. 'I've got to go. Just
talk to your father. He's a good man, isn't he?'

He hesitated, then nodded.

'OK then. Talk to him. Ask him.' I tried to sound
authoritative, knowing I was doing a terrible job. Then I darted
between tables to get out of there as fast as I could.

'Wait!'

I didn't, of course.

Outside I ducked around the corner. I didn't bother with
the trains, just headed for the Pacific Highway, a block away.
I hailed the first taxi I saw and jumped in. The taxi driver
looked askance at me. I wasn't surprised. I was pale and a bit
drunk.

I gave him my address and rested my head on the leather
seat. I still held the unclaimed Macca's docket. I dropped it to
the floor.

What have I done?

So much for Rik's directive not to talk to the family.

Stupid, stupid Kate.

PART IV

FOURTH OPEN HOUSE

SATURDAY, 26 JULY
MORNING

I called Mum to see if I could borrow Dad's car. I fed her a story about wanting to buy a floor lamp and a coffee table from IKEA, saying I couldn't fit them in my Hyundai. A believable enough excuse. Mum drove a two-door Beemer – her pride and joy. Dad's car was a Commodore station wagon. Practical and unexciting. And sometimes useful.

His car served two purposes, and two purposes only. The first to take him to golf, and the second to take his prized dachshunds – Fritz and Frieda – to a fenced dog park a couple of suburbs away. I wasn't sure why he bothered. They weren't very sociable, though Dad enjoyed chatting to the other dog people as Fritz and Frieda barked non-stop at every dog in the park.

Mum was so pleased at my new-found domesticity she jumped at me borrowing the Commodore, even though it was Dad's. He was playing golf (surprise, surprise) but would be home by eleven-thirty. Why didn't I call in for an early lunch before I went to IKEA? I agreed, saying I'd have to leave by twelve-thirty to avoid the afternoon crowds. A less believable excuse as IKEA was busy all day, but necessary as I had to be at the Harding open house by one.

She bought it.

Dad was in the double garage when I got there. When Fritz and Frieda saw me step out of my car, they rushed outside, their little legs bounding along so that their ears flapped up and down with each step, right up to my ankles as if about to nip me. At the last moment they relented but kept up the barking.

'Fritzy! Frieda! No! Leave Katie alone!'

The barking continued unabated. Fritz and Frieda never did a thing Dad said.

'Sorry, Katie, they're a bit excited because I just got home.' Puffing and red-faced, Dad bent over and grabbed the dogs by their collars, holding them back as though they were wild animals.

'That's OK. How are you?' I asked, leaning over his bent body and kissing him awkwardly on the cheek, which was cold and a bit sweaty.

'Good, good, sweetie. And you? You look well,' he spoke-shouted over the barking. 'How about you go in and I'll get these guys quiet before the neighbours complain. Bev and Jeff have been threatening to go to the council again, can you believe it?'

I made a sympathetic noise and left him to it, pleased to get away from the dogs' shrill yapping. If I was Bev and Jeff I'd probably have poisoned the yippy little things years ago. Dad should count himself lucky.

Unlike most people of a certain age who downsized when their children left home, Mum and Dad did the opposite. Five years ago they bought this monstrosity at Bella Vista Lakes, in north-western Sydney. Six bedrooms, four bathrooms, open-plan living. The estate even included its very own golf course. It was a good drive away around the lake, but it appealed to their snobby side – drinks at the club, fundraisers on the balcony with a view of the eighteenth hole.

'Mum?' I called, the word echoing over the tiled floors and bouncing off the bare walls.

'Here, darling, I'm in the alfresco area.'

'It's called a back yard,' I muttered as I tapped across the tiled living area and through the kitchen, which was the size of my entire apartment.

Half a dozen golf clubs were lined up neatly across the lawn, glinting in the sun. Mum was bending over with a club in one hand and a scrubbing brush in the other. She wore a polo shirt and long beige shorts and was lathered with soap up to her elbows. She glanced up, her face red and dotted with foam, and placed the club carefully on the grass. 'Hi Katie – Kate, I mean. Just cleaning my golf clubs,' she said.

'Yes, I can see that.'

She pulled another club from the bag. 'The seven iron,' she said, waving it fondly. 'I use this fellow all the time. Look at the state of him.' She shook her head, then straightened up, a hand at her back, and used the seven iron to lean on as she spoke. 'I was putting my clubs in the car for ladies' social day tomorrow when I saw how grubby they were. Betty Davidson – you know Betty, she's the club secretary, her son James was a year above you at school – anyway, Betty is just the sort to comment on someone's dirty clubs. And guess who I'm playing mixed foursomes with tomorrow?' She raised her eyebrows meaningfully. 'Betty.'

Jesus.

'Mum, I don't think I can stay for lunch, I really need to get to IKEA.'

'Oh. Yes, of course, Kate. I was just going to heat up some pea and ham soup, but, no, that's fine. I haven't even got it out of the fridge yet. You sure you don't want me to heat it up in the microwave for you?' Mum shook her hands to remove the suds but they were so thick it looked like she was wearing fluffy white gloves. She started to move towards the house.

'No, Mum, thanks, I'm fine. Really, I just need to get going.'

She stopped and looked at me.

'I'll get the keys from Dad. I'll bring the car back tomorrow. Or maybe Monday?'

'Yes, I'll come in with you,' she said, gathering herself and bustling inside, arms still extended. As I followed she threw words over her shoulder at me. 'So what sort of lamp is it? Something Swedish and modern? One of those bright-coloured ones? I saw one in the new *Home Beautiful*. It was turquoise, I think. Or was it teal? I get them mixed up.' By now she was at the kitchen sink, splashing water onto the suds, which appeared resistant to dissolving.

'Um. It's just a plain one. White.'

'Oh.' She sounded disappointed. Then her face signalled a change of subject. 'Did you see the article about Leah and Ellis in the *Herald*?'

I gave a curt nod and averted my eyes. I didn't want to talk about that now. Or ever.

'Look, Katie —'

'Kate.'

'Sorry. You know Leah, she didn't mean anything by it. She's just a little bit … thoughtless, you know?'

'Oh, I know.'

Mum's face softened. 'I did tell her if she wants to be friends with you again — and I know she does, especially with the baby coming — then she needs to put herself in your shoes.'

I had to bite my lip. My mother was not the most empathetic — or tactful — person to ever walk the planet. That's where Leah got it from.

'Give her another chance … Kate. She's your only sister.'

I'd heard that all my life. I was saved from having to answer by a slamming door.

'Barb?' Dad's voice came from the garage. 'You there? Katie's here; did she find you?'

'Yes, Keith. She found me.'

Dad padded into the living room in long socks. Fritz and Frieda trotted to keep up. They were – thank God – quieter and calmer in the house.

'Dad, can I have your car keys?'

He stopped and looked at me, eyebrows raised. 'What? What do you want my car keys for? What's happened to your car?'

'Oh, Kate, I haven't told your father yet. He was at golf.' Mum grabbed a tea towel to wipe her arms as she addressed Dad. 'Keith, Kate needs your car. She'll bring it back tomorrow. You can use my car if you need it. She's buying some lovely furniture at that really big Swedish shop, you know the one – IKEA? Judy and John went there a couple of months ago, bought all those bookshelves, remember? And other bits and pieces. It was so cheap! Just a few hundred dollars for the whole lot. Maybe we sh—'

'Mum.' She stopped. My mother tended to talk to Dad like he was a child, which sometimes aggravated the hell out of me, though occasionally I could see her point. Dad could be infuriatingly absent-minded. 'I'm sorry, I really need to go.'

'Yes, of course. I'll walk you out. The keys are in the car, Keith?'

Dad still looked confused, but he nodded. He bent down and gave each dog a quick scratch around the ears, then stood back up. 'Stay,' he said to them, his voice not at all authoritative; instead the dogs wandered out to the TV room to lie on the carpet in the sun. Dad watched them go fondly then turned to us. The humans in his life didn't have his heart the way those dogs did. 'See you later, Katie,' he said as he walked past, mind already elsewhere. 'I need a shower.'

As I climbed into the Commodore Mum pressed the button for the roller door, then appeared at the passenger window. 'Good luck, hon. I'd better go and heat up that soup for your father. The Lindsays are coming over to play bridge later and I need to clean the windows. I told your father —'

'Mum! Sorry, but I've really got to go.'

She looked surprised to be interrupted, though it was a common enough occurrence. Mum and Dad loved me. I knew that. But loving them back was hard work sometimes. They were so self-involved. And, compared to Leah, I'd always felt like I must be a disappointment to them. Except perhaps back when I had a famous husband and a gorgeous child they could dote over.

Now both of those were gone, I didn't have anything to offer my parents that Fritz and Frieda couldn't give them.

'I'd love to come over and see how your new things look,' Mum continued, almost shyly.

'Sure,' I said, already concocting an excuse as to why I wouldn't have a new lamp and coffee table. 'Do you want my car keys?'

'Oh no, that's OK.' She stepped back from the car. 'See you soon, Kate. Take care of yourself.'

I looked at the clock on the dash: 12.13 pm. Forty-five minutes to get to the Hardings. Should be plenty of time. I hit the ignition.

Time to see what had sprouted from the words I'd sown.

* * *

I sat across the road from the Harding house in my dad's car, hunkered down, wearing a cap and sunglasses like a private detective in some dodgy movie.

When Roger's Lexus appeared in the rear-view mirror, I crouched down further and hoped to God he wouldn't recognise me through the window. He parked just past the driveway and then was off through the gate, pulling his suitcase behind him as if the Harding house were an airport.

A magpie squawked, loud in the suburban silence.

What was happening in there?

Could I risk another look on foot?

Before I had a chance to think I was out the door and across the road. I ducked inside the gate. This time, I moved into the bushes running along one side of the driveway. I couldn't risk anyone seeing me. I crept towards the house, hiding behind the trees that masked the fence, my footsteps muffled by the damp leaves in the garden.

As soon as I could see the front door I crouched behind a large shrub. Roger was at the steps. The door opened as if someone had seen him approach. Roger faltered, just slightly – not enough that you'd notice it unless you were looking. I don't know if it was just me, but he looked like he was marching to his doom.

Maybe it was just me.

Pip walked down the front steps. She wore jeans, a white t-shirt, navy blazer and low heels, looking the epitome of smart casual. I could see the bandage on her wrist poking out from the sleeve of the blazer.

I did that.

Pip stopped at the base of the steps. A shape moved inside the house, coalescing into a person at the front door.

Brett.

He looked down on both Pip and Roger. His expression seemed tight, his mouth downturned. Dark circles underlined his gentle eyes.

Had I done that too?

Guilt joined the shame. But then again what did I know about Brett? Maybe the dark circles were the result of a busy week at work. Brett had paired his jeans with a shirt and black shoes. I guessed the Hardings were going out for lunch. They'd left it late. They should have gone by now – the open was starting soon.

My legs were burning from prolonged squatting, so I carefully lowered myself to the ground, wincing at the sogginess of the leaves beneath me. I peered through the foliage, mesmerised by the unfolding tableau.

The three of them stood facing one another. One above, two below. Then Roger said something I took to be a general greeting. Brett nodded and Pip smiled more naturally. She seemed to be the only one unconcerned about the whole situation. In contrast, Roger kept touching his helmet-hair self-consciously, while Brett shifted from foot to foot. Pip turned around and smiled at Brett, gesturing him to come and stand beside her. He walked stiffly down the steps as she continued talking. When he stopped she took his arm and leaned a little closer to him. Pip appeared to have nothing at all to hide. The only way Brett would believe Pip and Roger were having an affair would be from watching Roger.

And Roger wasn't a good liar.

Strange for a real estate agent.

He had a fixed smile on his face, but his body language gave him away. He stared at Brett for too long, then looked away as if realising he was behaving weirdly, before focusing back on Pip.

Just when things couldn't get any more awkward, Kingsley came to the doorway.

Roger looked past Brett and Pip and waved a greeting.

Kingsley waved back, subdued. I considered him, then his father, wondering if they'd had the conversation I'd urged him to start.

Had Brett told him?

Kingsley walked past his parents and grabbed his pushbike from where it was propped against a pillar. He slung a leg over the saddle and started off up the driveway. I ducked back, hoping I was well enough hidden. Kingsley pedalled along the drive and out the gate. I released the breath I'd been holding.

Brett and Pip walked around the roses to their car and as Brett climbed into the driver's seat Pip opened her door and then looked at Roger over the roof of the car for a long moment before getting in. I could only see the back of her head but I would have bet money she winked, simply because of the appalled look on Roger's face.

Brett started the car and I hunkered further down as they drove past. Just as I was about to stick my head out and see where Roger was, he materialised beside me, signs in hand to signal the start of the open. I almost felt sorry for him. Perhaps he'd bitten off more than he could chew with Pip Harding.

Roger soon returned and marched back towards the house, his smile now replaced by a worried frown. I watched him go inside and then counted sixty cats and dogs before making my way back through the garden to the road. Just before the gate I stepped out onto the driveway, brushing the leaves from my clothes and hair. I pulled up short when I saw a man and woman staring at me open-mouthed.

'Oh, sorry if I startled you,' I said quickly. 'Are you here for the open house?' When they nodded, I continued. 'Please, go on through, I was just finishing the gardening.'

I swept my hand along in a come-in gesture.

The couple walked on, giving me a wide berth, obviously not believing I was a gardener, or the owner, and probably wary of engaging in any conversation lest they catch something.

I got the hell out of there before the police were called.

Again.

SATURDAY, 26 JULY
3.13 PM

Kate. I know you were at the Harding open house today. This is your last warning. If I see you again I WILL call the police. Roger.

SATURDAY, 26 JULY
10.11 PM

Fucking Roger. Who does he think he is, anyway? He's not the boss of me.

The brash 80s music dictated my mood. 'We're Not Gonna Take It' was just finishing and I whirled furiously through the apartment. But when the first few notes of 'What About Me?' began, my shoulders slumped. I put my wine glass down on the benchtop, way too hard. I was surprised by sudden lightness, at the slivers glimmering across my hand. The stem of the glass, minus the rest of it, was still in my fist. Glass fragments littered the floor and benchtop.

Oh shit. Fucking glass. Stupid fucking granite benchtop.

I blinked, deciding what to do, then threw the stem into the sink where it bounced around, unheard over the soaring guitars.

More wine, I guess. And a fresh glass.

I tiptoed through the shards on the kitchen floor in my socks and found a new glass. After filling it with red, I crept back to the lounge, taking the bottle with me for good measure. Wine sloshed as I collapsed onto the cushions.

'Fuck!'

I tipped to one side as something sharp jabbed into my left bum cheek.

'Fucking fucker fuck fuck.'

Kingsley's dinosaur. How did it get into the back pocket of my jeans?

Moving Pictures wailed and I joined them, staring into the dinosaur's eyes. Its empty gaze made me think about the other mementoes I'd collected. I hadn't looked at them for ages. I stumbled into my room and grabbed the shoebox from my dresser then carried it back out to the lounge room. I sat on the floor and put the shoebox on the coffee table next to my wine.

I started removing items, trying to remember what house I'd taken them from. Most blurred together, a series of pleasant suburban family homes, cleaned within an inch of their lives before being put on display.

The largest souvenir in the box was the ripped-off cover of a *New Idea* magazine, with a blonde soapie-starlet and an article headline promising all the goss on Kim Kardashian's relationship with Kanye West. There were scraps of paper: shopping lists requesting bread, milk and – in one case quite specifically – four tins of smoked oysters. There were beer bottle tops, cigarette lighters, matchboxes, pens, a guitar pick, a few screws, a miniature bouncy ball, a takeaway menu from Shanghai Palace Chinese Restaurant, a handful of buttons, a used birthday candle in the shape of 21, some batteries and a battered playing card – the four of hearts. Nothing much of value, nothing anyone would miss.

Mostly.

Until … a tarnished and bent sugar spoon.

Oh, I remembered that one. I'd nearly left it behind, wondering if it was too valuable to pilfer. It had come from a gorgeous home: a deceased estate. The house had been about as un-styled as they came, all chintz and floral carpet and old-lady-with-too-many-cats smell. The smell of sadness. In the end I decided no one was likely to miss the spoon. For a while I'd kept it on my bedside table, but it made me too upset to see it every day and remember that the house was about to be sold; the old lady's things discarded.

Next, I picked up a brown Lego horse, standing the jaunty stallion on the coffee table beside the spoon and Kingsley's dinosaur. I remembered that house too. A basketball hoop was attached to the wall above the garage door and the kids' heights were marked in pencil on the laundry door frame – but the family had moved out and by the day of the inspection it was filled with double beds covered in pristine white linen. I found the horse on a shelf at the top of a built-in wardrobe. I had no idea how it had survived the open house cleaning frenzy and I took it as a sign I was meant to have it. To save it. It had been left behind by its family.

Forgotten.

I reached a trembling hand towards the little objects, my fingers hovering, hesitant.

My precious mementoes.

Part of me knew – of course I knew – that my souvenirs were junk, but another part of me understood they were so much more than that. They reminded me that every house – every family – was special. Walking around inside a family's home was special. Seeing their home and taking something small to remember it by gave me the gift of belonging. Just for a little while.

Sometimes the houses told me a lot; other times there wasn't much of their personality left. But I always took a memento. Some were good; some bad.

And some – I eyed Kingsley's black-eyed dinosaur – were perfect.

As Cyndi Lauper crooned about falling and catching, my eyes blurred with tears. I stared at the wine glass as if willing it into my hand, too tired even to pick it up but desperate for the oblivion it offered. Instead, I lay down on the lounge, closed my eyes and blacked out.

SUNDAY, 27 JULY
MORNING

A buzz woke me.

I was disoriented, stretched out on the lounge with a kink in my neck. My legs ached from overly energetic dancing. Thankfully for my neighbours the previous night's CD hadn't been on repeat. I groaned as it dawned on me the buzzing sound was the intercom.

I stumbled over to the handset on the wall near the door, tiptoeing carefully through the almost invisible minefield of glass in my sock-covered feet.

'Hello,' I rasped, lifting the handset to my ear as I peered at the clock on the kitchen wall.

9.32 am.

'Kate?'

Rik.

Shit. Rik was downstairs.

I rubbed my hair and stifled a moan. He must have heard from Roger that I'd gatecrashed the open house. 'Yes.'

'It's Rik McBride. I hope it's not too early for you?'

'No, no,' I said, looking around at the mess of my living area, the glass all over the floor, the empty wine bottles.

'Can I come up?'

Shit.

'Um, yes, sure. No problem. Come up. Just give me a couple of minutes if I'm not at the door – I just woke up.'

'OK, no problem.'

I buzzed him into the building, surprised it was even locked. Although maybe it had been open and he'd just used the intercom to be polite. Mind you, if he was being polite he could have called in advance. He had my number. I replaced the handset, wondering if I was about to be sick.

You'll be fine, Kate, just keep busy.

I'd feel right as rain, as my mother would say, once I drank some water. After a long moment well spent on repeated swearing, I tiptoed to the sink, turned on the cold tap and bent over it. I splashed water on my face then cupped my hand and gulped it down like it was going out of fashion – another of my mother's sayings. I stood up, gasping. *Fuck.* The effort of drinking water had exhausted me. I fetched the dustpan and brush from the cupboard beneath the sink then squatted, my head throbbing, frantically brushing shards of glass into the dustpan. After ten seconds I could see it would take all day to get every little piece of glass – it had gone fucking everywhere – so I changed tack and went for the biggest pieces. Surely Rik would be wearing shoes. Which reminded me, so should I. I took three large steps over the glass and ducked into the bedroom, slipping on a pair of flat shoes. As I emerged I stopped and looked in the mirror and nearly did a double take.

My hair was wild, my face red, eyes puffy and my lips a bright maroon from last night's wine. Oh God. I pulled my hair back into a messy ponytail. I wet my lips and rubbed at the stains with a finger until they were a little less obvious.

I stared at my reflection, thinking of Rik waiting in the hallway.

Nah, not good enough. Despite the pounding of my head, I had to do something about my appearance. And fast. I started by brushing my teeth, since my mouth felt like a used sponge. It made me feel so much better I decided to wash my face and swap my tracksuit for soft pants and a cotton jumper. I slapped on foundation, squirted some drops in my bloodshot eyes and decided that would have to do.

I swept up a few more shards of glass and raced around throwing bottles and other rubbish into the bin (wincing at the thought of Rik hearing the telltale clinking from the hall). I also chucked out the oranges Mum had brought when she last visited, now covered in white mould, and the tulips, which stank like a duck pond and drooped so low their faded blooms lolled on the benchtop, then glanced around and realised my mementoes were spread over the coffee table.

I couldn't let Rik see them.

I hurried over and grabbed handfuls at a time, thrusting them back into the box.

'Sorry dinosaur,' I muttered, shoving it in with the rest and cramming the lid on tight.

My stomach still churned but I pushed the nausea down, hoping it would stay there. I took a deep breath to compose myself and opened the door. Rik leaned nonchalantly against the wall opposite. This time he wasn't wearing his police uniform. Did that mean he was here on personal business?

Of course not. What personal business would he have with me?

'Hi Kate,' Rik said, pushing off from the wall.

He appeared leaner without the bulk of his uniform and all its accessories. He wore black jeans, an old Hunters & Collectors t-shirt and black boots. He looked good. Great, actually. Maybe, unlike me, Rik was a morning person. Although, once upon a time – before the incident – I used to enjoy getting up in the dark and heading out for a run. A yearning ache for that person rose in my solar plexus, a strange wistful longing for someone I could hardly remember being.

'You could have called first,' I harrumphed. 'And aren't you too young to know who Hunters & Collectors are?'

He smiled at my grumpy tone and his dimples flashed. 'I did call. You didn't answer so I decided to come anyway. And I'm not that young,' he added, sounding almost proud of the fact. 'I'll be forty in a couple of months.'

'Do you want to come in?' I asked, stepping aside.

'Yeah, that'd be great.'

I stepped back further to make room for Rik in the narrow entryway. He twisted slightly to get past me and I smelled his aftershave and, underneath, faintly, the fresh scent of his soap.

I closed the door and followed him inside, realising that the apartment stank. Just the usual stench of alcohol, stale air and the previous night's toasted cheese sandwich. As I opened the balcony door, Rik stood in the centre of the room and peered around.

'Nice place,' he said, though not with much enthusiasm.

I didn't blame him.

Why was he here? Did he have more news about Roger or Pip? Or both of them? Was I in trouble for going to the open house yesterday? Had he been – I went cold at the thought – following me? With an effort I pushed the thoughts aside, at last remembering my manners. 'Can I get you a tea or coffee, or a glass of water?'

'Ah, well, yes, maybe a glass of water, if it's not too much trouble,' he said, sounding a little bit nervous himself now, then stood awkwardly beside the lounge.

'No, of course not, please sit. I'll get us both some water.'

Rik sat down right in front of the box and I cursed myself for not having put it back in the bedroom. When I got back to the lounge room with the water, Rik was eyeing off the box. I gave him a glass and put mine on the coffee table.

'I'll just move this out of the way,' I said in a casual voice, bending over and grasping it with both hands. It must have been one bend too many, though, as I tasted bile in my mouth before I could straighten. 'Urgh.'

I dropped the box and ran for the toilet, slamming the door behind me.

Once I'd finished I felt much better, but I couldn't bring myself to go back out right away – the humiliation was too hot and sharp. I pictured Rik in my living area, listening to me throw up. Again. Maybe if I stayed in here long enough he'd just leave.

'Kate?' The word was spoken softly, just outside the door.

Oh shit.

'I'm alright. I'll be out in a minute.'

'OK.'

I hung my head, wiping the spittle from my lips with toilet paper.

Time to face the music, Kate.

I rose to my feet and lifted the toilet lid, throwing the paper into the bowl and flushing it again. I watched the water swirl and suck it away with something approaching envy. Yes, a new low: envying toilet paper. I washed my hands and walked back to the living room.

And found Rik riffling through the spilled contents of my box of mementoes.

'Why don't you sit down, Kate?' he suggested. 'I can tidy up this rubbish for you.'

'It's not rubbish,' I yelled, rushing towards him and snatching what I could from his hands. I righted the box and carefully began placing items inside: a bottle top, a pencil, an orange cigarette lighter. As I smoothed a crumpled receipt against the coffee table I realised Rik had gone silent. I looked up and found him watching me.

'What is all this, Kate?' He sounded predictably confused. But also concerned. I didn't know why, but his concern made it so much worse.

I looked down at what I was holding. Scraps of paper, screws and batteries, rubbish meant for the bin in most cases. Detritus of other people's lives. Seeing it now it looked dirtier, older. And yet I had found it and kept it. Searched for it.

Loved it.

I wanted to pick up everything in the box and hurl it out the window. To have a shower and wash the traces of other people's lives from my body. Another part of me wanted to pack everything carefully away, to look after it all like the treasure it was.

'Oh God,' I muttered, leaning against the door, averting my eyes from my secret shame, now exposed. 'You weren't supposed to see that.'

Rik was quiet. I couldn't bring myself to look at him. Instead I stared above the lounge at the blank wall. The one I'd never bothered to hang a picture on. I concentrated on that white space now and searched for a lie, for an explanation that didn't make me sound like a total and utter loony or a pitiable person with no life. But it was just too hard.

Time to tell the truth, Kate.

My hands were clammy so I wiped them on my pants. Resigned to saying it now, I bit the inside of my cheek, then started. 'I go to open houses – when houses are for sale, you know? I take something from each one. Something to … remember the house by, I guess. Just something small no one would want or even miss. Nothing valuable.'

I said the words unemotionally, then waited, still looking at the wall opposite.

'Wow, you have been to a lot of open houses.' There was the unmistakable sound of a smile in his voice and I looked over at him.

'Yes,' I said and shrugged.

'Why do you do it?'

'I don't know. I just do. It feels right. Although now I'm seeing everything through your eyes it feels a little bit less right.'

Rik didn't answer, but the look he gave me suggested he wasn't repulsed by my confession. He moved over to the balcony and peered out, as if to give me room to continue talking at my own pace.

'The first time I did it was in this nice place in Warrawee. I found a little Matchbox car sticking out from under a kid's bed. Remember Matchbox cars? A little red convertible, it was. Sasch – someone I knew – used to have one exactly the same. I slipped it into my pocket, something to remember the place by. I have another two boxes of stuff in the back of my wardrobe.'

I bit my lip, unsure what to say now I'd fully confessed my shame.

Rik turned to me, looking serious. Maybe I'd got it wrong, maybe he was disgusted by me. I braced myself. 'Kate, I need to be honest with you.'

Here it comes.

'I know who you are. I know what happened to you – to your husband and son. I've known since I first saw you and I didn't say anything.'

Rik's jaw tightened as if steeling himself to speak. My stomach lurched again, but from nothing physical this time. I couldn't catch my breath.

'I was young then, just a new recruit. I'd been posted to the inner west and been in the force for about ten months. I was there that afternoon. At the jetty.' He paused. 'I helped pull your husband and child out of Sydney Harbour.'

BEFORE

'Katie! Over here! Just a couple of questions for you.'

Camera flashes seared my eyeballs. My sunglasses didn't help.

'Mrs Bauer! How are you feeling?'

'Katie! Katie! Do you think the inquest will reveal anything new?'

Mum and Dad stood on either side of me, their hands under my arms the only thing keeping me upright as they helped me through the press pack.

Eleven months, one week and three days ago my son died.

Sascha would – *should* – my gut wrenched as I corrected myself – be over six years old now. His absence still regularly punched me in the stomach. Every morning I woke to a brief moment of not-knowing – of blessed ignorance – before being hammered with reality. I still ached for my boy; I longed for his smell, the feel of his skinny little arms around my neck, his fine curly hair tickling my cheek.

But he was gone.

For six days after the incident photographers lurked outside the apartment. I slept in Sascha's bed, wrapped tightly in his doona, staring sightlessly at the stuffed dinosaurs he'd lined up on his dresser. News vans swarmed the street like hyenas circling a wounded wildebeest. Every day Mum and Dad ran the gauntlet, dodging the cameras and microphones, bringing me food and checking on my parlous mental state. Then they moved me back to their house, finding it easier all round. The reporters followed us, camping outside the Pymble house until finally, since I didn't leave the premises, they gave up and the story fizzled out. For them it wasn't a story if they didn't have a face to splash across the TV.

The press found other tragedies to exploit – sorry, to *report*.

At some point I realised I'd never be able to face living in the apartment again. I sold it, cheaply and quickly, and bought the flat in Artarmon. I couldn't recall much about that time. Peter's taciturn sister – who I barely knew, having met her only once, at our wedding – came up from Melbourne and took some of his things, the rest I gave to charity. Most of Sascha's things I kept, Mum helping me box them up to store in her garage. I couldn't throw them away, but neither could I face seeing them every day. Mum found me the job with Imperial Real Estate. Life had moved on. Technically.

But now, eleven months later, the press was back.

I couldn't stay away from the coronial inquiry into the deaths of my husband and child. For some reason I had to hear a stranger describe and define what happened that day. I'm not sure why it mattered – as the cliché goes, nothing would bring Sascha back. Still, I had to be there.

For my son.

I ducked as microphones were thrust in my face. One reporter, ghoulish in her thick TV makeup, blocked my way. Her long nails gripped a microphone and her bright crimson lips formed words I couldn't decipher. Her eyes were emotionless. I lowered my head and pushed forward as if walking into a snowstorm.

She's just doing her job.

I could already picture how I would look on TV later that night: a grieving mother. A hounded victim. I kept my face expressionless, not willing to give them what they wanted.

I knew what they wanted.

My tears, my rage. My hate. They wanted it all on camera. They wanted to broadcast it on the six o'clock news, a story for people to tut at as they stirred their spaghetti bolognese and thanked God their family was normal, their children were alive and well. That they weren't like that poor broken woman on the screen.

I closed my eyes again, letting Mum and Dad lead me. The flashes faded and Mum murmured, *Up, up the steps, Katie.* I took off my sunnies and saw ahead the wide set of entrance stairs to the bland 70s State Coroner's Court building. We went down the corridor and into a large room. My bones were heavy and my nerve endings dulled. The room was packed. I shut my eyes tight and listened to the hum of the crowd. After a while the murmurs gave way to silence.

* * *

'The deceased were Peter Ian Bauer and his son, Sascha Jackson Bauer. Cause of death in both cases was drowning.'

The words jolted me from my anaesthetised state.

I looked over to the coroner. He resembled a friendly family dentist or a neighbour you'd wave to over the fence. He wouldn't have looked out of place cooking sausages at a school fete. His only distinctive characteristic was a deep and commanding voice that he used to great effect.

'Peter Bauer was the driver of the vehicle at the time it plunged from the jetty at Balmain into Sydney Harbour. Peter and his only child, Sascha, were inside the vehicle at the time and they drowned as it filled with water. Forensics have told us that – mercifully – death would have come quickly for both of them.'

He said the last sentence in a softer voice, and he glanced at me before continuing. 'Peter Bauer drove the vehicle from the jetty into the water that day deliberately. I have been well satisfied of that fact given the thorough investigation conducted by the New South Wales Police Force. My own determinations are that he did so to end both his own life and that of his five-year-old son, Sascha.

'Acceleration of the vehicle as it approached the water has been established by forensics. Peter Bauer had no existing medical condition that would allow us to attribute such actions to an involuntary reflex or medical episode, nor was any evidence found in the autopsy to support such a conclusion. In addition, testimony from his wife, Katie, suggests Mr Bauer's state of mind may have been unstable at the time of the incident. Although Katie Bauer was never explicitly told by her husband that he intended to harm Sascha, it appears – in hindsight only, it must be emphasised – that Peter may have been depressed or even suicidal after discovering she planned to leave him, which he might have predicted would limit his contact with the child for the foreseeable future.'

Hindsight. Explicitly. Harm.

He cleared his throat and continued. 'At the time the vehicle entered the water, Sascha Bauer was strapped into a child restraint in the back seat of the vehicle on the left side. According to his mother, Sascha was old enough to undo the restraints of the car seat and it appears he tried to do so, as the buckle had been released. In addition, Sascha was a proficient swimmer, having attended lessons since he was a toddler. However, investigations indicated the car would have filled with water extremely quickly – perhaps in just a matter of minutes – giving the child no chance of freeing himself and swimming to safety.'

No chance.

I looked down to see blood dripping down my wrists. My hands were clenched, my ragged fingernails piercing my palms.

'And now to my recommendations. There is only one. I recommend that the New South Wales government and local Sydney councils work together to review vehicle access to all Sydney Harbour jetties, with a view to restrict access of vehicles to the water, via appropriate physical means such as fences and bollards.'

He shuffled the papers on his desk before continuing.

'As to Peter Bauer. He may have been suicidal. His wife had left him and his enormous success as a first-time novelist had faded with his failure to produce another book. However, we will never know exactly how he found himself in such a dark place – a place so dark it would lead him to commit both filicide and suicide. Peter Bauer was an educated man, a doting father and a devoted husband. Perhaps if he had been able to find help or solace in the time leading up to the incident, this tragedy could have been avoided. Again, we will never know.'

His serious gaze fell on me.

'On behalf of the coronial team I offer my sincere condolences to the family of the deceased. In particular to Katie Bauer, who through no fault of her own in one terrible day lost both husband and son. Such a loss is something no one should have to bear and certainly not in such distressing circumstances. Also our condolences are extended to the grandparents of the child and all those who will grieve for the deceased and mourn their passing.

'I close this inquest.'

SUNDAY, 27 JULY
MORNING

I stared at Rik blankly.

'Seeing that car lifted out of the water … It was the worst day of my life,' he said. 'So I can't imagine what it was like for you.' He ran a hand over his bald head and I saw it was shaking.

'I don't remember you,' I said, the words thick in my mouth.

'We never met,' he said. 'Not personally. I mean, I was … there. On the day. But I was based in the inner west, and I was just a rookie.'

'You saw Sascha when he came out of the water?' I asked in a quiet voice, not wanting to know, but compelled to ask.

'I …' His face had paled and he looked wretched, as if he too felt faint. 'Yes.'

I fell more than sat down, my mind on my little boy coming out of the harbour, so cold. So lifeless.

Rik perched tentatively on the end of the lounge. 'I knew it was you as soon as I saw you at Northies. I'm sorry I didn't say anything sooner. I meant to talk to you about it at lunch the other day but, I couldn't. I … I wasn't sure you'd want to hear it.' He cleared his throat. 'Kate, I don't know if you want to hear this either.' The look he gave me was a strange mix of kindness and … something else. 'I don't know you well,' he continued. 'But I like you. You're funny and fun and honest.

And resilient. But … it feels like you might need some extra support right now. Like there's a lot going on in your life. I mean, what happened to you was the most terrible tragedy – I can't imagine how you've suffered. The fact you're still here is testament to your strength. But it seems like you're having a hard time at the moment. I'm concerned for your wellbeing.'

My *wellbeing*? He was concerned about my *wellbeing*? I looked away, the thought almost making me laugh aloud. Instead I met Rik's scrutiny. 'Please leave.'

The firmness of my voice surprised me.

Rik continued to look at me, his astute eyes now clouded with doubt, but he didn't argue. 'Of course. But, Kate, please get in touch if you need anything. Even just someone to talk to.'

He hesitated then walked to the door and let himself out.

I was alone.

BEFORE

I grasped my father's arm as we left the court. The media crowded on the footpath and lifted their heads like meerkats when they spotted me. But they were more subdued than earlier and we pushed through them easily. And as we walked around the corner they simply let us go. I don't know why. Maybe another grieving mother was about to arrive and they were waiting to accost her.

After we'd walked half a block my mother spoke. 'Katie, let's sit in here for a minute.'

I hadn't even noticed the franchised coffee shop to our right, patrons lined up inside and chatting at tables on the footpath. Mum was red-faced and looking at my father, whose pale face was covered with a sheen of sweat.

'Yes. Alright, sorry,' I said, wondering when – or *if* – I would ever feel emotion again.

We chose an outside table and I dropped into a seat and slouched forward, examining my palms and the thin red-brown lines marking my forearms.

Like Jesus on the cross.

My mother caught sight of the blood, a look of distaste flitting across her face. She pulled a hanky from a pocket and dropped it onto the table before me. 'I'll get coffees,' she said without further comment and made a beeline for inside.

I picked up the hanky. It was an old one of Dad's. Mum always kept one in her handbag. I used to use them to clean Sascha after he'd made a mess of an ice cream or a chocolate cake when the three of us had morning tea at the shops. He'd try to pull away, grizzling, until I blew raspberries on his soft cheeks and made him giggle.

A sob escaped me and I gritted my teeth, deciding it was better to stick with no emotion. Feeling nothing was infinitely preferable to remembering.

I licked my palm and used the hanky to rub it clean. Dad sat down beside me with a grunt that made me look up. His own hands were folded together on the table in front of him; his eyes red-rimmed.

Had he been crying in court? I hadn't noticed.

'Katie, I need to go to the bathroom,' he said in a shaky voice as he turned to me. 'Will you be alright here for a minute?'

I nodded and he waited a second or two longer as if convincing himself it was OK, then stood up and stumbled away.

I watched the cars as they zipped past, the drivers oblivious to my grief. All of them with their own lives; their own concerns and worries and joy. I couldn't comprehend such a carefree existence. The luxury of normality.

'Excuse me?' A matronly woman in her sixties approached the table. She had shiny eyes, and her generous bosom was sheathed in a bejewelled, baby-pink cardigan – the diamantes scattered across her chest glowed like stars. A lavender scent wafted from her.

Lavender is supposed to be calming. To me it had always smelled like death.

'You're the poor lady from the inquest, aren't you? The one who lost her son. And husband?'

I didn't say a word, so she took this for assent and prattled on in a tone that couldn't hide her macabre glee, even as tears filled her eyes.

'My friend Di and I sometimes attend the inquests, you see. A hobby of ours, I suppose you'd call it. We were there today – actually Di is just over there, finishing her cuppa.'

She pointed and I followed her finger to see a second woman nearby waving at me with the thrilled expression of a person who's spotted a celebrity. A tiny piece of cake was lodged in the corner of her mouth.

'And I said, Di, that's the poor lady from the inquest, I'll go over and tell her how sorry we are.' A single fat tear dripped from her cheek to land on the table. 'Such a terrible tragedy. Honestly, I said to Di, I don't know how I'd go on living if something like that happened to me. For your child to *die* …' She lingered on the word. 'Killed by his own *father*. It must make you wonder if you could have done anything to prevent it. I mean —'

'LEAVE!'

My mother appeared before me, brandishing a metal table number on a stand. The woman started, eyes even wider.

'How dare you?' Mum continued, her mouth contorted and made ugly with anger. 'You leave right now or you'll have this wrapped around your neck.' She shook the table number closer to the woman's face and the busybody backed away, terrified and affronted in equal parts.

'I was just giving this poor woman my condolences …'

'You were not, you ghoul! You were judging her! Well, you can just *fuck off*!'

My eyes widened. It was the first time I'd ever heard my mother use the *f-word*, which was what she called it.

Di, an equally portly lady with even more ample boobs, hurried over to join her friend. The cake had vanished from her lips, but she had crumbs sprinkled across her chest and her face had reddened at the scene she'd become involved in. Di passed a handbag to the bejewelled woman, grabbed her arm and half-dragged her away. I watched them hasten down the street, heads close together, occasionally turning back to us, happily horrified. They'd dine out on this story for years, I thought, still unable to rouse any strong feelings either way.

My mother watched them go, then turned to me. 'It's not your fault, Katie,' she said fiercely and flopped onto a chair, setting the table number down with a clang. 'It's not.'

But I knew the woman was right.

It *was* my fault.

It was my fault my son was dead.

SUNDAY, 27 JULY
AFTERNOON

I spent the rest of the day moping around the house, moving from bed to lounge to fridge. I couldn't make sense of my feelings – my feelings about what Rik had told me, how I felt about what he'd said. And I kept imagining him holding Sascha's pale little body in his arms. Cold and wet and lifeless. But I didn't want a drink. If anything, the thought disgusted me. It disgusted me almost as much as the box of rubbish spread over my coffee table.

In the early evening I set the box upright and shoved everything back inside, not bothering to put the lid on. I picked it up, planning to take the whole lot down to the bins and get rid of it once and for all. But as I grabbed the door handle something held me back.

Perhaps I didn't need to throw it away right now. Not yet.

I glanced down. Kingsley's dinosaur lay on its side on top of an old shopping list, its blank black eye accusing me.

It wasn't as if the box took up much space. There was no need to throw it away right this second. I set it beside the door. Just for now.

I picked up the dinosaur.

When I went to bed that night – early, exhausted – it watched me from my bedside table. I slept like a log.

MONDAY, 28 JULY
MORNING

I called in sick. And for once it wasn't because I was hungover. I'd slept for twelve hours straight. For the first time in months I woke up feeling … pretty good. When I looked in the mirror my face appeared less puffy, the usual black circles under my eyes slightly diminished.

I called in sick anyway.

I had other things to do.

By nine I was sitting in my father's car outside the Harding house. Hoping for what? I didn't know. I'd expected Pip and Brett to be at work, but the gate was open and Pip's car was parked on the street. So perhaps she was home alone? Surely Roger wouldn't be here on a Monday morning. Although, thinking about it, I supposed a daytime tryst while Brett was working probably wasn't out of the question. I glanced around suspiciously, suddenly expecting him to appear at my window.

Nothing. Thank fuck for that.

Blustery wind shredded leaves and whipped dust up and down the street. The sun shone, though the day was cool. I'd called my parents earlier, talking briefly to Mum who was just back from her usual sparrow's-fart walk. I told her the lamp was out of stock and more were due at the store later today. Could I keep Dad's car until tomorrow?

'Tomorrow's fine.' I could hardly hear her over the dogs. 'I'm just giving Fritz and Frieda their breakfast. Quiet, you two! Your father went to a four-ball best-ball early today. David Brunhill picked him up, so that was no trouble. I'll be at tennis until six tomorrow night, but you could drop it back after that, if you like?'

'OK. Thanks, Mum.'

I hung up before we got started on other things I didn't want to discuss: work, my drinking, Leah, babies. It was a pretty long list.

So now here I was. I'd parked across the road from the front gate, in a spot that allowed me to see partway down the drive.

I munched on an apple, virtuous about eating fruit *and* not being hungover. Just when I decided I'd have to risk heading into the bushes again, Pip emerged. She wore workout clothes: long tights and a singlet, all black. Her ponytail was whipped up by the wind and lashed across her face as if imparting some sort of punishment. As I watched she plugged headphones in her ears and jogged away. I ate a banana. Forty minutes later she was back, a little redder in the face but still looking pretty bloody good. She slowed to a walk and disappeared down the driveway. It was actually very relaxing sitting inside the warm car.

* * *

I woke with a start.

1.51 pm.

Shit.

I'd slept for a couple of hours.

Pip was pruning bushes along the driveway, barely a dozen metres from where I sat. She'd changed into baggy jeans and a grey jumper and wore gardening gloves. My stomach growled, loud enough to be heard back in Artarmon, and I held my breath until Pip walked away. She returned pushing a wheelbarrow and left it by the gates. She started to prune the plants along the front fence. I sat low in my seat but she didn't appear to have any inkling I was there. Even doing mundane chores, Pip was effortlessly graceful – even her old clothes looked stylish.

Despite being hungry, I must have somehow dozed again, because I jerked wide awake as Brett's car pulled into the driveway. I fumbled to check my phone.

3.35 pm.

Stupid, stupid Kate.

Pip stopped pruning and smiled at Brett as he passed. He didn't return the smile. His mouth was a thin flat line. The Mercedes moved out of sight down the driveway. I stared at the house, willing Brett to come out but dreading it too. I jumped when he reappeared and walked stiffly towards Pip, his suit jacket flapping open so I could see a shirt stretched tight across his middle. Brett's thinning hair was made comically tufty by the wind, although the glare he aimed at Pip was anything but funny.

Pip put a hand on her hip and wiped her brow with the back of her other hand. She seemed about to say something then must have taken in his demeanour because she stopped talking and dropped her hands so they hung loosely by her sides. Her wrist was still bandaged. Brett moved in very close so his face was right up in hers, like opposing boxers before a bout. My skin prickled.

C'mon, Pip, can't you see he's angry? You need to leave.

Now.

Brett grabbed Pip's arm, pulling her close even as she tried to shrink back. His face was twisted with rage.

I'd wanted to break up Pip and Roger. I didn't want this. And though I might have fantasised about hurting Pip myself – actually, shamefully, I *had* hurt her, I realised with a lurch – I certainly didn't want Brett to harm her. I leaned closer to my open window but the wind snatched their words away, though they were only metres from me.

Suddenly Brett's voice rose and he shook her as he spoke. 'WHO ELSE KNOWS?'

Pip didn't reply. She flinched but otherwise seemed more surprised than scared. Instead she put a hand on his arm and spoke quietly to her husband.

Fuck.

What was she doing? Would Brett hurt her?

During my sessions with Dr Evans we'd talked at length about the type of person who hurt – even murdered – others. Given my circumstances, the subject came up often. We'd listed psychopaths, sociopaths, sadists, those with one of several mental illnesses, plus people who were just pure evil. We'd tried to categorise Peter but couldn't come to a definitive classification. Peter had been intimidating, yes. He was certainly a control freak. In hindsight, perhaps he was a psychopath. But he'd rarely been violent towards me. I'd had no warning of what he planned. It worried at me – constantly, like an infected tooth or a stomach ulcer – that I'd been married to someone who could do what he did. That I didn't know what kind of man he really was.

That I didn't do enough to stop him.

But it was too late by then.

I didn't know Brett well enough to categorise him. Perhaps he was just extremely angry. But rage – pure rage – well, that was just as deadly as any psychological condition.

Had I – stupidly and unwittingly – put Pip and Kingsley in danger?

I clenched my fist then realised I still held my phone. I stared at it dumbly. I couldn't just sit here and do nothing. Should I call the police? Or would calling the police make it worse?

Rik.

I could call Rik. He'd know what to do. My fingers hovered over the keypad, unsure.

Brett stopped talking. He still held Pip's arms but she shook him off. She glanced around and motioned for him to follow her inside. Partway down the drive she turned back to face him, a pleading expression on her face.

Oh, Pip, it's too late for that.

A flash of movement in my rear-view mirror drew my eye away from the argument unfolding before me. Kingsley was riding along the pavement towards Pip and Brett.

Shit.

Not again. Kingsley didn't need to see this. I glanced back at the Hardings but they were engrossed in their drama.

If Pip couldn't protect her son – or herself for that matter – then I would.

I jammed on my cap and sunnies and climbed out of the car. I didn't look towards the Harding house, just hoped Pip and Brett were too busy to notice me as I crossed the road. I broke into a jog as soon as I was out of their sight and ran towards Kingsley.

At first his eyes slid away from me – of course, he had no interest in a strange overweight woman wobble-running along the footpath. But then he looked again and his legs started slowing. Finally, an expression of affronted recognition came over him and he stopped. I saw now he wore a navy blazer and grey pants, his tie a little loose. On his back was a heavy-looking school-issued backpack he carried with apparent ease.

'You!' he said accusingly.

I stopped, puffing, put a hand to my chest.

Now's not the time to have a heart attack, Kate.

'I …'

'What are you doing here? Are you following me?'

'I … no. I need to talk to you.'

'That's what you said the other night.' His eyes narrowed in suspicion, then he glanced towards his house. 'Have you been to see my parents?'

'No. I just —'

'Then go away,' he spat, his blue eyes flashing. 'I don't care what you have to say. No one does. You need to go away and stay away. Leave my family alone.'

His animosity shocked me. We were supposed to be friends. This was all going horribly wrong. 'What?'

'I spoke to my mother about you.'

His *mother*? *Oh, shit.* I'd told him to talk to Brett.

Not Pip.

'I told her what you said. She told me she knew who you were. That you knew her from back when you were both at art school together.' He regarded me with narrowed eyes. 'She said you are a sad, lonely lady who is jealous of us. She said you wanted a family like ours to replace yours. And she said you have "mental health issues".' Kingsley made air quotes with his fingers as he said the last three words. 'Mum told me to keep my distance and to call her if I saw you again.'

I couldn't breathe. *Mental health issues.*

He started to ride around me. 'I'm going to tell her you're here. You'd better leave.'

'No,' I called out, following him. 'Don't go in there!'

'Watch me!' he called over his shoulder.

I stumbled after him, still winded from his words.

They were so fucking … *true.*

Kingsley was nearly at the gate when Brett emerged. He must have heard us. I faltered and stood for a second, trying to catch my breath. As Kingsley reached his father and turned to point at me I took off to my car, running faster than I had in years. I yanked open the driver's side door as Kingsley tried to pass his father. Pip was no longer in the driveway.

As I slammed the door shut, I saw Brett grab Kingsley's arm. He appeared to be questioning him closely and he gestured at me. Kingsley shook his head and tried to pull away. The boy glanced at me, the look fleeting. At first I couldn't put my finger on the expression I saw in his eyes. He spun away from both of us.

I started the engine and made my escape. And then it hit me what I'd seen in Kingsley's eyes.

Fear.

Why was Kingsley so scared of Brett?

TUESDAY, 29 JULY
4.43 AM

My teeth clattered together hard enough I thought I'd shatter the enamel.

So. Fucking. Cold.

I opened my mouth and salty water rushed in. I coughed and gagged, kicking out with my legs and breaststroking my arms. But something held me back; something heavy pressed me down. I opened my eyes but it was dim; shapes reared up before me in a way that didn't make sense. The water tasted of brine and faintly of sewage. My arms ached but I didn't stop, aiming upwards, my fingernails tearing at something soft but unyielding half an arm's-length in front of me. I gave up pulling at it and pressed against it, pushing back instead of up. It didn't help. I was stuck.

Nothing existed but the need to breathe. I pressed my hands to my head, feeling them shake – in terror or from the iciness of the water, I couldn't tell. Water bubbled up my nostrils and I sobbed, sucking more of it into my mouth. Stars burst before my eyes. I couldn't do it. It was too late. I opened my mouth, trying to yell, to scream, to beg someone to come and help me.

'Mummy!'

I jerked up, the word torn from me like a wounded animal's yelp of pain.

My heart thudded wildly and my whole body was slick with sweat. I blinked. My bed. My flat. All OK. All normal. I tried to calm my heart.

Deep breaths, Kate. The Dream. Just the fucking Dream.

But this time it had been different. It wasn't my normal dream. It wasn't just me drowning under some random body of water. It was him. My boy. This dream was the day he died. The day Sascha needed me.

The day I wasn't there.

I started sobbing. Wailing. Like I hadn't since the month he died.

It was all my fault.

WEDNESDAY, 30 JULY
1.22 AM

'Hi Rik. It's Kate. Sorry to call you so late. I guess you're asleep. I … ah, I just wanted to apologise for the other day. I was … *upset*. But I guess you know that. I … um, I thought maybe we could catch up sometime. Perhaps not just yet though – I'm trying to get my life back together. I haven't had a drink in … (*laughs*) well, this is only the second night – and it's not morning yet (*laughs again*). But it's a start, you know? Anyway, I'll call you in a couple of weeks. (*Pause*) I hope you'll take my call. Bye.'

WEDNESDAY, 30 JULY
EVENING

That evening was clear and cold. By the time I arrived home my breaths were puffs of fog in the darkness and my nose was running. I walk-jogged from my car to the apartment block on a path lit by dim streetlights, as unprepared as always for one of Sydney's rare frosty nights.

'Hi Katie.'

A figure emerged out of the gloom. My heart rate zoomed sky high, then I realised who it was.

Leah.

My sister stood near the entrance to the building. Under the too-dim security lights I could just make out her face, her features more angular than the photo in the paper had suggested. Her hair was like mine again, back to its normal waves, slightly out of control. But Leah's ready smile was missing. Her whole body was shivering and she clutched her large handbag to her belly.

'The baby's gone.'

Her voice was flat. I couldn't see her eyes.

'What?' I replied. 'Gone? What do you mean, gone?'

'I mean, gone. I miscarried. I'm not pregnant any more.'

A familiar cold began in my fingertips, working its way along my arms and right through my body.

Gone.

'Come upstairs.' I walked past her and unlocked the door. We didn't speak on the way up in the lift and Leah didn't stop shaking.

Once inside the flat my sister wandered into the kitchen, apparently in a kind of daze, and stopped near the bench. She didn't look at me. With her handbag still held tightly over her stomach she started to talk. 'I knew on Friday something was wrong. I'd had spotting during the day, but the books all say that can be normal so I tried not to worry. Then it got heavier and heavier and when I went to the toilet there was a lot of blood. And cramps and … other stuff.' She stopped and took a breath. 'Ellis took me to hospital about 1 am that night. They told me I was having a miscarriage and sent me home the next morning.'

She turned and opened the fridge, lifting a carton of milk from the shelf and staring at it before putting it back.

'So the baby is … gone,' Leah continued in a monotone. 'There's still some bleeding. Some pain. But he's gone, I can feel it. I don't know for sure if he was a he, but that's what we've been calling him. Jack, actually. That was his name. Jack.' She finally looked at me. Her eyes were dull. I remembered what that was like. 'You're the first person I've told.' Leah shut the fridge door, walked over to the lounge and sat down. 'I haven't been able to face telling Mum. She called me yesterday but Ellis fobbed her off.'

I swallowed. I knew how thrilled Mum was at the prospect of another grandchild. She'd probably given up on the whole idea years ago. Then unmaternal Leah fell pregnant.

And now this.

I bit a cuticle on my pointer finger, ripping a chunk of skin free.

Why did Leah come to me?

Mum would know what to say. Why not go to Mum? Or a friend. Leah had loads of friends, most of them socialites or celebrities but still. They were her *friends*. We were barely on speaking terms.

'You should be at home with Ellis. Recovering.'

'I can't be at home, Katie. I just think about the baby.'

I understood that at least. The last thing Leah wanted was to think.

She sat up straighter, looking at me differently now, her eyes huge – searching – and I realised perhaps she didn't want sympathy. She spoke in a pleading voice. 'What do I do now? I don't know who else to talk to.'

I sat down with a thud next to my baby sister. It was my turn not to meet her eyes as I spoke. 'They'll tell you time will heal your pain. They'll tell you you're young, you'll have another child and the memories of this child will fade over the years. That you will – eventually – feel better. That you will miss your child forever but the grief that fills every moment now, that consumes you, won't last forever. That you can be happy.'

I finally met her blank gaze, holding them with my own. 'They're right, Leah,' I said fiercely. 'Please, let them be right. Don't end up like me.'

THE MOMENT MY SON DIED

I was at the multiplex, sitting in a darkened cinema with a dozen strangers giggling at something inane Ashton Kutcher had just said.

Of course, I don't know the exact moment my son died. But I worked out it was around midway through the movie. That morning I'd bought some new running socks and a ten-dollar costume jewellery necklace with a unicorn on it – I knew Sascha would love it. I'd had a coffee and a toasted sandwich in one of my favourite cafés while I read the newspaper.

Then I'd taken myself off to the first movie I'd seen in months. A chick-flick that required no real thought. I'd enjoyed every minute of it.

While my son died.

Without me there.

FRIDAY, 1 AUGUST
EVENING

I put my joggers on and went for a walk for the first time in ... well, I couldn't remember the last time I'd walked for pleasure or exercise. Months. Though, if I was honest, I'd only decided to get some exercise because I couldn't face cleaning my apartment again. I'd never been a neat freak but over the previous few days I'd used every distraction I could to stop me drinking.

So far it had worked.

Yes, it had only been five days – this was my sixth – but that was a record for me. Since Sascha's death anyway. I'd gone a day or two at times, sure, but not five days. Five days. Really, it was sad. How proud I was of something so many people managed most weeks of the year.

Early evenings were the worst. That's when I was at my most vulnerable – straight after work. My usual drinking time. So I scrubbed the shower or folded washing or even, yesterday, resorted to cleaning the blackened oven. Now you could see through the glass and the house reeked of chemicals that made me gag.

But more than any of those things I checked Facebook, sometimes refreshing it every thirty seconds.

What was happening with the Hardings?

Not knowing was killing me. How had I become so invested in their lives so quickly? So fully? Even sober they were always in my thoughts.

Especially Kingsley. He'd been so dismissive when I'd bailed him up outside his house. Didn't he know I was just looking out for him?

Trying to protect him?

Leah was never far from my thoughts either. After my little speech on Wednesday night I'd used her phone to call Ellis. He was out of his mind with worry and said he'd be right over. When he rang the intercom, Leah wandered down to him as dazed as she'd been when she arrived, as if she didn't know where she should go or what she should do with herself.

I knew I should call her and see how she was doing.

I wondered if she'd told Mum and Dad yet.

I thought of Rik. I wanted to call him again and tell him I wasn't drinking. I often brought up his contact details on my phone, but never quite found the courage to press the button and do it. I thought I'd sound lame, calling when I'd only been off the grog for a few days. Five days without alcohol shouldn't be worthy of celebration. But it was, sort of. And even that was ironic. How to celebrate not drinking without having a drink?

How to commiserate, to socialise, to get through a fucking Friday night, without a drink?

But I was also scared to call him. It had been a very long time since I'd met a man I liked. I hardly remembered the feeling, let alone knew how to act on it. And what if he was only being nice to me out of pity?

But it was more than that. Rik had been with Sascha, had held him, when I could not. I couldn't articulate how that made me feel.

So now I was out walking along the main street of Artarmon. I was so deep in thought I didn't notice I'd reached the pub until I stood right in front of it. The doors were shut but I could hear muffled laughter. I could imagine the warmth inside, the familiar stale smell of beer. Reluctantly, I turned away.

By the time I got home I was sweating, despite the cold. I used the stairs in the spirit of my health-kick and I was panting as I fumbled with my keys. Once inside, I walked straight to the fridge. I didn't realise until I'd been standing there for ten seconds or so that I was reflexively searching for something with alcohol in it. With a determination that surprised even me, I shut the door.

Instead I put the kettle on and put a teabag in a mug. I was unashamedly using chocolate as a wine substitute and had bought a box of half-price soft-centres from the supermarket as a no-drinking reward. I would get even fatter but I needed something to replace the alcohol.

One vice at a time, Kate.

While I waited for the kettle, I took the chocolates over to the lounge, fired up my sleeping laptop and opened Facebook. I typed in Kingsley Harding without really thinking, my mind half-focused on choosing between a strawberry or a mint chocolate.

Then I saw what he'd posted and I forgot all about the virtues of one chocolate over another.

Trust. When it's gone, what's left?

That was it. The post had 87 likes and several comments, most along the lines of *You alright, bro?* One comment from Max Garrett, a kid from school, read, *Is this about me? You shitty with me about the thing in science last week?* This was the only comment Kingsley had replied to. *Nah course not mate. We're cool. It's my parents. Never seen Dad so mad. Probably shouldn't have posted anything. See you on Monday — if I make it through the weekend. Ha ha.*

His words were light but I was sure there was something beneath them. Maybe my meddling had been a mistake. If Brett lashed out at Pip, Kingsley could get involved. Brett might hurt him.

Pip couldn't protect her son. Like I couldn't protect Sascha.

Fuck. It's all my fault.

I closed the laptop, wondering if Kingsley had friends to support him. He seemed popular when I saw him with his friends at Macca's. And on his bedroom wall he'd chalked a reminder for a friend's sixteenth birthday party he was obviously planning on attending.

Hang on, Kate.

Kingsley's bedroom wall.

It hadn't exactly been a series of Snoopy cartoons. I frowned, remembering. He'd drawn heads in a row. Including a monster. Now that I thought about it, there were a number of drawings about darker issues. The skull and crossbones. A crying girl. A heedless mouse sleeping on the back of a cat.

Was his wall a cry for help? Was he in danger?

I froze, cold down to my bones.

From himself? Or someone else?

Perhaps he was scared. Surely he wouldn't *hurt himself?*

No, that was reading too much into it. I pulled out my phone and scrolled through the photos I'd taken at the Harding house. Other drawings were less threatening: planets orbiting the sun, animal portraits. No, it was just my overactive imagination.

Kingsley was just a normal teenager, exploring the things he found interesting through art.

Surely that was all it was.

A sharp physical ache for the deadening effect of white wine hit me. I picked up the chocolate box. Chocolate released serotonin into the bloodstream, didn't it? If I ate enough of them, I'd feel great in no time, for sure.

Kingsley's face swam into my head.

I picked up my phone and found Rik's name. My fingers hovered over the screen.

No, I was overthinking it.

The last open house was tomorrow. I'd watch from the car, check they were all alright. Which they would be. Maybe not perfect any more but alright. Brett might throw Pip out of the house. Or maybe they'd be one of those strange couples who stayed together after infidelity, telling all and sundry how one partner having sex with a stranger *made our relationship stronger*. Who knew?

Yes, I'd go tomorrow and find out everything.

PART V

FINAL
OPEN HOUSE

SATURDAY, 2 AUGUST
MORNING

I'd kind of expected to sleep like a baby once I stopped drinking.

Turned out it didn't work that way. I'd tossed and turned the night before the final open house, playing numerous different scenarios out in my head. Brett and Pip arguing. Brett and Pip making up. The Harding house echoing with Brett's rage and Pip's sobbing. Kingsley eavesdropping from the top of the stairs or hiding out in his room with headphones on, rap music blaring. In the worst of them – the most preposterous – Brett pulled a gun and killed a shrieking Pip, a tear-streaked Kingsley and then himself. In the middle of a sleepless night this seemed perfectly possible – even logical and somehow likely.

Little did I know.

Around midnight the wind grew stronger, until the windows shook and the trees of the leafy north shore swayed. I considered scenarios where trees fell on my apartment, wiping me out. These I relished, playing them over and over in my head, drenched in self-pity. Annihilation by tree was what I deserved after the Hardings had all been gunned down.

I woke at seven, groggy and achy. The gale continued unabated and I stumbled out of bed and over to the window, lifted a flimsy metal venetian blind and peered outside. The street was strewn with leaves and twigs. It looked like God had shaken the city's trees in a fit of rage. But none had toppled over and there were no large fallen boughs – or none that I could see anyway.

Shit day for an open house, though, that's for sure.

The open was at 1 pm. Six hours. I gnawed at my thumbnail. What the fuck would I do for the next six hours? It seemed an interminably long wait.

I checked Facebook.

Nothing of note had been added to Kingsley's post.

I made tea, drank a few sips, then walked to the balcony door to stare at the whipping branches. I tipped the cold tea out and made more. I turned the TV on, but the chirpy commentators annoyed me. All my CDs suddenly sucked. I made and then wasted a third cup of tea.

When I checked Facebook at ten, I saw that one of Kingsley's friends had tagged him in a photo about a soccer game and that Kingsley had liked the comment. I released a deep breath. He was alive. I didn't realise how concerned I'd been for his welfare.

Stupid Kate, it's just your imagination running wild.

I calmed down a bit and drank a whole cup of tea, even managed some toast. And then somehow it was after twelve and time to go to the open. I grabbed my jacket and keys and headed down to the lobby, taking the stairs again in the spirit of healthy living.

Through the lobby windows the weather appeared even more wild. The rain had intensified. No umbrella could stand up to this kind of wind so I didn't bother. Once in my car I sat for a moment, shivering, before starting the ignition and blasting the heater.

The trip to Wahroonga was eerily devoid of people. Leaves littered the usually busy highway. There were a few branches down but most of these had been moved off the road by diligent council employees or by drivers who came across them. But most people it seemed had sensibly decided to wait this out in the safety of their homes and the roads were relatively empty. It felt like the end of the world.

About twenty minutes before the open I coasted slowly past the Harding house. Pip's car was parked on the street. The gate was open. I parked a little further down the street and watched for comings and goings in my mirrors, ready to make a quick getaway if necessary. I was nervous to be back in my yellow Hyundai. If the weather had been better I would have parked a block away and loitered behind another car on foot, but fuck that. Not in the wind and rain. I'd just have to hope Roger was keen to stay out of the weather and wasn't watching for me.

I settled in to wait.

The street was empty but it wasn't quiet. Trees trembled, their leaves blanketing the ground and vehicles, camouflaging everything. Maybe my car would be hidden that way, I thought, after a foot-long branch landed on my bonnet, making me jump. The open was going to be a bust, for sure. Even the Harding house would have trouble luring people out in this weather.

One o'clock came and went. No sign of Roger.

Maybe they'd cancelled the open.

Two other cars had braved the weather and parked on the street near me. I assumed they were here for the open house, because in both cases the occupants remained in their vehicles, apparently not ready to face the wind and rain until it was obvious the agent had arrived. But at 1.08 pm a tall balding man from the car nearest me could wait no longer. He dashed from his sedan to the front gate, pausing briefly before racing down the driveway out of sight.

He was gone a minute, maybe two. I waited impatiently, biting a nail. Just as I readied to follow him, the man scurried out onto the street again, not looking pleased. Rain dripped from his bald head as he ran back to his car. He flung open the car door, dived inside then slammed it shut. Thirty seconds later he screeched away from the kerb and drove past me. A woman in the passenger seat held a mobile to her ear and gestured unhappily with her free hand. Maybe they were calling the agency? The man conducted a jerky three-point turn and sped past me again, heading towards the highway. The second vehicle followed them, clearly having watched them and deducing the open house had been cancelled.

I checked the street. No one in sight. I gnawed harder at my nail, ripping it free. Maybe the whole family had gone out earlier that morning? Gone away for the weekend? Blood seeped from the cuticle of my throbbing digit and I sucked it, tasting metal.

Last night's nightmare – the one where Brett pulled a gun on Pip and Kingsley – replayed in my head.

No, surely not.

Those people in the cars would have been complaining to someone from McQuilty about their wasted trip.

I wouldn't have long, I thought, chewing the inside of my cheek.

Fuck it.

Leaving my handbag and even my coat behind, I grabbed the keys and beeped the car as I ran for the house. I sprinted, head down, now more than ever glad to be a flat-shoe wearer, as I fought wind and rain and slippery cobblestones. Finding Roger's car parked on the turning circle – rather haphazardly – nearly made me turn around, but I'd come this far, there was no turning back now. There was no sign of Brett's Mercedes. I sheltered under the front portico, dripping wet and dishevelled, to catch my breath.

Was Roger inside? If so, why wasn't the house open for inspection by now? And if he wasn't here, then why was his car parked outside the house?

I made a decision.

I shook myself off like a dog and wiped my feet on the doormat, then pressed the doorbell. The ring echoed inside. Silence. No footsteps. No voices. Nothing. I glanced behind me then moved to the keypad, and entered the four numbers of Sascha's birth year. Then I pressed the hash key. A buzz told me the code had worked. Sweet relief. In my rush I pressed hard on the heavy front door, which swung open so easily I almost fell forward. I pulled up just over the threshold and shut the door behind me.

No sound but for the ticking of a clock. No sign of Roger. Or anyone else.

'Hello?' I asked in a small voice.

I crept forward, the squeaking of my shoes on the floorboards terrifyingly loud in the silent house. It was no warmer in here than outside.

Where the fuck is everyone?

The door between the foyer and the kitchen sat ajar and I pushed it open, sticking my head through.

No one.

I backed out of the kitchen and went upstairs. I darted into the master bedroom, then the guest bedrooms and finally

Kingsley's. No one. The rooms were neat and empty. I walked to Kingsley's window. Rain lashed the glass. From there, Roger's car looked even more askew. Where was he?

I jogged down the stairs and hurried through the rest of the rooms before returning to the kitchen. I walked over to the glass doors overlooking the pool and peered into the maelstrom. The sky had darkened and it felt more like early evening than the middle of the day. The pool was filled with dirt and leaves and the water level had risen. It certainly wasn't inviting. I scrutinised the water more closely, apprehension sliding into me, further chilling my already cold limbs.

A shape.

There was something big in the pool.

Menacing somehow, like a crocodile submerged, still and watchful, in the dark waters of a billabong.

Just a tree or a fallen branch? Maybe. I knew I should take a closer look but I hesitated, uneasy about the murky pool and bemoaning the sodden walk down there. Did I really need to confirm a tree had lost a branch? What was the point in getting saturated again?

Then I recalled the rage on Brett's face and remembered my gun-toting nightmare. I had to check.

I flicked the lock above the handle on the back door and slid the door open. There was a roof over the balcony but the wind was strong and rain came at me sideways. I shivered. Shutting the door behind me, I moved swiftly along the balcony then down the path to the pool. Trees slapped me with wet tendrils and I stepped over puddles. I wrestled with the slippery child lock on the pool gate for a moment, swearing at it, then entered, the gate clanging behind me with force enough to shake the fence.

As soon as I looked at the pool I saw it.

A body.

In the shallow end.

Pip Harding.

* * *

I stood in the driving rain, rigid with shock.

Pip's hair floated on the top of the water like ink-black seaweed, matted but still somehow beautiful. The rest of her was invisible but there was no mistaking that hair.

I started to shake so badly I thought I might collapse. Reaching behind me, I gripped the cool glass of the gate, turning from Pip to lean on it. My breath came shallow and fast.

Oh God. What had Brett done?

And where was Kingsley? It was only the thought of him that made me turn back to the pool, and I forced myself to scan the area. I could see Pip from the corner of my eye but refused to look directly at her. A branch – a gum tree branch – had fallen into the deep end of the pool, further away from me. It was long, half in the pool, half out. The jagged end, as thick as a person's thigh, rested on the pool's edge with its leafy offshoots stretching across the water, green-blue in the dim daylight.

And then I saw it. Under the branch, just visible beneath the foliage.

A second body.

Kingsley. Brett's killed his child.

I spun away and vomited onto the fence, watching the thin liquid splatter across the glass and drip down onto my boots.

Not again.

I tried to get air into my lungs.

Brett had drowned them both.

Drowned.

Just like Sascha.

I shivered. Water dripped from my nose, from my chin. My palms pressed into my thighs, trembling and sweaty despite the rain.

I focused on my feet. An earthworm made its way through my watery vomit, contracting and releasing as it moved towards the lawn on the other side of the fence. There were dozens of them. The rain had forced them from the soil in search of oxygen and now they were at the mercy of the elements. They moved in all directions, wriggling over leaves and twigs, undeterred by the wind and water in their path.

I kept watching them, unsure if I could turn around and face the cold bodies in the water. I thought of Sascha, in the car as water seeped inside, strapped in, unable to free himself, trying frantically to escape.

My nightmare.

And now Pip and Kingsley.

I knew they were dead. I knew, but I had to be sure. I couldn't just leave them there without checking.

Sucking in air, I clenched my jaw and walked the few steps to the shallow end of the pool. I reached in to grasp Pip's hair. It was silky smooth, belying its matted appearance. I tugged it gently then let go and Pip floated my way, rolling over at the same time. A moan escaped me when I saw her blue lips, the usual red lipstick washed away. Pip's eyes were closed – thank God for small mercies – and her pale skin was now tinged grey; her eye sockets bruised and dirty. A fingernail-sized green leaf adhered to her cheek and I wiped it off with a finger, shivering at her skin's chill and sogginess, as if the water had started to seep into her body, already claiming her as its own.

I swallowed.

Was this how Sascha had looked when Rik pulled him from the harbour?

Like everything that had once made him human was gone?

Pip had red abrasions around her neck. Had she been strangled before she hit the pool? I brushed a few strands of hair from her forehead. She began to float away, her face dipping below the surface of the water. I let her go. Moving quickly before my courage faded, I stood up, walking to the deep end of the pool where the branch was partly submerged.

With a grunt, I picked up the thick jagged end and, walking backwards, dragged the branch free from the water. I wiped the dirt from my hands as I walked back to the edge of the pool, knowing there was no chance Kingsley was alive.

Peering into the water, I realised my error immediately, ashamed at the relief that flooded through me.

It wasn't Kingsley in the water.

It was Roger.

* * *

Of *course* it was Roger. I'd seen his car parked out the front.

My initial relief that Kingsley was alive then morphed into something else. Pip and Roger were dead. *Dead.*

Had Brett caught them together? I sucked in a sharp breath. Was this my fault?

Think.

Call the police. Call Rik.

I stuck a wet hand into my soaked pocket. Nothing. My phone was in the car.

Fuck fuck fuck.

I stepped back and examined the second body again. It was definitely Roger. Orange tanned skin, now sallow in death. The distinguished grey hair somehow still holding its shape, even underwater. He wore the same jacket and pants he'd worn to previous opens, or they looked the same at any rate. Roger had kids too. His girls were just babies really. I held in a sob at the thought, trying to think what to do.

Two dead people in the pool.

The police would come.

Panic rose in me with a shot of adrenaline. I wasn't meant to be here. Roger had banned me. And I'd attacked Pip at the pub. I'd been to so many of the Harding open houses. I'd followed Kingsley. I'd hidden in the garden, for fuck's sake. Stalking, they'd call it. They'd take my phone and find messages from Roger. *This is your last warning. If I see you again I WILL call the police.* Or they'd find his phone and see them on that. They all knew me as the unhinged woman whose husband killed her son and who, everybody knew, drank too much.

Fuck.

I sat down on the pavers with the earthworms and the vomit, and let the rain wash over me. Brett had done it. I knew that. Surely the police would believe me.

My brain snorted at me with derision.

Me.

A known drunk. Found dirty and wet at the house. A stalker. I rested my head on my hands, let the rain beat my skull.

I was screwed.

Unless.

Unless, if I left now, no one would ever know I'd been here. No one had seen me. I could go around the side of the house. It could work, if I was careful.

Fuck, was I the type of person to flee a crime scene?

I had to.

For Kingsley. Because if they caught me – if they arrested me – who would be left to save him from his father?

I scrambled to my feet and walked to the pool gate. As I lifted the safety latch I stopped, thinking about fingerprints. I'd been to open houses here before and surely no one would know if my fingerprints were from today or two weeks ago. I was hazy on the science but it seemed unlikely. I looked around. What had I touched today that was different?

The bodies.

Well, I hadn't touched Roger, and only Pip's hair. Pulling the branch from the water – could they take fingerprints from wet bark? That also seemed unlikely. They would probably be able to tell it had been moved, but I guess that didn't point to me any more than anybody else.

Pip's face was still to the sky, her forehead the only part of her above water. I couldn't see Roger under the branch.

'I'm sorry,' I whispered to them. 'The police will get him for this, don't worry.'

My words seemed silly and empty as the rain and wind howled around me.

I let the gate slam and started jogging, realising someone from McQuilty was bound to be here soon. I needed to leave here fast and to report this so Kingsley didn't discover his mother and her lover dead in the pool.

I made my way across the back yard and around the side, soaked through to the core. My boots squelched with every step. I slowed as I emerged at the front of the house, looking for cars.

As I crept down the driveway, ready to dive into the bushes at the first sign of a vehicle, a prickling sensation spread across my shoulders.

Was someone watching?

I spun around and looked back at the Harding house, still so beautiful under grey skies. The upper storey windows looked down at me with a sinister watchfulness. For a moment I thought I saw a shadow at Kingsley's window.

No. Just my imagination.

I glanced at the front door, still closed.

Shit, the keypad. My fingerprints.

I ran over and climbed the steps, rubbing at the numbers with a tissue from my jeans pocket that was so drenched it barely held together, before turning on my heel and heading for the gate.

I sped off in my car, water pooling under me on the upholstery and in the footwell.

I drove up the highway, looking for a payphone. Ten minutes up the road, I saw one on a side street and pulled over, looking around as I entered the booth, and dialled triple 0, and anonymously reported hearing suspicious noises at the Harding house. I hung up with shaking hands and wiped down the phone with my sodden jumper.

As I drove away I thought of Kingsley and bit the inside of my cheek hard enough to taste the sharp metallic tang of blood.

He'd lost one parent. The other one was a murderer.

What would happen to him now?

* * *

I huddled on the lounge, blankets piled on me. As the wind and rain battered the apartment building I shivered, unable to warm up. I flicked from channel to channel, finally seeing the story on the five o'clock news.

'The bodies of a man and woman were found in a back yard pool on Sydney's north shore this afternoon ...' The brunette newsreader wore a sorrowful expression and lipstick that was – ironically – the colour of blood. A live cross to the Harding house replaced her onscreen. Its wrought-iron gate was open as usual, though nothing else about the scene was usual. The house was lit by flashing lights, and dozens of uniformed and plain-clothed police carrying various pieces of equipment swarmed up the driveway and poured out onto the street like ants at a picnic.

The newsreader's smooth voice continued over the video footage. 'Police have not released details of the shocking crime other than to confirm two people are dead and that they are treating both deaths as homicides. Unconfirmed reports have been made that the male and female were both prominent local figures in the north shore community, pillars of society who will be sadly missed by their families and many others. We will bring you more information as it becomes available throughout the evening.'

I hauled myself to my feet, knees creaking like someone decades older. My thoughts raced. Why hadn't the police arrested Brett yet?

I shuffled over to a cupboard in the kitchen like a zombie and reached into the far back corner where I'd put a bottle of 'emergency' wine. This was clearly an emergency. The wine was cheap and white – and warm – but I cracked it open and drank straight from the bottle, wincing at the taste but drinking it anyway because cheap warm wine was what I deserved.

How many deaths were on my head now?

My son died because of me. Now another woman's child was motherless.

I should never have become involved with the Hardings. I was bad news.

I started crying. Crying for all the people in my life I'd let down. Mostly Sascha, of course. And now Pip and Roger. They were innocents, despite their affair. They didn't deserve to end up dead in a swimming pool.

It was too late for them. There was only Kingsley left to worry about now. Should I go to the police, tell them everything, for his sake? I had to, didn't I? Even if it made me look bad. They needed to know about Brett so they could catch him. I wiped my cheeks and took another long drink as I walked over to the lounge.

I was exhausted, right down to the bone.

What chance was there the police would believe me?

How likely was it they'd suspect the mild-mannered husband with the kind eyes? No, they'd be far more likely to point the finger at the crazy, drunken stalker who 'just happened' to be at the scene of the murder and then fled like a criminal. The one who had harassed the dead people less than two weeks earlier. The one who drank too much. The one with a chip on her shoulder about her own son's death, furious with the adulterers for screwing up another child's life.

I could hardly blame them. Even to me I looked guilty.

Far more guilty than Brett.

I lay back on the lounge, gripping the bottle of wine like it was all I had left in the world. I glanced at my phone. The police hadn't called. That must be a good thing. I lay back again and started to drift off, lulled by wine and the drone of the TV.

Just before I fell asleep a thought came to me and I sat bolt upright.

Fuck.

I'd thrown up all over the crime scene. Was it raining hard enough to wash all traces of my vomit away? I didn't know. I rubbed my face. This was such a mess. Rik had been right. I should have stayed out of it.

The buzz of my phone vibrating along the coffee table set my heart racing.

I peered at the screen.

Rik.

As if my thoughts had conjured him up.

'Hello?' I said tentatively.

'Kate. It's me, Rik. Senior Constable McBride.'

'Yes, I know.'

There was a moment's silence then he continued. 'Look, I'm downstairs. Can I come up? I need to talk to you about something. Something … important.'

Shit.

I was in tracksuit pants and a jumper. I mentally shrugged, supposing Rik would have to cope with my poor fashion choices. At least I was dry.

'Yes, of course. I'll buzz you in.'

'Thanks. Don't worry about the door, it's already open. I'll let myself upstairs.'

I rolled off the lounge and stumbled towards the front door, opening it and leaving it ajar, then walked over to the sink and splashed water on my face. I shuffled back over to the lounge and sat down, trying to slow my breaths.

'Hello?' Rik called out from the front door.

'Come in,' I said, voice wary.

He was wearing his full uniform and I felt a spark inside me go out.

An official visit then.

I don't know what else I'd expected.

Of course he was here about Pip and Roger. All the local police would be on the case. And Rik had been there when I'd confronted them at the pub. He'd have to come and talk to me about it.

He had dark smudges under both eyes but stared at me as keenly as ever as he took in my inebriated and unkempt state. His eyes flickered to the wine bottle on the coffee table in front of me.

'Kate,' he said, a little stiffly. 'How are you?'

I laughed, a bitter sound. 'Am I drinking again, do you mean? Well, I wasn't. Until tonight. I guess you could say I've had a bit of a relapse.'

He frowned and moved a few steps closer, making no comment on my ... setback. 'You heard then? About what happened at the Harding house today?'

'Yes,' I said, unsure how much more to say. I wanted to ask him about it. I had a thousand questions, but I didn't know what was safe. Did they suspect me? Had they found Brett yet? Then I remembered I wasn't supposed to know the identity of the dead people. 'It was Pip, wasn't it? They said it was a man and a woman. Who was the man? I wanted to call you to ask about it but I thought you'd be busy working.'

Plausible lie, Kate.

The look Rik gave me was cryptic. He blinked then seemed to deflate a little. He gestured at a dining chair and I nodded. He sat facing me, looking almost as miserable as I felt. 'Yes, it was Pip Harding. And Roger Bailey.'

His eyes stared into mine, but I couldn't tell if it was with suspicion or sympathy.

'So who killed them?' I asked. 'They didn't just drown in the family swimming pool, I take it? Was it Brett? Did he find out about the affair?'

'You know I can't tell you that, Kate,' he said, but my stricken face must have made him soften. 'Look, at this stage we don't have any strong leads. We're on it, though. We'll find the killer.' Rik clenched his teeth so hard a knot of muscle bulged on each side of his jawline.

Suddenly, an image of me bent double as I vomited onto the pool fence popped into my head. I felt light-headed.

'Are you sure you're OK, Kate?' Rik asked. 'You look pale.' He watched me intently and when he spoke again there was a note of steel in his voice I'd not heard before. 'Is there anything you want to tell me?'

'What? No.' I fiddled with my sleeve then forced my hands to be still. Sweat broke out on my upper lip. I swallowed, trying not to let the intensity of Rik's gaze unnerve me totally.

'Kate. Look. I'm here in an official capacity, obviously. We're currently working at Hornsby Station to help out with this case. Doug – Senior Constable Lindsay – was supposed to come in with me while we talked, but I called in a favour and he agreed to wait downstairs. I thought it might be easier if we spoke alone. I wanted to see how you're doing, but I also need to make sure … to find out … if you'd been back to the house. You haven't, have you? You didn't see anything?'

'You told me to stay away from them. Remember?'

He nodded and his body relaxed. 'Good. That's good.'

I cleared my throat, scared to ask my next question. 'What happened to their son? Is he safe?'

'Kingsley? Yes, he's safe. He's staying with his father in a motel.'

'With Brett?' I felt my blood freeze again.

'Yes, why?'

'Is that ... wise?'

The look he gave me was sharp. 'Do you know something – something specific – about Brett or Kingsley that we don't?'

Fuck.

I opened my mouth to tell him everything. That Kingsley seemed scared of his father, that Brett was the killer, that I had been at the Harding house that day and had called the police.

But before I found the words, Rik spoke. 'Kate, I shouldn't tell you this, but ... it appears Brett has an alibi. Both he and Kingsley do, actually. So we're focusing our efforts on other suspects for the time being.'

My heart thudded. Brett had an *alibi*? How was that possible? Other *suspects*? My head spun.

Who?

Me?

Well, I knew it wasn't me who killed Pip and Roger. So who else could it have been?

I squinted, regarding Rik with a keener eye. He was paler than usual. And those black smudges under his eyes made him look older. Perhaps he was just overworked; stressed. That made sense. Rik's eyes slid from mine.

No.

Not Rik. He was the perfect man. Wasn't he? A thought flashed into my brain.

That's what you thought about Peter.

I obviously wasn't a great judge of men. But why on earth would Rik kill Pip and Roger? I was being paranoid.

My mind slipped back to the confession he'd made when he was here last. *I helped pull your husband and child out of Sydney Harbour.* What sort of a coincidence was it that he'd been there on the worst day of my life and now here he was again?

Had he been watching me? Stalking me? Was that why he was so forgiving when I vomited on his boots that drunken night in Manly?

I pushed the thought down, remembered his kindness, how he'd been so understanding.

No, Kate, not Rik. He's one of the good guys.

'Kate?' he continued. 'Are you feeling alright?'

I nodded and smiled, though I felt queasy.

'We have them both under police protection if that's what you're worried about,' Rik continued. 'They're both perfectly safe, we're watching them 24/7. No one can get to either of them. We'll make sure of that.'

'That's good to know,' I said in a small, croaky voice.

Rik stood up and spoke without looking at me. 'Kate, I wish I didn't have to ask this of you.'

I somehow knew what he was going to say.

'My bosses want you to come down to the station tomorrow and give a statement.' He rubbed his face. 'And a DNA sample. Forensics found some … biological matter at the house and we need to rule you out. It's just to eliminate you as a suspect.'

'Yes, of course,' I heard myself reply, as if from a long way away. 'Just to rule me out.'

To eliminate me.

SUNDAY, 3 AUGUST
MORNING

I woke early, still on the lounge.

Ever since Sascha's death I'd dreaded waking. Each morning there was a split second when everything was like it was *before*: when I was still Sascha's mum and he was down the hall in his own bed and I knew I'd soon be hearing him wake up, pad down the hall and jump in with me. A split second. Immediately after that came the realisation he was gone. That knowledge hit me hard – like the very first time – every single morning.

Today was different.

Today I woke knowing.

There was no split second. No moment of normality. I knew he was gone. I knew they were all gone. Sascha. Roger. Pip. Even Peter.

Gone.

I lay unmoving, willing everything away. It was quiet, the sort of quiet that made me think something was wrong, and it took several seconds to realise the storm had passed. Sunlight strobed through the venetian blinds. I had a headache – too much warm white wine will do that – and a kink in my neck. Not as much pain as I deserved. I wished I was nauseous. Throwing up would have made me feel better.

I spent most of the morning on the lounge feeling sorry for myself. I didn't drink. Or even eat. I just lay there. Dozed, on and off. Cried, on and off.

At one point I woke up in a cold sweat after a dream where I rolled Pip's body over, her floating silky hair exposing her face, her lips now blood-red. *You did this*, she hissed, her smile a rictus.

I'd told Rik I'd meet him at the station at noon. To give a statement and provide some of my DNA for comparison. He'd explained they couldn't force me to give a sample but it would look better for me if I did.

But he didn't know I'd vomited my DNA all over the Hardings' pool fence, so I had a strong suspicion nothing was going to look better for me after today.

What worried me most was that if I was arrested for Pip's and Roger's murders, Kingsley would be left alone.

With Brett.

Because despite Brett's alibi I still believed he was the killer.

SUNDAY, 3 AUGUST
AFTERNOON

I parked on a back street and with heavy feet approached Hornsby Police Station, feeling like a convicted criminal being led to the gallows. That sounds melodramatic, I know, but given I was about to offer up my DNA then be arrested for a crime I didn't commit, which would in turn set a murderer free to live with his innocent child, melodrama seemed appropriate.

I ran a hand through my hair, belatedly realising I probably should have washed it. That's how they took DNA, wasn't it? Apparently they only needed a single strand of hair. Was it protocol to have clean hair before giving DNA? Probably. I didn't want to gross Rik out.

Rik.

I pictured his face when he told me he'd pulled Sascha out of the harbour.

Rik might just believe me.

Perhaps I could tell him everything.

I must have been deep in thought because when I turned the corner to the front of the station I was surprised to be confronted with a mob of people. No, not people.

Journalists.

Journalists, with the hefty cameras and intrusive microphones

I remembered so well. They chatted among themselves convivially, as if partaking of a rather pleasant morning tea.

But I was pretty sure that wasn't why they were here.

'Yes, Sandra,' said a voice to my left, 'a press conference is set to begin here inside Hornsby Police Station any moment now. The officer in charge of the case, Detective Inspector James Avery, is due to appear with the family of Philippa Harding and the wife of Roger Bailey.'

I turned and saw a brunette with a serious expression in a shift dress, jacket and heels nodding to a camera only a couple of metres away. I doubted I was in shot, but stepped to one side just in case.

The woman spoke again, in answer to a question. 'That's correct, Sandra. My sources tell me the press conference has been called to appeal for witnesses, rather than to present any findings. As yet, no one has been arrested for committing these horrendous murders.'

A press conference?

Brett was *here*?

My jaw tightened. The sheer gall of the man. How dare he come and *appeal for witnesses* when he was the one who'd killed his wife. My body shook with anger and I clenched my hands into tight fists in an effort to regain control. Then another thought hit me.

Would Kingsley be here?

My heart lurched at the thought of seeing him. He must be suffering so terribly and craving his mother and she wasn't there to help him, just when he needed her.

My poor boy.

The police station door opened and a uniformed officer called 'come in' before spinning on his heel. The journalists moved as a pack towards the door and I was swept along with them, up the stairs and into the building. I didn't fight it, deciding I might as well hear what the police – and Brett – had to say. And maybe see Kingsley too. Perhaps if he saw me here he'd be happy to know he had a friend in the crowd. Someone who understood him. We moved through the busy lobby and then into a large room. Chairs had been set in rows facing a long table on which sat three microphones. The journalists started jockeying for good seats, pushing and shoving towards the front of the room. Camera operators set up noisily, blocking the views of others. I moved to sit on the end of a row at the far side of the room.

Several people entered from a door near the table and the media quietened. The first was a broad-shouldered, balding man in black-rimmed spectacles. He wore a dark suit: Detective Inspector Avery, I presumed. He took a seat in front of the microphone at the centre of the table. Following him were Brett and Kingsley.

Brett – unshaven, his eyes bloodshot – wore a rumpled business shirt, the sleeves rolled to the elbow as if he was about to perform some sort of manual labour. His hands were clasped before him and he twisted them together with such force the veins in his forearms stood out.

Kingsley wore the shell-shocked expression of a war veteran, but resembled a young James Dean: handsome, world-weary and stoic in the face of tragedy.

Following a beat behind the Hardings, as if not wanting to be associated with them, was a woman with ash-blonde hair I recognised from Facebook as Roger's wife, Stephanie. Her pale eyes were clear and her gaze sharp as it ranged across the assembled journalists. I wouldn't want to be on the wrong end of that stare. If Stephanie was upset about Roger's murder it was hard to tell. Her daughters weren't with her, she had no mother or friend for moral support, but she seemed unfazed by the room full of journalists. I kind of admired and feared her at the same time.

Did she know – or care – about Roger and Pip's affair?

The three of them hovered near the door until a female police officer entered and directed the Hardings to one side of the detective inspector, and Stephanie to the other. Kingsley sat a little further from Brett than seemed necessary. Neither looked at or acknowledged the other.

Finally, another uniformed officer emerged. Rik.

He closed the door and remained standing, his back to it as if his job was to stop anyone entering or leaving. Perhaps it was. His gaze settled on me. I nodded to him but he didn't respond and I felt myself colour. Perhaps he sensed my discomfort as he gave an almost imperceptible nod before looking away.

Professionalism, I supposed. It still stung.

Detective Inspector Avery bent over the central microphone. His dour face reminded me of a bored schoolteacher, but when he spoke – quietly and firmly – the image was soon dispelled. In an instant, he had the press pack eating out of his hand.

'Welcome, everyone. As you know, yesterday two people were murdered not far from here. We hope this press conference might help jog the memory of someone out there.' He waited a beat then continued. 'We believe the victims were known to the killer and we are currently investigating a number of possible leads. In addition, there are several persons of interest assisting us with our inquiries. However, it is our hope someone saw something. Any information you may have could be useful to our ongoing investigation and help bring the murderer to justice.'

Several persons of interest.

I shrank down. I knew what that was code for.

The detective inspector glanced to his left before continuing. 'With me, I have two of Philippa Harding's family members – her husband, Brett, and her son, Kingsley. I greatly appreciate their presence here today. I know they are grieving over the loss of their wife and mother. To sit with me, in such circumstances, to help us find those responsible is a difficult thing to do and we appreciate it.' He turned fully to his left now. 'Mr Harding, what would you like to say to the public?'

Brett was silent, almost as if he didn't hear the question. After a moment he looked up, slightly dazed. He cleared his throat and spoke in a husky monotone.

'Ah. Yes. My wife, Pip – Philippa – is … *was*, a beautiful woman, inside and out. I will miss her every day of my life. I have no idea who would want to … take her from us' – his voice almost broke – 'but I am appealing to people for any information that might help us find out who did this so they can't destroy any other lives.' He looked at his son, then the detective inspector. Then back at the journalists. 'Please. If you know something, contact the police.'

Tears filled his eyes. Kingsley reached out a hand and placed it on his father's laced fingers. Brett's response was to gently pull his hands away.

I frowned.

Brett continued to stare across the assembled media, the very picture of a grieving husband, while Kingsley sat back and stared at his father, a bewildered look on his face. Detective Inspector Avery watched Brett with an inscrutable expression.

I shifted uneasily. Up at the table, Kingsley caught the movement. He saw me and his brow furrowed.

I gave a nod, trying to communicate that I was here to support him – to help him. Like a mother would.

'Thank you, Mr Harding,' Detective Inspector Avery said, then turned to the media pack. 'Also with me today is Roger Bailey's wife, Stephanie. Stephanie would like to say a few words.'

Stephanie remained quiet for a few uncomfortable seconds as her gaze raked the room. 'Thank you, Detective Inspector,' she said, her voice crisp enough to cause a ripple through the assembled journalists. 'Roger was, at heart, a good man. His daughters will miss him greatly. They are just children – children who will now never really know their father. I have faith that the police will find my husband's killer, nevertheless I appeal for any information the public may have to bring that person to justice.'

She nodded at Detective Inspector Avery, who regarded her with what seemed to be renewed interest.

The press muttered. It was obvious they found Stephanie's manner brittle. I didn't want to jump on any Lindy Chamberlain bandwagon, but Stephanie did appear rather hard-hearted at the death of a man I assumed she'd once loved. The father of her children.

But then I berated myself. I knew firsthand that grief was not always of the textbook kind.

Just then Stephanie glanced at Brett and I had an answer to my earlier question.

She knew about the affair.

The disdain in her eyes made that abundantly clear. Before I could ponder that further, the detective inspector returned his focus to the room and spoke in a tone that made clear the press conference was concluded. 'We *will* find the person or persons responsible for taking the lives of these two individuals, I am certain of that fact. Thank you, everybody.' He pushed his chair back in one fluid movement and stood up, gesturing to the others at the table to do the same.

Reporters immediately called out, 'Detective Inspector!' and 'Mr Harding!' but one voice carried louder than the others: 'Detective Inspector Avery – should the public be concerned for their own safety, with a murderer on the loose in the city?'

The detective inspector scowled at the gathered journalists, unhappy with the question. He sat back down. 'Absolutely not. We do not believe these deaths were random attacks. The victims were targeted. We do not hold any fears for the safety of the general public. Thank you and good afternoon.' He stood up again and made his way towards Rik, who stepped aside and opened the door for him.

Brett looked at Stephanie with what appeared to be curiosity. She returned his gaze evenly and he looked away, now scanning the crowd, almost immediately noticing me. He cocked his head, then I saw the penny drop. He must have remembered seeing me at his home a week earlier, arguing with his son. His mouth opened and for a second I thought he might call out to identify me. I froze in place, but before Brett could act the female police officer ushered him and Kingsley towards the door. Rik waited for Stephanie to go through the door as well, then he followed, shutting the door behind him, though not before flashing me a penetrating look.

Had he seen both Brett and Kingsley notice me in the crowd?

The journalists grew louder, jostling to do their piece to camera or calling editors to file stories, but I sat still, my heart beating too fast, trying to make sense of it all.

Kingsley had noticed me. Brett too. Stephanie knew about the affair. Meanwhile, the detective inspector spoke as if he might know who the killer was – and yet Brett sat right beside him. Not in chains. Apparently not a suspect.

How was I going to fix this?

I needed to get out of there. Get some fresh air. Do some thinking. I walked around behind the journalists and left the room, heading back through the lobby and outside. At the top of the steps I stopped and took in a lungful of air.

I hadn't yet formulated a plan when I heard a voice in my ear. 'Hello there. I thought it was you.'

* * *

I turned slowly, willing him away, but it didn't work.

Brett.

He must have rushed out of the station to find me. I suppressed a shiver, my feet rooted to the ground. Up close, Brett's eyes were rimmed with red. Puffy black bags underneath them added ten years to his age. He didn't look at all like the man I'd seen from the rose bushes laughing with his wife and son about going to the football.

I tried to look calm and unconcerned. Which was difficult, as Brett stared at me with an intensity that suggested he was searching for something.

Did he know I'd been at his house the day before?

I thought of the presence I'd felt as I ran down the driveway. Had that been him, watching me?

Brett put a hand on my elbow and pulled me away from the door as two uniformed officers exited the station, glancing at us as they passed. The skin on my arms broke out in goose bumps at his touch.

He stopped several metres away on the station verandah, positioning himself facing the door so that my back was to it. I couldn't see who was leaving or entering. Again, he cocked his head to one side and regarded me, eyes opaque. That intensity. It reminded me of Peter. My throat felt dry as I recalled the last time Peter had looked at me that way.

He'd killed my son soon after.

'I saw you talking to Kingsley last week,' Brett said. 'I've always had a knack for faces. You know I'm Brett Harding. Can I ask who you are?'

I swallowed. 'I'm Kate Webb.'

His eyebrows knitted together, considering this. 'You were outside my house. And now you're here. Should I know you?'

Shit. Shit. Shit.

'Ah, no. Not really. I, ah, I knew your wife at university.'

His eyes widened. 'It was you who injured her wrist!'

My mouth fell open.

Pip had told him about me. *Told him the truth.*

Why would she do that?

'You're the woman whose child died, aren't you?'

So she had told him about the incident too. And instead of being angry I'd hurt his wife, his eyes now suggested sympathy. I opened and closed my mouth, completely flummoxed. 'Yes,' I finally managed.

'I'm very sorry for your loss,' he said, sounding sincere.

'I'm sorry about Pip. About everything,' I said, the words drawn from me somehow.

'Thank you,' he said.

The whole situation was very weird.

Brett sighed. He lifted a lined hand and rubbed his bald head. He'd aged. Seemed smaller. Now he didn't look like the type to hurt Pip and Roger. Or Kingsley.

But then I recalled how Peter had smiled as he'd driven away with Sascha strapped into the back of our car. I pictured my boy's grin, his excited wave goodbye, the plastic dinosaurs in the purse gripped tightly in his little hand.

I narrowed my eyes at the man before me. I couldn't afford to trust Brett Harding.

I'd trusted Peter and look where that had got me.

Brett touched my arm again then spoke, tears in his eyes. 'Goodbye, Kate. I need to go and find my son. Kingsley's all I've got now.'

He walked back inside the station. I took a few deep breaths and decided to leave. Fuck the DNA testing. I couldn't handle this. I started down the stairs.

'Kate.'

Too late.

Rik jogged after me, taking hold of my elbow. 'It's time to give your statement.'

He led me back into the busy station lobby. Police moved purposefully in all directions, carrying sheafs of paper or talking on phones. I shivered to see so many dreaded uniforms in one place. Rik propelled me down a wide corridor, past several closed doors and into a basic interview room containing a table and several chairs.

He gestured for me to sit. He didn't quite meet my eye and I felt something was off between us. Something had happened since last night.

Was I now a suspect? Or did he know something about Brett – or someone else – that he wasn't telling me?

Rik had just pulled out a chair when another cop opened the door.

'Kate, you remember Doug, don't you?' Rik asked, and I nodded, recalling that night in Manly. I reddened at the memory.

I didn't – for obvious reasons – remember Rik's partner very well. I noticed now that he was tall with a pronounced beer belly. His smile put me at ease, which was surprising given my current state of mind.

'Good afternoon, Kate,' Doug said.

Doug took the lead while Rik sat back and observed. It wasn't anything too difficult. Doug asked questions guiding me through the history of my relationship with the Hardings and Roger.

Obviously I didn't tell him everything.

I failed to mention any of my online stalking – of course, I'd been kidding myself to think that it was anything *but* stalking – praying it would never get to the point where my computer was seized and examined. I wouldn't come off looking very good there.

Otherwise I tried to stick to the general truth. I admitted Roger had banned me from open houses. It was only when talking about the fifth and final open house that I lied outright, telling Doug I'd not gone to the Harding house that day.

Roger, after all, had told me to stay away.

After I'd finished, Doug produced a swab and I wiped it around the inside of my mouth. Rik bagged the swab. No hair was taken. I recalled my concern that Rik would see my dirty hair and reddened again. What possible interest would Rik have in me once my DNA linked me to the crime scene? He then escorted me over to another area of the station, a short walk but one excruciatingly devoid of conversation, where my fingerprints were taken – all computerised, not like the messy ink I'd seen on countless American TV shows. Rik and I took a seat on a hard bench in the waiting room while we waited for Doug to prepare the statement, but within moments a moustachioed man approached him, leaning over and speaking in an undertone. Looking annoyed, Rik excused himself, asking me to stay put for a few minutes. My thoughts swirled over and around what I'd seen and heard at the press conference, trying to make sense of the pieces of the puzzle.

'Well, I don't buy the husband's alibi.' The voice belonged to one of two uniformed officers who strolled into the waiting room, his mouth half-filled with some sort of pastry. 'The guy has to be guilty. His wife was cheating on him. Hey, she was a looker, wasn't she?'

I lowered my head and made a show of examining my phone.

'You can bet Avery is checking up on the client he was supposed to meet. Dodgy as hell if you ask me.' The men continued on without sparing me a glance.

So Brett's alibi wasn't as tight as Rik had suggested.

I knew it.

Five minutes later Rik and Doug returned, presenting me with a typed document which I read and signed.

Done and dusted.

Now I just had to wait for them to arrest me. Until that time, I supposed I was free to do whatever I wanted.

'I'll show you out, Kate,' Rik said, as Doug took a call and nodded a goodbye.

We walked back to the station entrance without speaking. As he reached the door Rik cleared his throat. He lifted his eyes to meet mine. 'Kate, I did get your voicemail the other night, by the way. I was really pleased to hear it.' He smiled a little. 'I'd really like it if you got in touch with me. I would certainly take your call. Whether or not you stop drinking, I mean.' He paused again. 'And whatever happens with this case.'

I just stared at him.

'I like you,' Rik continued. 'I think I can help you, or at least be a support. A friend. So please do call me, OK?'

I nodded, unable to speak for the giant lump in my throat. Not to mention the guilt I felt for suspecting him — even briefly — of being the killer.

'But, please, stay away from the Hardings, alright? Avery knows his stuff. He'll get the murderer. In fact, I'm sure he already has a hunch about who's guilty. He just needs more time to make sure of it.'

I wanted to believe the detective inspector suspected Brett. That he'd have him in custody by the end of the day. Especially after what those officers had said about Brett's dodgy alibi. But I couldn't help being pessimistic, especially given the cops now had my DNA and were bound to tie me to the scene.

Was it Brett they'd suspect?

Or me?

'Avery's organised a meeting for this afternoon and he's promised to fill us in on everything,' Rik said, his eyes on mine. 'I'm sure the culprit will be behind bars very soon, Kate.'

'Thank you,' I whispered.

Rik gave me one last searching look then turned. I watched him walk away, trying not to feel guilty for what I was about to do.

I couldn't sit around waiting for Detective Inspector Avery to catch Brett. I needed to warn Kingsley about his father now.

I couldn't put his life at risk. Not when I'd made so many mistakes already.

But how was I going to manage that?

* * *

As it turned out, contacting Kingsley was rather easier than I'd expected.

I saw him as I reached the bottom of the stairs.

Kingsley stood alone, leaning against a signpost on the street corner. His body language suggested nonchalance, though there was something stiff about him too. Something tense.

Poor boy, trying to be so brave.

He caught my eye and subtly motioned me over to him.

I walked over, trying to act normal. Difficult, given the circumstances.

This was not a normal day.

'Kate,' he said.

'Hi Kingsley,' I replied. 'I – I'm so sorry about your mother.'

He nodded and looked away as though embarrassed to reveal his emotions. My heart went out to him. What else could I say?

I remembered the useless things people said to me after Sascha died.

You'll have another one.

Time heals all wounds.

It wasn't your fault.

What a crock of shit.

I regarded Kingsley for a long moment. How could I help him through this?

'Where's your dad?' I asked. 'And the police? I thought they were looking out for you.'

'I ducked out without telling anyone,' he said. 'I needed to see you.'

'Oh. Why?'

'You know something,' he said. 'Tell me.'

I couldn't read the look he gave me, though I couldn't miss the determined set of his jaw. He really did want to know. I searched his face, taking in his wavy hair, so like Sascha's. As I watched he lifted a slender hand and twisted a lock of it around his fingers.

Just like Sascha used to.

But Kingsley's chin was patchy with light stubble and he was several inches taller than me and still growing, no doubt. Kingsley wasn't Sascha. He wasn't a child.

He was old enough to know the truth.

'You've wanted to talk to me about Mum and Dad for a couple of weeks now,' Kingsley continued, his brow furrowed again. 'So, what was it you wanted to tell me? Is it related to her death?'

I took a deep breath. 'You're right, Kingsley, there's something I need to tell you.'

How was I supposed to do this?

Your father is a murderer.

Could I say it?

I had to. I had to keep Kingsley safe.

I opened my mouth to speak, but Kingsley stopped me.

'Not here, Kate. We need to talk privately.' He blinked nervously. 'Somewhere we can be alone.'

I looked around and couldn't see a soul. 'We're alone now; can't we do it here?'

'No, not here. I feel like Dad and the police are constantly watching me – I just need to get away from them for a bit. Will you help me?'

He stared at me with anxious, puppy dog eyes. Another lump formed in my throat. Kingsley had no one else to talk to. The poor kid needed his mother. Tears prickled and I blinked them away. Well, I wasn't his mother but I could be there for him when he needed me.

'Of course. Whatever you want.'

'Can you meet me tonight at that Macca's where we first spoke to each other? 11 pm. I'll slip away when Dad's asleep.'

I wasn't sure about this. Why so late? Why the secrecy? I'd have preferred to get it over with, but the terrified look on Kingsley's face made me nod. 'See you tonight.'

'Good.'

He pushed away from the pole and headed back to the police station. I watched him go, his head slightly bowed as if the events of the past two days had physically weighed him down.

I had to support Kingsley through this. And I had to keep him safe.

SUNDAY, 3 AUGUST
EVENING

Kingsley was late.

I stood outside McDonald's, checking my phone in case he'd messaged to tell me why he wasn't here. Which was stupid, as he didn't even have my number.

Please come, Kingsley. I need you to be safe.

Seconds later Kingsley stood directly in front of me, within arm's reach.

He smiled slightly but sadly and we moved inside where he slipped into a booth and sat with his back to the wall, facing the entrance.

I slid onto the bench opposite.

'What information do you have?' he asked.

I was taken aback by his directness, though I guess if I was him I'd want to know too. 'Look, Kingsley, I don't want to scare you, but I think your father might have been … involved in your mother's death.'

His eyes widened. 'What?'

'Did you know your mother was having an affair with Roger?'

He cocked his head at me, the gesture so reminiscent of his father it was uncanny. 'You aren't serious?'

'Yes. I saw them. I … saw them in a pub in Manly a couple of weeks ago. Kissing. I'm really sorry. I hate to tell you this now, but I'm scared for you.'

Kingsley's shoulders slumped. I'd wanted to tell him about the affair but this was terrible. I hated being responsible for causing him pain. I wanted to protect him. 'Is that what you were trying to get me to ask my dad about?'

'Yes. I told your father about the affair. I just wanted your family to work it out.' I stopped to breathe. 'I had no idea your dad was a violent man – that he would hurt Pip – kill her. I mean, I'd never have got involved if I'd known that.'

He shook his head and the look he gave me was rightly angry. 'Who do you think you are to interfere in our lives like that? We don't even know you!'

I looked at the table. 'I'm sorry,' I whispered.

We sat in silence, guilt a pillow pressed against my face, suffocating me. Finally, I couldn't bear it any longer. I reached out a hand to Kingsley's. It was shaking. I lifted my head and stared into his eyes.

He leaned forward, holding my gaze. 'I think you're right about Dad,' he said in a low, urgent voice. 'I think he killed my mother. And Roger.'

I exhaled.

Kingsley's long eyelashes were wet with tears. 'I can't go back to him. Can I come to your place?'

* * *

We took the train home.

Kingsley didn't want to take a taxi. He was worried that a driver would recognise him from the news. I doubted it but didn't want to argue. What I really wanted to do was to call Rik and fill him in, but when I told Kingsley that I had a cop friend who could help, he asked me to wait until we got home. He seemed subdued, trying to process what I'd told him about his mother and Roger. My heart went out to him.

It was late, maybe 11.45, when we arrived at my apartment.

'I'll call Rik,' I told him, pulling out my phone as we walked out of the lift on my floor.

'Do we have to do it right now?' he asked, following close at my heels. 'Let's just get inside. Can you lock this door? Is it secure?' He sounded tentative, as though embarrassed to be afraid.

'Of course.'

Kingsley watched me walk back to the door and set the deadlock. When I turned around, I could see his shoulders visibly relaxing. I hadn't realised just how terrified he was of his father. I pointed out the bathroom in case he needed it, and also just to keep talking, to distract him – but his whole life had changed so much in just a day or two I'm not sure that was possible. He was even polite enough to say my apartment was nice.

It's no Harding house, I wanted to say, though now wasn't really the time to discuss architecture.

I poured myself a wine and drank it as I made Kingsley a cup of tea, before finding some blankets and setting up the lounge for him to sleep on. Kingsley watched from the kitchen table, running his finger over my Little Miss Naughty mug, now half-filled with lukewarm tea.

I tucked the blanket in and straightened up. 'Now I really do need to call Rik – I mean, the police,' I said.

Kingsley pushed the chair back from the table so quickly its legs squealed on the tiles. 'Can I get myself a glass of water

first? We can call them after that.' Tears welled in his eyes. 'It's
been so hard. I can't believe Mum's gone. I just need a little bit
longer, OK?'

He seemed so young again with his dark hair curling at the
ends, like Sascha's. Kingsley needed me now more than ever.
And I needed to look after him, just as if he were my boy. If
he wanted a bit more time then I owed him that. 'Of course,'
I said. 'The glasses are in the top cupboard near the sink.'

He stood up and walked to the kitchen. I went to my room
and grabbed my second pillow – I didn't have a spare – pulling
the used pillow slip off and slipping on a clean one as I walked
back to the living area.

'Here.' Kingsley stood at the table, a glass of water in front of
him. He held my refilled wine glass out.

'Thanks,' I said, dropping the pillow onto the lounge and
taking it, thinking how well brought up he was. I drank deeply,
then added, 'We really do need to call the police now, Kingsley.'

He nodded slowly. 'I know. But it's hard. He's my dad.'

'Of course. But we need to protect you, and I don't think
you're safe while he's out there.'

He nodded again. I sipped, then yawned. It was late and
I longed for sleep but a lot had to be done before I could climb
into my comfortable bed. Once I called Rik the police would
come and I'd have to explain everything. I wasn't looking forward
to it, that's for sure. It was going to be a long night. But Rik
would know what to do to help Kingsley. We sat quietly for a
couple of minutes, me drinking wine, Kingsley staring into space.

'He's always had a temper, you know?' Kingsley said, breaking
the silence. 'I just didn't believe he could ever do anything like
this.'

I nodded.

'Not to Mum. I thought he loved Mum. I can't believe he'd hurt her.'

I understood how it was to be blindsided like that. I wanted to agree with him but it was too hard to form the words.

'Do you think he wants to hurt me too?' Kingsley asked, then continued without waiting for a response. 'I'm scared. But for some reason I feel safe here with you, Kate.'

My eyelids drooped and it was suddenly too hard to stay awake, though at the same time I felt surprisingly relaxed, even happy. It was so nice to be sitting on the couch with someone who needed me. To feel so comfortable. But maybe a little nap would do me good.

The last thing I saw before passing out was Kingsley's face as he leaned over me.

He was smiling.

* * *

I woke up in the bath.

I peered around the bathroom, blinking, my breathing ragged and amplified by the small tiled space. Why was I here? I tried to sit up, my brain foggy.

How much wine had I drunk?

I lay back against the end of the bath, feeling odd. I looked down at my body and realised I was fully dressed: still in my jeans and t-shirt. Why would I have a bath in my clothes? The water was very hot — far hotter than I would usually bathe in — but I felt calm. Almost peaceful. I blinked, thoughts coming slowly, as if my brain was filled with cotton wool.

The bathroom door swung slowly open. Kingsley popped his head around the door jamb.

'Oh, Kingsley,' I said weakly, relieved. 'It's you. God, I'm so sorry. I seem to have drunk way too much.'

He smiled, an echo of the smile I caught just before I passed out. Despite the steam rising from the bath I felt a chill. 'Kate,' he said. 'Or Katie. I prefer Katie, I think.' He stepped into the room, looking somehow different. Taller. Menacing. But also strangely … *happy*.

What the fuck was going on?

'Katie Webb,' he continued. 'Or, once upon a time, it was Katie Bauer, wasn't it? I did some research. Mum wouldn't tell me much, she just said you had a sad past. I needed to find out more.' Kingsley leaned against the tiles facing me, so relaxed.

I blinked at him, confused. He appeared to be *enjoying* himself.

'She didn't tell me you had "mental health issues", either,' he grinned, using his fingers to make air quotes around the words as he had before. 'I made that up. She felt sorry for you, can you believe it? I mean, she was pissed off you'd hurt her wrist. Not that she told me how it happened. You'd be surprised how much I figured out myself. Some from eavesdropping – Mum and Dad always spoke too loudly when they thought I wasn't around. And, of course, the internet is so useful for research, isn't it?'

A flash of guilt flickered through my fuddled brain.

'You had a son, Katie, didn't you?' he continued in an indifferent tone. 'A little boy?'

Ice blossomed in my chest.

'He died, didn't he? Killed by your husband, the kid's dad.' Kingsley's hair was slicked back. Neater than usual. He looked nothing like my Sascha now. 'That's gotta hurt,' he said, then smiled. 'A sad little story. For a while I felt sorry for you. Then you kept sticking your nose in where it didn't belong.'

At last I found my voice, the words thick in my mouth. 'I was trying to help you. Trying to help your family!'

'By butting into our business?'

'By telling you the truth!'

He shook his head. 'Katie, Katie, Katie. I *knew* the truth. I've known for years. Even Dad knew the truth – though he never admitted as much to me. Did you really think that smarmy shit Roger was the first guy Mum had an affair with? There've been at least five other guys over as many years – perhaps a few more she managed to keep secret even from me.'

I tried to sit up, but couldn't. 'What?' I whispered.

'Yes, there was Julian, the publicist from her art gallery – he was the first I knew about. I thought at the time that it would be the end of my parents' marriage. I was only eleven and naive as shit. Next was a barista from the café she went to after yoga. Ten years her junior, what a cliché. The next one was the landscape architect, I think, or it could have been the artist from the UK. He was only here for a week so I get the dates mixed up. Then there was the pool guy – another fucking cliché. Oh, yes, and the last one was the dad of one of my best friends. That's six. And, like I said, there could have been others.'

Roger wasn't Pip's first. She'd done this before.

'You and your dad knew about the affairs?' I asked, looking into Kingsley's disdainful glare.

'Katie, I just told you – of *course* we knew. Dad probably didn't know as many of the gory details as I did. I don't think he wanted to know.'

'Why wouldn't he?'

'Fuck. Have you seen my mother? She was so far out of his league; he was just hanging onto her shirttails with his pudgy little fingers. Dad buried his head in the sand and hoped she'd stay with him. She fucked everything that moved, but no one knew. They all thought butter wouldn't melt in Pip-fucking-Harding's mouth. With her slutty ruby lipstick and tight sweaters.' Despite what he was saying Kingsley's tone was conversational. 'She wasn't a proper mother. She didn't give a shit about anybody else. Certainly not her son. For a year after I first found out about her slut behaviour, I sided with Dad. I thought he'd make her stop. But he did nothing. *Nothing.* By the third affair I thought, well, maybe *now* he'll leave her. But he still did nothing. Sweet fuck all. I caught him watching her once, when she was on the phone to the landscape architect – it was so obvious they were fucking – and Dad looked over at me with those sad, hangdog eyes, and I knew he would never leave her. He fucking loved her. How pathetically lame is that?'

I tried to lift my arms but it felt like they were buried under a pile of bricks.

'And then, finally, Mum decided it was over. Just like that. She talked Dad into a divorce, after all those years of him putting up with her shit. And they decided to sell the house. Without consulting me.' He frowned and I blinked, trying, my mind working sluggishly, to equate this furious Kingsley with the one I thought I knew. He continued, anger in every word, every gesture. '*My* house. Dad wouldn't live there without her. Even though the house had been in his family for generations. He could have just given her cash. Kept the house.' He clenched his jaw. 'Highfields,' he said the formal name with a reverence that contrasted with his anger, 'is *mine*. If they thought I'd sit around and watch them sell it off, well, they were sorely mistaken.'

Despite the scalding water, cold seeped into my bones, into my blood. I stared at Kingsley, seeing him anew. Some of the fog in my brain lifted. 'What did you do, Kingsley?'

'I killed them, of course. Dad was too big of a pussy to do it, so I had to. I hated him for not standing up for himself, for letting Mum cheat on him, make a fool of him. So I killed them both.'

The words pounded their way into my brain like Kingsley had hammered them in there. I tried to sit up but my whole body felt enervated and frail, like I'd been sick with the flu. 'What did you do to me?' I whispered.

Kingsley laughed. 'Rohypnol. Roofies. Heard of them? Mum has insomnia. She's tried everything for it but nothing works so she's got a whole drawerful of drugs at home. The roofies worked like a dream.'

Oh God, Kingsley, what are you?

'Considering what an alco you are – I overheard Mum tell Dad that too – and given all the *tragedy*' – he emphasised tragedy in a mocking tone – 'you've had in your life, the police will be quite happy to chalk your death up to suicide. I doubt they'll do toxicology tests in time to find the roofies. Even if they do, they won't link it to me: the poor boy whose mother recently died.' He pushed off from the wall and paced back and forth in the small space. Two steps one way, swivel, two steps the other way. 'Crazy alco woman kills a pair of adulterers she'd become obsessed with. Yes, it works better than framing my dad, I think. Then, the sad, alco woman decides to off herself, so she drinks some wine and climbs in the bath. Voila! One less waste of space in the world. And given how your husband and son died, there's some poetic justice in the whole drowning thing. Not to mention how Mum and Roger were dumped in the pool. It all fits together so well, don't you agree?'

He really was enjoying himself. This new Kingsley was far more talkative than the one I knew. I preferred the old Kingsley, the seemingly non-psychopathic one.

'Anything you want to ask me, Katie?'

Was I dreaming? Surely this couldn't be real? Kingsley couldn't be a monster, a psychopath. He was the perfect boy.

Oh God.

My gut twisted.

Kingsley wasn't like Sascha, he was like *Peter.*

How did I not know? How could I not have seen it?

'Oh, and I found this,' Kingsley pulled the parasaurolophus I'd taken from his bedroom out of the front pocket of his jeans, 'on your bedside table.' He looked genuinely puzzled. 'It's mine, isn't it? Why did you take it, Katie? Where did you even find it?'

'Under your desk,' I whispered.

'Huh.' Kingsley turned over the dinosaur in his hands as he spoke. 'Mum dumped boxes of toys in my room for me to sort. But she was crazy if she thought I'd help her get the house ready to sell. I tipped that shit out all over the place, left it for the housekeeper to clean up. This one must have been missed.' He laughed. 'Anyway, it's weird, you taking it. And illegal. And what about this?' Kingsley produced my phone like a magician and I could see the photos of the drawings in his bedroom on the screen.

'How'd you open that?'

'Der. Your thumbprint. Fingerprints don't disappear when you're unconscious, Katie. And I really don't appreciate you photographing my art. My art is personal.' He shook his head and tutted at me. 'Honestly, Katie. The first rule of committing a crime is to always cover your tracks. Taking stuff from houses? Photos? Really? I wouldn't keep, oh, I don't know, a lock of your hair, would I? Once you're dead that ties me to you. Police love that shit. No, when I killed Mum and that tanned idiot, I dumped them in the pool, cleaned myself up and left.

No one can tie me to their deaths.' He smiled at me, setting the parasaurolophus on my sink. 'It was a nice touch, don't you think, putting them in the water. You appreciated that, I hope? You certainly seemed to, vomiting up your breakfast the way you did.'

I stared at him in horror and his grin widened.

'Yes, I set that little scenario up for you, Katie. Well, I hoped it would be you. I couldn't be sure. But I did know what a stickybeak you are and I was pretty sure you wouldn't be able to resist it when Roger didn't show up for the open.' He squatted down beside me and looked at me with cold eyes. How could I have ever thought them beautiful? And *kind*? 'I didn't realise you had the house code, though,' he continued with some admiration. 'I assumed you'd come round the side. You're more devious than I realised, Katie Bauer. And then you came into my room! I had to scurry into the cupboard like a little cockroach. I know it was a little bit stupid to stay, but I couldn't help myself.'

'The police said you had an alibi.'

'Ah, yes, the alibi. I was at the library that morning. The librarian knows me well. The poor dear can't resist a smile and a chat from a hardworking youngster who always asks after her pet cockatiels. I just set up my books on a table and then ducked outside through the staffroom. I came back in the same way. She had no idea I'd ever left and if she did notice she'd have assumed I was searching for a book.' He smiled again. 'So, Highfields won't be sold now. No one will want it, not after dead people were found in the swimming pool. Dad and I will stay. And, should something happen to Dad, say, just after my eighteenth birthday, well, then the house will be mine.'

'But, Kingsley —'

'No more questions,' he said, reaching over the bath. His beautiful face blocked the light and moved closer to mine until his blue eyes were all I could see. His cool hands touched my shoulders. His expression was detached, as though he were conducting a science experiment. It was as if I wasn't a real person, just a thing to be taken care of. 'Relax, Katie, it will all be over soon.'

He pressed me down. Water gushed up my nose and I gasped and swallowed some, tried to snort it out. This was my Dream. The bathtub. Drowning. But the Dream was not the same as reality. Nowhere near it.

Reality was far worse.

Reality put all my Dreams to shame.

* * *

I was almost surprised to discover I didn't want to die.

I thrashed and kicked and burst from the water for a lungful of air. Kingsley's face darkened in anger. He hit me – a hard, stinging slap across the cheek.

As I went back under the water, my ears rang. Peter had hit me like that, once. Only once, about a month before Sascha's death. I hadn't fought back. I'd let him strike me, thinking soon enough I'd leave, take my son with me, never see him again.

Look how that had worked out.

Rage coursed through me like a wildfire. I rose up, shoving Kingsley backwards, my hands on his chest, pushing him with all the strength remaining in my weakened body.

It was pure luck I caught him off-balance.

The fact he was squatting on slippery bathroom tiles worked in my favour too. So when I shoved, he teetered, then fell to one side, using a hand to stop his fall. It only gave me a second, but I took it, adrenaline giving me the strength to stand. I was seeing double and my head was pounding, but I knew this apartment. Water splashed everywhere and my clothes weighed me down, but I skidded and slipped from the bathroom into the living room.

I could hear Kingsley behind me, swearing; coming fast. I raced to the front door, slammed into it. My fingers fumbled with the locks I'd taken so much care to set earlier. As I grabbed the deadlock, I was wrenched away from the door – Kingsley's thirty-years-younger arms around my chest. I thrashed my head and arched my back, tried to twist my shoulders free. But Kingsley's grasp pinned my arms against my sides, my legs up off the floor. He was too strong.

'Help m—' I started to yell, but his hand slapped over my mouth.

'Shut the fuck up, Katie,' he hissed in my ear. 'You will *not* ruin this for me, you hear me? Not now.'

Kingsley half-carried, half-dragged me – his arms tight, my ankles dragging along the carpet – towards the balcony. His hand covered my nose as well as my mouth and I grew light-headed from lack of air. I ceased struggling, getting weaker. He briefly removed one arm from around my torso to fling the balcony door open and switch off the living room light. Freezing air hit my soaked clothes, then I felt a dull pain as my heels struck the raised metal edge of the balcony door frame. I started shivering. Kingsley dragged me to the edge of the balcony and turned me around to face the glass balustrade. He flung me over it roughly, so my chest and head hung over the other side and my toes lifted off the tiles on the balcony floor. His hand was back over my mouth. I stretched my feet, scrabbling to find something solid.

'Without the lights on, no stickybeak neighbours can see us,' he whispered, close to my ear. 'So the plan's going to change. Instead of drowning in the bath like a sad alco, you'll jump from the balcony like a sad alco. It works for me. I'm nothing if not adaptable.'

I shivered, water dripping down my face, which rested against cold, smooth glass. I was suddenly so tired again. It was too late. All too late.

I stopped struggling.

I was done.

Without warning, Kingsley grabbed my shoulder and pulled me back onto the balcony, spinning me around to face him. I could barely stand; I desperately wanted to sit down. My knees buckled and I started to slump. 'Katie! Listen when I'm talking to you.'

Kingsley grabbed my neck and held me upright. He leaned forward, his face a dark space, darker than the night sky. I blinked, tried to focus. 'You really should have stayed out of it, shouldn't you? Stayed in your little loser world of drinking too much in your little loser apartment and kept the hell out of other people's lives.' His teeth appeared, ghoulishly white in his dark face. 'I didn't want it to come to this. I bet you were a good mother to your boy.' His hands tightened and I felt a fresh surge of terror as I tried and failed to swallow oxygen. 'Not like Pip.' He spat her name, squeezing my neck even further. 'You certainly grieved for your boy more than my mother would have grieved for me. Not that it matters now.'

I couldn't speak; couldn't take a full breath. My head pounded worse than any hangover and I saw stars. Kingsley smelled incongruously of aftershave, a familiar scent. The aftershave was similar to one I'd bought Peter, back when we were young and in love.

Kingsley let go of my neck and I fell, banging my knees on the tiles. I gulped in air through a burning throat. He pulled me up to standing. 'Sorry about that, Katie. I lost it for a minute there.'

Hope pierced my grogginess.

Maybe he'd let me go?

'I'm supposed to be helping you jump from the balcony. Strangulation wasn't part of the plan.'

I tried to struggle but my limbs were too heavy.

Kingsley grabbed me around the waist, lifted me towards the balustrade.

I made to scream but it came out as a groan.

'Don't fight, Katie. Accept it,' he whispered. I felt his hot breath on my cheek. 'Maybe you'll see your son soon, who knows? Maybe you'll see Sascha.'

It was hearing his name that did it.

I lashed out, elbowing Kingsley in the stomach and yanking free of his grip. Adrenaline pumping again, I turned and kicked him hard in the balls. He moaned and doubled over in pain, but before I could open the balcony door, he rose up like something out of a nightmare, his face contorted in rage as he rushed at me. We both slipped around on the wet tiles, our arms flailing. I lunged for the chair in the corner, somehow sliding around to put it between us. Kingsley reached for me and I ducked behind the chair. He growled his anger, stepping onto the seat as if to climb over it and leap on me. I moved to one side and he turned, off-balance. And at that moment, I shoved him. Not hard but enough.

Kingsley fell, windmilling his arms as he disappeared over the glass balustrade. He had time for a final blood-curdling scream before it was cut off with a thud as his body hit the footpath below, and I collapsed, exhausted, onto the cold tiles of the balcony and passed out.

* * *

'Kate? Can you hear me?'

The voice came from a long way away. I shivered, half-awake but wanting to go back to sleep.

'Kate? It's Rik, can you hear me?'

Rik? What was he doing here? My eyes fluttered open but I was too tired to keep them that way. I glimpsed a face but couldn't decipher features.

'That's it, Kate. Stay with me. The ambulance will be here soon. What happened? How did Kingsley fall?'

Kingsley.

My heart beat faster as the fear returned. I tried to open my eyes again, tried to move. It was no use.

'It's OK, Kate.'

'I killed him,' I said in a low raspy voice.

It hurt to speak. It hurt to move.

'I pushed him over the edge.'

WEDNESDAY, 6 AUGUST
7.31 AM

'— depends on many —'

'— lack of oxygen can cause brain impairment —'

My eyelids fluttered open. The room was bright and white. I shut them again.

'She's awake! Nurse!'

Beeps and flurries of air came from my side.

'Kate. Kate!'

Rik's face appeared, creased with concern.

'Rik?' My voice was as hoarse as a geriatric with emphysema and my throat felt as rough as brand-new sandpaper. 'Where am I? You look like shit.'

I didn't mean to say that out loud, but it was true. Light stubble covered Rik's chin and he had tired eyes. He opened his mouth to speak, but a brassy-haired nurse in her fifties swished open the curtain beside the bed, frightening me.

'You're awake!' she said, immediately taking my pulse with one eye on her watch. 'How you feelin', love?'

'OK,' I managed, and then obeyed her orders to open my mouth, look at the light and so on. I tried to peer past her at Rik but she blocked my view – deliberately, I thought grumpily as she shoved her head in front of my wandering eyes.

She smiled and patted my arm. 'Lookin' great. Considering. Rest up. The doctor'll take a look at you once he's finished his rounds. This just here' – she picked up a small button with a lead attached – 'is for pain relief. Don't be afraid to use it, OK?'

I nodded.

She turned to Rik with a wagging finger and her words were stern. 'Don't wear her out.'

He lifted his arms in surrender, but they shared a conspiratorial smile.

And she was gone.

I blinked, trying to focus. I smelled lilies – my favourite. 'Where am I?' I asked again.

'You're in hospital. God, it's good to hear your voice – what's left of it,' Rik said, and rubbed his face, the sound scratchy over his stubble. 'We've all been worried.'

'All?'

'Yes, it's been quite a gathering. Not in here, out in the waiting area. The nurses have been very protective of you. Let's see, visitors. Your parents. Your sister and her husband. Your boss and a younger woman – the receptionist maybe? Jenna. Michelle. Michelle even brought her kids – who ate all the biscuits in the kitchen. Crumbs *everywhere*. The nurses were *not* happy. We've all been coming and going, keeping an eye on you.'

I must have looked as surprised as I felt because he laughed.

'It appears you don't realise how many people care about you, Kate Webb.' He sat down and I turned my head to keep him in sight, the movement making me cough and then gasp with the pain of coughing. 'You alright? Want some water?'

He reached over to the tray beside the bed, poured me half a glass from a plastic jug and passed it to me. My hands shook as I took it from him. It was hard to swallow but it was good.

'My parents were here?'

'Yes, they left about an hour ago. The nurses let them come after visiting hours. I think they feel sorry for them. They've been out of their minds with worry.'

My pleasure in my parents' worry was swiftly replaced by guilt for worrying them in the first place. Perhaps it was time I cut them some slack and occasionally stayed to eat the pea and ham soup in the McMansion, instead of dashing off to avoid their concern. 'And you? How are you still here outside visiting hours?'

'Ah, I'm a policeman, see? Special privileges.'

I attempted a smile, coughed again instead. My throat was almost swollen shut. Every breath hurt. I fumbled for the morphine button and pressed it, then tried to remember why I was here.

Kingsley.

He'd tried to kill me.

Rik took my hand and held it in his own and I saw I had a cannula inserted in my wrist. A tube from it led up and away to an unfamiliar beeping and flashing apparatus.

'It's OK, Kate. You're going to be alright.'

'What day? What … what happened?'

'You've been out of it for more than forty-eight hours. We've pieced together most of it. We know you arranged to meet Kingsley at McDonald's.'

'Oh.'

'The detective inspector suspected Kingsley almost right from the beginning. He thought his alibi was flimsy. Avery's done a lot of work with psychopaths in the past. I think he suspected Kingsley was one from the moment he first met him. And Brett confirmed he'd had concerns about his son's behaviour for some time. For a long time, in fact. But he had no idea Kingsley was capable of murder.' Rik shook his head. 'Luckily for us, Avery knew what he was looking for. I never would have pegged Kingsley as a psychopath in a million years. He was a clever bugger.'

'Was?' I managed.

'Yes. Was. He's dead,' Rik replied. 'Avery had cops watching Kingsley and Brett that night and they saw him leave the hotel. He was followed to McDonald's, then both of you were seen going back to your apartment. Despite Avery's suspicions, we still didn't really believe you were in serious danger.' He gave me a wry smile. 'Then we heard sounds of a struggle inside. My main regret is that we waited as long as we did before knocking the door down.' Rik's thumb brushed my knuckles. 'You were unconscious,' he said, his voice quieter now. 'I thought we'd lost you.'

'You knocked my door down?'

'Yeah, sorry about that. It's been replaced now. Promise. You just concentrate on getting better. You'll need to talk to Avery, of course, to give an official statement. But that can wait till tomorrow.'

We sat in silence for a moment. There was so much to process and my head was fuzzy from the morphine.

'I'd seen Brett talking to Pip and Kingsley just the week before,' I said. 'He was so angry. He looked like he'd kill them. I was sure it was him. So much for my meddling. I couldn't have stuffed things up more if I'd tried.'

'You weren't to know.'

I appreciated the absence of a well-deserved *I told you so*. All of a sudden I was bone-weary. Flattened.

My eyelids fluttered. 'I'll leave you to sleep, Kate,' he said.

I started to demur, opened my mouth to say, 'Stay with me,' but no words came out. My limbs pressed heavily onto the starched sheets and I slept.

BEFORE

The squeaking bed alerted me to the intruder, pulling me grumpily from a restless sleep.

Sascha's hot, wriggly little body slipped between the sheets and into my arms. He snuggled back against me, taking the small spoon position, and I curved around him, using one hand to brush his sweaty curls from his forehead. His dinosaur pyjamas were damp but I hugged him close.

The sofa bed in my parents' spare room had a hill in the centre, forcing me to tense all night lest I fall out. I hadn't had a decent sleep in two weeks. Peter was picking up Sascha to go to the zoo in a few hours and I would head back to our apartment for the night. I didn't relish the thought of returning to our marital home, although I was hanging out for our king-sized bed and the expensive linen sheets Peter had always insisted on.

Of course, there was another reason for my tiredness.

Sascha's breathing became rhythmic, telling me he'd gone back to sleep. I twisted my head and was able to just make out the time on the alarm clock. 6 am. Wow, he'd slept in. Perhaps knowing he'd see his dad today had done him some good after all. I breathed in unison with my son.

Leaving Peter was the right thing to do. I hadn't felt this calm in months, maybe years. Sascha would be alright. Peter and I would work together to put him first, I was sure of that. He would be better off in the long run.

Just then, Sascha flung his head back and whacked my boob, the pain ricocheting up and into my collarbone and shoulder. I bit my lip to avoid crying out, but Sascha sensed me stiffen and he squirmed, turning around and somehow managing to elbow me again in exactly the same spot.

'Holy sh—' I bit the swear word off.

'Are you awake, Mummy?' Sascha asked, oblivious.

'Yes, mate.'

'Can I take my dinosaurs to the zoo today?' he asked.

'Sure, but just the little ones, OK?' I said, marvelling at his single-mindedness where dinosaurs were concerned. I rolled onto my back and gingerly checked my breast for serious damage. 'I'll find you a little purse for your favourites,' I continued, as Sascha sat up and regarded me seriously. 'It'll be a big day, you don't want to carry too many around or you'll get tired and won't be able to see all the other animals.'

'I need to wee,' he announced, and clambered off the bed, padding out of the room to the toilet.

I'd just drifted off when he returned.

'What's this, Mummy?' he asked.

I opened my eyes and swore internally. 'Sasch, honey, you really shouldn't pull things out of the bin, OK?'

He nodded but continued to examine the plastic stick with frank interest.

'Look, that's just a mummy thing, OK? I don't need it any more. That's why it was in the bin. Can you put it back there, please?'

He nodded again and ran out of the room, losing interest.

'And wash your hands after touching that. With soap!'

I lay back, staring at the ceiling as I heard the tap turn on, full bore.

Pregnant again.

It wasn't ideal – *understatement of the year, Kate* – but it was a *baby*, a miracle. We'd been trying for more than two years now.

The timing could have been better, but, no matter what, I would have this child.

Sascha raced back and jumped on my groin area. I laughed, in pain but unable to resist Sascha's exuberance.

How – and when – was I going to tell Peter?

I had no clue. I just knew that it wouldn't be today. I wouldn't tell him today.

It could wait.

THURSDAY, 7 AUGUST
AFTERNOON

As far as hospital rooms went, this one wasn't too bad.

Sure, it smelled of antiseptic – and the intermittent beeps from adjacent rooms were constant reminders of the nature of the place – but it was pleasant enough. There was a window, for one, undoubtedly the room's best feature. From my squeaky vinyl chair I overlooked a courtyard with a stone-bordered garden as its centrepiece. The garden was bursting with geraniums, all one single colour.

The look-at-me red of Pip's lipstick.

I sighed.

Poor, poor Pip.

It was lunchtime. Outside, doctors and nurses sat on benches, eating sandwiches and checking their phones, while a group of orderlies smoked, stomping from foot to foot in the cool air and lifting their faces towards the weak winter sun. I'd had an official visit from Detective Inspector Avery that morning and told him everything. Well, almost everything. Some things were better left unsaid. He'd been polite and surprisingly kind.

I still didn't really think I deserved kindness.

'So you were pregnant at the time of the incident?' Rik asked.

I glanced at him, sitting in the chair next to mine, and looked back outside, admiring the glorious blue sky, not a cloud visible. The sort of clear and perfect day that made telling Rik about those other days – the worst of my life – not only possible, but necessary.

It was time.

'I was. I lost the baby, of course. I was barely pregnant. And the grief ...'

Outside, a willy wagtail fluttered against the glass, its black and white feathers so lustrous they sparkled in the sunlight. What could he see of us from out there? Or was he looking at his own reflection, watching his tail flick jauntily from side to side, hoping to befriend the satiny bird before him? His perfection made me wish I had my camera with me.

At my request, Mum had brought in a couple of my old photo albums that she kept at her place. Mostly photos of Sascha I'd taken at the park and at the beach. Another was filled with landscapes and close-ups of tree trunks and plants I'd taken at art school. Looking at them had woken something in me. I'd jotted ideas on a notepad begged from a friendly nurse, feeling a once-familiar excitement rise.

Perhaps I could ask Rik to collect my camera from home. Practising with the settings would give me something to fill in the long hospital hours. I could take candid portrait shots of some of the nurses too.

It was the first time I'd thought of using my camera in years. Perhaps I'd even take up Vivian's offer and do some photos for our brochures. Might be the first step in a new career. It wouldn't be fine art, but would that be so bad?

I smiled.

The willy wagtail up and vanished in a flurry of wings.

I looked back at Rik. 'The grief of losing the new baby got all mixed up with the pain of losing Sascha.' Saying the words aloud brought a tightness to my throat.

Rik shook his head, leaning forward to pick up my hand in both of his. 'You've been through so much.'

'I never told anyone. It was so early. No one guessed. The baby just ... disappeared.'

'Oh, Kate.'

I shrugged, trying not to tear up.

Disappeared.

That wasn't quite right. No matter that my baby had barely existed, I grieved for him or her more than I would have thought possible.

Just as Leah grieved for her child.

Rik told me that Leah had visited while I was unconscious and was coming back to see me today. Perhaps I could talk to Leah about my other lost baby. At last.

'Kate?'

I turned to Rik, hearing a different tone to his voice. His warm, dry hands remained folded over one of mine. Perhaps his touch was the reason I felt so calm.

'Yes?'

'Brett Harding wants to see you.'

I thought I'd feel something more. Some stronger emotion. Instead, it seemed right. I needed to apologise to Brett for the trouble I'd brought to his family. Perhaps it wasn't all my fault, but I needed to take responsibility for at least some of it.

'OK,' I said.

Rik raised an eyebrow. 'OK?' he asked. 'Just like that? You're alright with it?'

'Yes, I'd like to talk to him.'

Rik smiled and shook his head a little. 'You have courage, Kate Webb. You don't mind tackling the difficult subjects, do you?'

'Actually, that's not me at all,' I replied, surprised. 'I've always been terrible at confrontation. I hate awkward conversations.'

He laughed. 'Then maybe you've changed, Kate.'

I smiled tentatively at Rik. Perhaps he was right. Maybe I had changed. One thing was sure, though. I liked the crinkles in the corners of Rik's eyes when he smiled.

FRIDAY, 8 AUGUST
MORNING

I almost didn't recognise Brett Harding.

His skin was grey-tinged; his face hollowed out to gauntness. His shoulders were rounded and he shuffled, more than walked, into the room.

Brett had become an old man.

He looked at me, his face blanching at the purple bruises now changing to green and yellow across my neck. His gaze met mine and I saw an apology in his eyes.

Rik had left us to speak alone.

Brett stood beside the bed until I asked him to sit. The air whooshed out of the seat as he sank into it. 'How are you, Kate?' he asked, no doubt taking in my pallor and the darkness around my bloodshot eyes.

'I'm fine, thank you.'

And it was mostly true. Despite the traces of Kingsley's attack I felt better than I had for years.

More alive, ironically.

Brett's words came in a rush of breath. 'I'm so sorry. That my son could do this to you. I knew what Kingsley is – what he was,' he stumbled over the tenses then carried on, 'but I swear to you I didn't think he was capable of murder. I swear it.'

Parents always wanted to believe the best of their children. To protect them, if they could. I understood that.

'He'd always been … manipulative,' Brett said. 'But charming. Even as a child. But to kill … I mean, the *violence*. I just never thought he had that in him. I know Kingsley was shocked when we decided to sell Highfields – he loved that house – but Pip and I thought he'd come around. But this …' He shook his head, his devastation clear. Then he looked me directly in the eyes. 'Kingsley had planned it all out, you know? He emailed my office pretending to be a new client and set up an appointment for me so I'd be out of the house. The client didn't show, obviously, and my alibi was shaky. He tried to frame me.' Brett rubbed his beard, the sound scratchy in the quiet room, and I noticed his hand was trembling. 'I loved my wife, Kate. I mean, she certainly wasn't perfect. Pip had had affairs before, I knew that. But Roger was different. She really loved him. I finally understood we were over. I just … I just can't believe she's gone.'

His voice cracked on the words and his shoulders sagged.

It was my turn.

'I need to apologise to you too, Brett. I should never have got involved in your life. Perhaps if I'd stayed out of it, none of this would have happened.'

He shook his head emphatically. 'No, Kate. This was my fault. Mine and Pip's.' His voice cracked on her name. 'We should have done more. We should have taken responsibility for what our son was.' He sat back and shook his head again. 'It's all my fault.'

We sat without talking for a long moment.

Brett bowed his head, defeated. Bereft. He'd lost everything.

I knew how that felt.

Then he spoke, keeping his eyes on his hands, which he twisted subconsciously. 'Pip was so sorry for what happened to your son, you know? We talked about it after ... well, after her wrist was injured.'

By you, he could have added.

He stopped wringing his hands and lifted his gaze to meet mine with eyes that were watery. Bloodshot. 'My son deserved to die, Kate. Yours didn't.'

PART VI

AUCTION DAY

SATURDAY, 9 AUGUST
MORNING

I was released from hospital on what was to have been the auction day.

Of course, the auction had been cancelled. Mum and Dad arrived at the hospital first thing, as they had every day. Mum stood near the small wardrobe, pulling out the unworn clothes she'd put there a few days earlier, folding them and putting them back into the suitcase Dad had lugged from my place. She insisted on packing for me.

'You need to rest, Kate,' she said, ignoring me when I told her I was actually feeling much better. She smiled as she folded a bizarre long white nightgown I had never seen before. She must have bought it for me to wear in hospital. 'Are you sure you don't want your father and me to drop you home, darling? It's no trouble, is it, Keith?'

'No. No trouble,' Dad said, from his regular spot by the window, the paper over his knee. 'We need to pick up Fritz and Frieda from Ruth Brinkley's house by eleven, but we have time …'

Mum gave him an annoyed glare and was about to say more but I got there first. 'No, I told you Rik was going to do it, remember? You didn't really need to come in this morning – I told you that too. Rik said he'll get us out of here without alerting the journalists. Reckons he knows a back way or something.'

Mum's face softened at the mention of Rik. 'Oh, well. If Rik says he knows a way then I'm sure he does. Policemen are handy like that,' she added, nodding sagely. 'And I wanted to come to the hospital this morning, darling. To make sure you were ready to head home and to help you pack. We'll visit you at the apartment later, though. Bring a few groceries around. I don't expect Rik to do that. That's a mother's job.'

I smiled.

As if mentioning his name had conjured his presence, Rik appeared at the doorway. 'Good morning all.'

'Rik! We were just talking about you.'

'All good stuff I hope, Barb?'

Mum gave a girly laugh.

Was she flirting with him?

Dad stood, leaving the newspaper on the chair, and crossed the room to shake Rik's hand. 'Senior Constable,' he said, his voice serious.

'I told you to call me Rik, Keith. Besides, I'm off the clock today.'

Dad gave a little laugh, but I knew he'd call him Senior Constable again next time they met.

'How are you feeling, Kate?' Rik asked.

'Pretty good,' I said. 'Itching to get out of here.'

Which was true. For the first time in years I had a strong urge to do something. I wasn't yet sure exactly what it was, but I knew the time for sitting around was over.

It seemed to take an age to get the paperwork sorted and farewells made to my parents and hospital staff before Rik was pushing me out of there in a wheelchair, a hospital orderly dragging my suitcase along behind us.

'I feel stupid in this thing,' I muttered.

He laughed and his voice came from so close to the top of my head I felt his breath in my hair. 'Hospital policy. Enjoy it while you can, you'll be walking soon.'

'It can't come soon enough. God knows, I need to get some exercise. I really want to lose some weight,' I continued.

'Lose weight?' Rik sounded surprised. 'Why?'

I laughed. 'Isn't it obvious?'

'Not to me, it isn't,' he replied. 'You look great, Kate. The only thing you need to lose is the bruising. Black and blue are not your colours.'

I grinned. 'Well, I totally agree with you there.'

There was a lightness inside me that felt like … youth. I almost laughed aloud.

As we descended in the lift to the bowels of the building, my concern returned that the press pack would find us. But Rik was true to his word. Once the orderly stowed the bag in the boot and departed with the wheelchair I stood at the passenger door, my hand on the handle. 'Did you bring it?'

'Yes.'

From his jeans pocket he pulled out the small plastic dinosaur. I'd asked Rik to have a look in the bathroom for me, the last place I remembered seeing it. I'd also asked him to throw away the boxes of mementoes in my bedroom. I knew I didn't need them any more.

I held out my hand and Rik sat the parasaurolophus on my palm. Its blank eyes regarded me with something like … understanding. I nodded my thanks and climbed into the car.

He did the same and spoke to me across the centre console. 'What do you want it for?'

'Can we make a detour on the way home?'

He looked mildly puzzled but said OK. 'Where to?'

'Balmain.'

He twisted his head to look at me, though I kept my gaze in front. I sensed his scrutiny without turning around. 'Alright.'

I liked that he didn't try to talk me out of it. We were silent on the twenty-minute drive, but it was a comfortable silence. Rik took the Sydney Harbour Bridge route, perhaps because it was the weekend. I was grateful. The sun glinted off the water – yet another brilliant winter's day. You could always tell the locals from the tourists by the way they rushed along the bridge's pedestrian path, not ambling and taking selfies.

We headed to the inner west. Traffic slowed along these narrow streets where terrace houses worth millions competed with their neighbours for the most expensive-looking-but-not-flashy renovation. Sandstone and brick in natural hues with intricate metal fences. The Harding house would have fitted in around here, but as a big brother to these smaller homes. A worker in high-vis stopped us at roadworks on a street with multi-million-dollar views of the Harbour Bridge.

'Almost there,' Rik said.

'Thanks for everything you've done,' I said. 'I don't deserve —'

He interrupted me as the worker flipped the 'stop' sign to 'slow'. 'Will you give it a rest already, Kate!' he said, smiling but exasperated as he drove off. 'I'm doing this because I want to. You really need to start to understand that people are allowed to like you. They want to help you.'

'Everyone's been so nice to me. Supportive. I can't believe it.

Vivian came in and gave me as much time off as I need. And I saw Leah.'

Leah and I had talked about our miscarriages. We'd both shed tears. I knew she was still the same thoughtless Leah; she wasn't perfect. Then again, neither was I. I wasn't totally on Team Leah, but had decided to give her a chance, see if we could get along at least. My attitude to her had changed.

My attitude towards a lot of things had changed.

'I was such an interfering idiot and I caused so much trouble.'

Rik pulled over in front of the driveway of one of the rare stand-alone two-storey houses in the area. 'People make mistakes, Kate. We forgive them. We move on with our lives.'

'You make it sound so simple.'

'It is. Look, I'm not saying it's not hard. It's bloody hard. But we make choices. The people in your life are in it because they want to be. It's that simple.'

Ahead I saw the jetty.

I'd never been there before but I knew that was it.

The place where Sascha and Peter had died.

On this gorgeous day it seemed innocuous enough. The jetty ran in a straight line from the end of the road, which was a cul-de-sac allowing cars to turn around. It was nearly fifty metres long, with a series of bollards across it to stop cars from driving out onto it. Thanks to the coroner. Back then, apparently, there was no such barrier.

I waited for the emotion to hit me, expecting a wave of grief or a flood of tears. It never came. The sadness was still there. It probably always would be. But it was a manageable sadness, not the desperate suffering of a crazy grief-stricken mourning mother.

At a large family gathering on the grass nearby women wore hijabs and men smoked pipes. Upbeat music in a language

I didn't know blared from portable speakers. The group lazed on rugs and ate food that smelled of smoke and garlic and made my stomach rumble in appreciation. Another family strolled past them. Kids chased one another, throwing sticks into the water. An elderly couple held hands.

On such a beautiful day, the atmosphere of the place was more party than memorial.

I smiled.

'What do you want to do?' Rik asked.

'I need to say goodbye. Will you help me?'

'Sure.'

We got out of the car and I pointed towards the jetty. He raised an eyebrow in the way I liked, but didn't say anything.

We walked down onto the jetty and I paused for a moment, thinking of my son and what had happened here.

I'm sorry, Sascha. I miss you every day.

I'll always miss you.

I heard a child's laugh and for a moment I felt Sascha was close. I looked around and saw a pair of little girls, both around five years old, giggling over something in a private game. I smiled at them and they grinned back.

I kept walking along the jetty, sensing Rik just behind me. Halfway along, we passed a father and son, sitting on fold-out camping chairs with fishing rods in their hands. Then at the end we were momentarily alone. Rik stood close enough for me to feel his arm against mine. I looked into his calm eyes and then out at the harbour, glistening in the sunlight.

The dinosaur was warm and sharp in my hand and I remembered my boy: his laugh, his smile.

This is for you, Sascha.

I threw the dinosaur into the water.

ACKNOWLEDGEMENTS

Thank you to all those who took a chance on *Other People's Houses*. I'd particularly like to thank my agent, Melanie Ostell, who believed in me and guided me through the publication process like the true professional she is. Her advice has been invaluable.

To my publisher, Anna Valdinger at HarperCollins – the nicest person in publishing – and her faith in the novel, and me. To my brilliant editor, Madeleine James, who fixed so many of my errors and made the book a far better version of itself. Thanks to Kimberley Allsopp and all the publicity team at HarperCollins for their patience with an introvert who's allergic to attention. Also to the design department for the brilliant cover; it's such a thrill to have my name on something so beautiful.

Thanks to those who saw potential in *Other People's Houses* over the past four years. To the Faber Academy for their 2016 scholarship, granted for little more than an idea. And to Queensland Writers Centre and Hachette for including me in the manuscript development program where I received invaluable feedback from Kim Wilkins, Brigid Mullane and Jane Novak, among others.

Thank you to my family. Mum and Dad for supporting me. Anna – my sister and my best friend – and her family. My friends, who have helped me more than they probably realise over the past couple of very rocky years. And Matt's family – my family – Fritz, Shell and Chris and the girls. We are lucky to have you.

A huge thank you to my kids, Asha and Dusty. We've been through stuff lately no one should have to go through, and without you both I'd have been lost. You are two of the best people I know.

Can I thank a dog? Dexter was seriously the best dog ever and he slept at my feet while I wrote much of *Other People's Houses*. I still can't open a cheese slice wrapper without expecting to hear your feet tapping across the floorboards, Dexter.

And finally this book would not have been published without Matt. My husband died less than six months before I signed the contract with HarperCollins, so the publication of *Other People's Houses* has been a strange time for me. The joy of knowing I'd be published after so many years of writing has been tempered with the knowledge that Matt wouldn't be here to see it, just like he wouldn't be here for so many milestones to come.

So, Matt, thank you. For supporting me for so long when we had no idea if I'd ever achieve my dream of having a book on the shelves. For being my best friend. For your writing advice, which usually consisted of 'yeah, that's sounds like a real book'. For how much fun we always had, and how much we laughed.

We miss you.

ASK NO QUESTIONS.
TELL NO LIES.

ALL
SHE
WANTS

KELLI HAWKINS
BESTSELLING AUTHOR OF *OTHER PEOPLE'S HOUSES*

**Ask no questions. Tell no lies. The utterly compelling
new novel from the bestselling author of
Other People's Houses.**

Lindsay just wants to be a mother. And when she discovers her
partner is leaving her for another woman, her dreams are left in
tatters. He was her last chance at a family ... or was he?

Then she meets Jack, they fall hard for each other, and
suddenly everything seems perfect. But why is his sister Natalie
so strangely protective of him, yet eager to pass the responsibility
to Lindsay? Who are these siblings, why did they really leave
the UK, and what terrifying secrets lie in their past?

And does Lindsay really want to know?